WHEN THE KISSING HAD TO STOP

CONSTANTINE FITZ GIBBON

UNABRIDGED

D1328760

PAN BOOKS LTD : LONDON

First published 1960 by Cassell & Co. Ltd.
This edition published 1962 by Pan Books Ltd.,
8 Headfort Place, London, S.W.1

*Printed in Great Britain by Richard Clay and Company, Ltd.,
Bungay, Suffolk*

... As for Venice and its people, merely born to
       bloom and drop,
Here on earth they bore their fruitage, mirth and
       folly were the crop:
What of soul was left, I wonder, when the kissing
       had to stop?

'Dust and ashes!' So you creak it, and I want the
       heart to scold.
Dear dead women, with such hair, too—what's
       become of all the gold
Used to hang and brush their bosoms? I feel chilly
       and grown old.

      Robert Browning: *A Toccata of Galuppi's*

The soundest strategy in war is to postpone operations
until the moral disintegration of the enemy renders the
mortal blow both possible and easy.

               V. I. Lenin

FOR MOYRA AND FOR ROGER

PART ONE

1

THE WAITER was, in fact, waiting, with his trolley of liqueurs and his boxes of cigars.

"Would you care for a brandy, Mr Cuthbertson? Or a cigar?" Patrick asked his guest.

The big American glanced rapidly at the mass of bottles.

"Just a glass of Vichy water," he said, addressing the waiter. "Do you have any Upman cigars?"

While he chose one from the box, Patrick, sixth Earl of Clonard, glanced with polite speed at his watch. Not quite two-fifteen. Nora had told him that they wouldn't get to Trafalgar Square before three, so there was plenty of time. He said to the waiter:

"And a small Calvados for me."

The American blew out a cloud of smoke, speaking through it:

"I hate mixing politics and business. It usually leads to bad politics and worse business. On the other hand, you know the feeling in this country. And, hell, if we give you the account it's up to you to give our product the most efficient form of advertising you can think of."

"I'm quite sure we must stress that this is a British product," said Patrick. "At least to begin with. Since the Sioux City disaster, the people here are firmly convinced that any American-made reactor is likely to blow up. They'll get over this, of course, but for the time being I'm quite sure that you will sell five times as many of your motor-cars if we advertise them as an intrinsically British product. I would propose to start the campaign with a series of brief TV sequences with a recurring slogan: Fuelless to Stratford: Fuelless to Oxford: Fuelless to Scotland. Completely familiar scenes, you know the sort of thing, Anne Hathaway's cottage, the dreaming

7

spires, grouse moors, which will reassure the public. Into each of these we will insert your atomic car."

"I thought only Americans saw England in those terms nowadays," said the American with a smile.

"Oh no, I assure you three-quarters of our population believe that England still exists—only they just don't happen ever to have gone there. It's a cosy little dream. By putting your car into that dream, the fear of the unknown will gradually vanish."

The American nodded, Patrick went on:

"And I think it's as well to insist from the very beginning that this is a people's car, not a luxury product."

"So it is. The cheapest damn thing on four wheels ever built."

"Exactly. But what I mean is that we should insist that this is a car designed and built for the little man, not a rich man's car that is offered for a miraculously low price. In fact, the little British car, in which the little British family can tour the little British Isles safely, cheaply and in comfort."

"Check," said Mr Cuthbertson. "I like that."

"Because you must realize that the fear of anything connected with atomic energy is now very great here, and to judge by the propaganda that's being given to those people, it's likely to go on getting greater. Nuclear and atomic are dirty words. Therefore we must emphasize that your product is British, domestic and safe."

"I'll call New York this afternoon. So far as I'm concerned, Patrick, the account is yours, but naturally I must check with G. W. As you know, we start production just as soon as we've cleared with Home Office and Treasury and all the other ministries that seem to want a hand in this. But I hope we'll have the first British Fuelless Car on the market in twelve months. So the sooner we get the advertising campaign rolling, the better. How soon can your agency let me have a plan?"

"Six weeks?"

"Fine, Patrick, fine. I must be getting along. I've got to see three politicians and a journalist this afternoon. God, I hate mixing business and politics."

"Say as little as you can to the journalist, Mr Cuthbertson."

"He's only interested in the financial side. But I'll play up the fact that this is a British concern. As you advised me."

The waiter had brought the bill, and Patrick scribbled Clonard across the bottom. Then, passing between bent, black-coated figures murmuring *"Bonjour monsieur, bonjour milord,"* they were out into the bright sunshine of Charlotte Street.

"Can I drop you anywhere?" asked Cuthbertson, as the taxi drew up.

"No, thanks," said Patrick. "I'll walk."

He felt moderately pleased with himself, as he limped down Rathbone Place, and waited for a break in the endless traffic in order to cross Oxford Street. He had never suffered many illusions as to why Jack Beaulieu had taken him into the agency ten years ago, when he returned from the Korean War with one leg slightly shorter than the other, and a minute pension. There were still prospective clients likely to be impressed by a title, even a title as obscure as Patrick's and with no money or country house to back it up. But gradually he had persuaded his bosses that in fact he was more than a walking object of snobbery, and had been given increasing responsibility. This was the first really big account to be entrusted to him, and there was certainly no question of Mr Cuthbertson or the British heads of Fuelless Cars being impressed by titles handed out a hundred and seventy years ago in order that Irish country gentlemen might vote the right way in the Irish House of Lords. And, he told himself as he entered Soho Square, he was well on the way to pulling it off. It would be very big. A million dollar deal he thought with a smile. Who knows, maybe a billion dollar deal? He glanced at his watch. A quarter to three. Plenty of time.

He stopped outside the entrance to a drinking club, beneath the sign that said STRIPTEASE and DANCE WITH NAKED LOVELIES, to glance at the pictures. A naked girl with very good breasts writhed on the floor of the small club stage, while another girl, dressed only in boots and a Sam Browne belt, stood over her, brandishing a toy whip. A nervous-looking boy of perhaps seventeen years sidled past him into the club. A second picture showed one naked girl undressing another. She had reached the stage of unrolling her friend's elastic girdle. But the real attraction of these places was that the customers could actually touch these well-developed young women, though only, he understood, on the dance floor. And a third picture showed an improbable-looking fellow, more like a tailor's dummy than a real human being, gliding across the dance floor with a tall, sinewy and supercilious blonde, stripped to the buff, in his arms. And looking at their faces Patrick remembered a word that had been current some years ago. Never, he thought, had he seen a more toffee-nosed couple, he in his pinstripe, she in her skin.

A couple of elderly men, laughing heartily, walked past him into the club. One day, he thought, he really must go into one of those weird places and see what actually went on. The only problem was that it would be so shameful to be seen by friends, coming out. It would be bad enough, even, to be surprised looking at the pictures. And he walked on.

The thing to do would be to go with a girl. He wondered if it would amuse Nora. The trouble was that Nora was so well known, perhaps about the best-known face on the London stage today. She would certainly be recognized even in such a place as this. Still he'd ask her, after the meeting. And he walked on into Shaftesbury Avenue, where the traffic was in its usual state of total immobility. Some of those cars, he thought, might well have been standing there ever since they started rebuilding Piccadilly Circus as a square, two years ago.

In Gerrard Street he saw a knot of Mediterranean-looking men at the next corner, and prudently crossed over to the other side of the street. There had been several nasty murder-robberies in this area in recent weeks, a couple in broad daylight, and though there were usually police about, there was none in sight today. Presumably they were all at the mass meeting in Trafalgar Square. So he crossed over, just to be on the safe side, and walked briskly enough to discourage the two elderly prostitutes gossiping outside the post office.

There were, indeed, a great many policemen standing about at the various entrances to Trafalgar Square, more policemen, really, than people drifting towards the meeting. He saw Black Marias parked down side-streets, and quite a few of the new, armed, crash-helmeted Mobile Guards, with their black motor cycles, as well as the familiar mounted police upon their beautiful horses. They must be expecting quite a fracas, he thought, which was odd considering that this was primarily a pacifist demonstration. Still, the police were very odd these days. 'I think your British police are wonderful!' He wondered if anyone ever said that now, as he passed a group of steely-eyed, iron-jawed, law enforcement officers, their thumbs tucked into their belts.

As he entered Trafalgar Square, he realized why there had been so few people coming to the meeting. It had already begun, and old Braithwaite was in the middle of a speech. Yes, and there was Nora on the platform beside him, at the nearer end. As always, when he saw Nora, his heart lifted. Even when she was as far away as this, even when she was upon a platform at a political meeting, she was gentle elegance. He moved on into the square.

". . . it is not for our own sake alone that we make this demand," Leonard Braithwaite was saying, his voice amplified by twenty loudspeakers, "not for our sake, but for that of our children, yes, and of our children's children." He stopped briefly for applause, and since there were so many microphones dotted about the square, the closing words were magnificently multiplied into 'children's children's children's children', reminding Patrick of those chapters in the Bible where somebody begat somebody who begat someone else again, for verse after verse.

Not that there was anything Old Testament about Leonard Braithwaite's leonine old head, with the mane of white hair falling over the collar of his open-necked white shirt, nor in his voice with its strong West Country burr that he must have had some trouble preserving throughout fifty years of political life and strenuous London journalism.

"We believe," the Grand Old Man of the Left was now saying, "that this government is pursuing a policy of suicide. Very well. If a man wishes to commit suicide that, in my opinion, is a matter for himself to decide. I have campaigned for years, inside and outside Parliament, against the punishment of would-be suicides. But this is very different. If a man attempts to commit suicide by blowing up a cinema in which are seated several thousand people, including old people and children, as well as himself, then I say that that is a crime. And I say that the continued fabrication of nuclear weapons is just such a crime. The children . . ."

But this time the echo did not come, lost in a great volume of applause, and at the far side of the square Patrick saw the policemen's horses shifting sideways.

Children had always formed a staple ingredient of Leonard Braithwaite's oratory, even before the Spanish Civil War. His own son, doubtless persuaded by his father's magnificent oratory that this war was a conflict between the forces of good and those of evil, had volunteered to fight with the Communists on the Republican side, and had been killed at the age of eighteen. Thenceforth Leonard Braithwaite had been able to refer to children and to the tragic sacrifice of their young lives from a personal angle as well. He had seldom failed to do so.

"Children," he began again, as the applause rippled into silence, "yet unborn are being sacrificed on the altar of national stupidity by this warmongering government. And this is a subject on which I can speak with great personal feeling. Nigh on thirty years ago my own son, outraged by the monstrous rebellion of that very clique of Fascist brigands and reactionaries with which our government today is so anxious to sign a treaty of alliance, chose the nobler road. But, my friends, he *chose* it, he was not conscripted, let alone mutilated by decisions taken decades, perhaps centuries, before his birth. I say to you . . ."

Again there was a roar of applause, in which several people on the platform joined. Patrick saw Nora hesitate, then clap her hands with the others. He slipped closer towards the platform, through the crowd.

Braithwaite, he thought, was speaking not only about children, but also, to a large extent, at them. It was easy to distinguish the marchers from the Londoners, or rather those who had marched from those who had walked or come by bus

12

to this meeting. The marchers, many with rucksacks and some with walking sticks or even crooks, looked in most cases as though they were scarcely out of school, their expressions tense and rapt, even when the boys in their leather jackets stood with one arm about the shoulders of a pretty girl, free of lipstick and tanned by the long hike from the missile bases on the Yorkshire coast. The girls, with their pony-tails and tartan slacks, seemed even more hypnotized by the old man's oratory than were the boys. Patrick wondered if any one of them might speculate concerning Mrs Braithwaite's feelings over the past quarter century, as her dead son was produced, year after year, in support of cause after cause.

"Strontium 90," Braithwaite was saying, "and other poisons, some of them far more vile, many of them so far unidentified by science . . ."

Patrick stopped listening, as his eyes moved across the platform immediately beneath Nelson's Column, now only twenty yards or so away.

Nearest to him sat Nora May, her eyes focused on a point several feet above the heads of the crowd, a slight smile upon her lips. This smile he knew was, with her, a sign of faint embarrassment, as when she found herself at a quite unsuitable party or being the recipient of fulsome and exaggerated compliments. She had, indeed, only come here to please her sister, Antonia May, the novelist, who was seated at the other end. All her life Nora had had to make amends to Antonia for the fact that whereas she, Nora, was a beautiful, charming child who grew up easily into an even more beautiful, more charming and talented woman, Antonia had only had the talent. All her life she had praised Antonia publicly and flattered her in private, and when Antonia's novels had a small success, she proclaimed, and perhaps even believed, that her sister was the greatest writer and thinker of the age. Therefore when Antonia telephoned her and asked her to take part in the march and to lend her fame and beauty to this great cause, she had felt obliged to agree. She had put down the telephone, turned to Patrick, and said: "She's the brainy one. If she says I must go, then go I must." But Patrick knew that that was not the real reason for Nora's presence on the platform.

The real reason lay long in the past, when the sisters had been children evacuated to New Hampshire during the war, and their foster-parents had so obviously preferred the company of the pretty, gay child to that of the morose and plain one. It was in part repayment of this unpayable debt that Nora now sat on the platform beneath the victor of Trafalgar, Copenhagen and the Nile, a smile, which perhaps only Patrick recognized as one of embarrassment, playing about her lips.

She was clapping now as, to tumultuous applause, Leonard Braithwaite sat down, mopping his brow, and Canon Christian rose to address the meeting. He started by turning his head, with a queer, jerky movement, first to the right and then to the left, so that all might enjoy his open, manly smile and his fine, aquiline profile. Then he began to speak in his deep, melli-fluous voice.

"My friend Braithwaite and I disagree about many matters." He glanced down at his friend Braithwaite, who was glaring at the Union Jack bedraped table, his chin resting upon his fist in an attitude reminiscent of Rodin's 'Thinker'. "I am a Chris-tian, not only by name, but also by belief." He waited for his little joke to be taken, and a few people must have found it amusing, for a slight titter passed through the crowd. "Braith-waite is a staunch humanist. But there is one belief that we have in common, and that is the paramount dignity of man. Now I say to you that the soul of England demands that we get rid, once and for all, regardless of the cost, unilaterally if need be, of these monstrous weapons of mass destruction. I say to you that the soul of England . . ."

What odd theology, Patrick thought. Did this clergyman really believe that communities could possess souls, or, for that matter, that the dignity of man was paramount? In any event Canon Christian was quite prepared to quote the founder of Christianity, for Patrick heard something about a millstone being tied about the necks of the government, who should then be cast into the depths of the sea. So he too was play-ing the children theme. Patrick glanced at the other two mem-bers of the committee.

Seated between Antonia and Braithwaite was the round and rosy figure of Victor Cockshore, the famous scientist and

Nobel prizewinner. He had won the Nobel prize for his brilliant research into metallurgy and kindred subjects, but had achieved far wider publicity in England only a couple of years ago when, with maximum publicity, he had resigned from his position as part-time scientific adviser to the Ministry of Defence, on the grounds, as he said, that they were debasing pure science by asking for his advice in the construction of missile casings. Never, he wrote in a book that became something of a best-seller and on which Antonia May had collaborated, never would he let his genius be so prostituted as to be used for the making of weapons of mass destruction. Others said that immediately before resigning he had asked the Ministry to raise his pay as part-time adviser from three to four thousand a year, but this, Patrick thought, was probably a malicious invention by his enemies. Scientists, he knew, could be just as jealous and bitchy as the members of any other profession.

And finally there was the youngish man seated next to his darling Nora, elbows on his knees, his finger-tips coming together and parting in time with the oratory of Canon Christian's peroration. The Canon, who was now invoking the sufferings of Christ upon the Cross, which he compared to the mental sufferings of all good Christians as they observed the rush of the Gadarene swine towards the abyss of nuclear war, was obviously drawing to a close.

For a moment Patrick failed to recognize this man, who was approximately his own age, about thirty-five. Then he turned and spoke briefly to Nora, and Patrick realized that this too was a familiar face, but where, when? And then, suddenly, he saw that face, little changed, for already it had been lined and leathery, above a black suit and stiff collar, standing at the end of a school corridor, shouting for a fag. Yes, there was no mistake about it, this must be Rupert Page-Gorman. And of course it was entirely logical, indeed perhaps inevitable, that he should be here. He was speaking to Nora again, who shook her head and smiled, as Canon Christian sat down again amidst vast applause. Now Page-Gorman got to his feet and stood, impassive and ready, waiting for silence. It came, and he began to speak.

"You have heard," he said, "from British science." He bowed towards Cockshore. "From the Church of England,"

and another bow. "From British literature," and he waved towards Antonia, who nodded at the crowd. "From humanism and journalism, that guardian of our freedoms, I mean from our President, Leonard Braithwaite." This was greeted by prolonged applause. "The stage, too, is represented upon this platform in the person of Miss Nora May." More clapping. "But she has asked to be excused from speaking, since she has a sore throat which must be protected for her performance this evening." This was news to Patrick. She had had no sore throat when he had left her flat at nine that morning. "But I myself speak as something quite different. I speak as a politician. . . ."

And so, thought Patrick, he should. Rupert had been a politician almost from the day he could speak, and perhaps even before then, for his father had been a Liberal minister in the last Lloyd George administration. While Patrick learned a little at Sandhurst, Rupert had been President of the Oxford Union. Elected to Parliament as a Conservative at a very early age in the 1951 Election, he had disagreed with his political leaders about Suez, and had resigned his seat. Almost immediately he had made a great name for himself as a television interviewer, and his decision to stand as a Labour candidate in 1959 had caused considerable excitement in political circles, since so quick and total a change of allegiance had not been seen for many a year. He had stood for a marginal constituency in south London, chiefly on an Anti-Nuclear Bomb platform, and had been returned. He was known at Westminster as 'The Anti-Nuclear Bomb', and a great future was foreseen for him by those who foresee great futures for young MPs. Patrick had not met him since they were at school together. He hadn't cared for him much then.

"I speak to you," Rupert was saying, "as a politician, but above all as an *English* politician. And I ask you, and I ask myself, who is in charge of this England of ours? Is it the government down the road there?" He pointed towards the equestrian statue of Field-Marshal Earl Haig. "Is it the men whom you, whom we have elected? Or is it some altogether different group of men, living in Grosvenor Square, men we have not chosen, men who are not of our nationality or even

of our continent? Is it the Americans who are in charge here?"
Protracted groans came from the crowd. Was Mr Cuthbertson
in charge here, Patrick wondered? In a way he supposed that
he was, at least of the British Fuelless Car Company. "Their
money pours in," Rupert went on, "and they believe that they
can conquer and subdue us by the power of the mighty dollar,
by a policy of take-over bids, by the exploitation of British
workers in the interests of American capitalism. I say to you
that this is monstrous." He waited for the applause, which
came full-throated. "But that is not all. They are menacing
our very lives. It is their atomic bases that ring our coasts.
You who have been to Yorkshire on this great historic march
have seen, as I have seen, American military police standing
behind the protection of our own British police against the
justified wrath of us, the British people. I say to you that this
is shameful!" Again there was a great applause. "If they
believe that their security depends upon these diabolical con-
traptions, then let them take their beastly weapons and install
them in their own country. We don't want them here!" Now
the crowd was really roaring. "Must we die that the Pentagon
generals may live?" "No," roared the crowd, "No! No!
No!" "We wish to live in peace with all the world. How
the Americans arrange for their self-defence is their own concern, but WE DON'T WANT THEM TO DO IT HERE." The crowd
was verging on hysteria. "Come, let us march to Grosvenor
Square, as we marched from Yorkshire, and tell them that we
don't want them here, that we refuse to die for them, that they
must all GO AWAY. Who follows me?"

Nimbly he jumped from the flag-bedecked platform, and
headed towards Pall Mall, the crowd parting to let him through,
then falling in behind. For a moment he paused, and Patrick
saw the other members of the committee struggling to join
him. Nora was last. Then the crowd came together again, and
they all vanished from his view, as he fought his way through
the angry mob towards the woman he loved. They were
raising the banners that had rested on the ground during the
speeches, and one caught Patrick's eye. It said MALTESE
BAKER'S UNION. And he saw the mounted police closing the
exits from Trafalgar Square.

2

AT TEN-fifteen that evening Patrick Clonard was having a brief chat with the stage-door keeper at the Globe, while Nora and the rest of the cast took their curtain calls.

"That's a terrible black eye you've got, sir," said the old doorkeeper.

"I'm lucky not to have a broken arm," he replied.

His arm was in a sling, badly bruised but intact.

"Horrible people, the police these days," the old man commented. "If you ask me, sir, Miss May never ought to have been there at all. She's not the sort for vulgar brawls, not at all the sort."

His wizened face expressed the utmost disapproval, and Patrick wondered what sort of a scene he could imagine that they had been involved in—perhaps some latter-day Mafeking Night. But their conversation was interrupted by the sound of quick footsteps and voices in the corridor.

"There they come now, sir."

"Right," said Patrick. "I'll go on up."

At the same hour a small group of men in Prague were discussing the vulgar brawl in the drawing-room of a hotel suite. They were seated at a round table covered with a brown cloth, and beneath an overhead lamp with a very large pink cotton shade. A man called Kiesinger had almost completed reading a report from the Czechoslovak Embassy in London, translating into Russian as he went:

". . . in conclusion, a positive gain, possibly of major importance. The identification of the police with the American forces will be entirely to our advantage. Questions are certain to be asked in Parliament, and there is every prospect of further demonstrations, perhaps even this evening, in which case the total of arrests and casualties will certainly exceed the figure aimed at, namely 250 and 50. However, our friends here do not consider that the time is yet ripe to announce our open support of the Braithwaite group."

Kiesinger laid down his report, and looked across the table

at General Nikitin. Nikitin was a heavily built man with astonishingly broad shoulders and a ruddy, healthy complexion. He wore the uniform of the RKK (which was the new name for NKVD since the death of Khrushchev) and many medals. He took off his heavy, horn-rimmed spectacles, thought for a moment, and then glanced at O'Mahony, the melancholy-looking, long-jawed Irishman.

"The Braithwaite group?" he asked, briefly.

O'Mahoney was equally laconic. It might even be that he modelled his manner on that of the general.

"Liberals," he said, with evident disgust. "From a world-historical point of view, nonentities. But useful."

"That," said the general, with a note of sarcasm, "I had already realized. Discipline?"

"I said that they were Liberals," replied the Irishman, somewhat stuffily. "However, our people inside the movement can and do give it considerable guidance."

Nikitin got up, walked across to the window, drew back the heavy rep curtain, and glanced down at the glittering river. Far away a searchlight was moving back and forth rhythmically across the sky. Then he turned back into the room.

"We will continue," he said, "to give these people maximum support, but without identifying ourselves with them and, indeed, if need be, disclaiming them. Meanwhile I should like a full report, as quickly as possible on this man . . ." He went over to the central table and glanced at a piece of paper, ". . . this man, Gorman. That is all, goodnight."

The others got up and left the room. The general waited until the door had closed behind the last of them, and then walked across to the table in the corner. He poured himself a glass of brandy, which he swallowed in one, neat. After glancing at the three telephones he picked up the middle one, and said:

"Moscow."

Nora sat at her dressing-table, in a wrapper of towelling which she had bought in Paris, removing the grease-paint, while her elderly dresser fussed about the little room.

"It's quite true, Mary," she was saying. "Lord Clonard

19

absolutely saved my life. If that truncheon had come down on my head instead of on his arm. . . . How is your arm, Patrick?"

"Aches," he replied, and sipped his drink, leaning against the corner wall and trying to make himself as little of a nuisance to the dresser as possible. He knew that she didn't approve of his being here at all.

"Well, if he hadn't grabbed me and put his arm over my head, that nice little Susan Anne would have got the great chance that every understudy dreams of."

Mary Parker cluck-clucked.

"Have you ever been in a crowd charged by the police, Mary?"

"Certainly not, Miss May," she replied, in the same tone that she would have used if asked whether she had ever committed adultery. And there was much too much of *that* in the theatre. The stories she could tell. Not that she ever would. Take this nice Miss May, wasn't she married herself? And young lords hanging about leading ladies' dressing-rooms were no novelty to Mary. Not that this one was particularly young, nor did he look at all like a stage-door johnny. "I leave politics to *Mr* Parker, Miss May."

"And I think I shall leave them to Lord Clonard in future. The faces, twisted, distorted, terrified and terrifying. Like, like . . . the French Revolution, I suppose. Paddy, would you leave the room while I just slip into my dress?"

Mrs Parker nodded her approval.

The supreme master of the Soviet Union was a puffy-faced man of fifty-two, who had learned his Kremlin politics as assistant secretary to Josef Stalin. By the time that Khrushchev was no longer there, re-Stalinization had been in all essentials completed. Kyril Vassielivitch Kornoloff, had, however, symbolically reintroduced many of the forms that had prevailed in Stalin's lifetime. One of these was to make his decisions very late at night, after a fairly heavy meal and copious glasses of Crimean champagne. Kornoloff had an extremely strong head. Some of his colleagues had not. This gave him an advantage. He never missed taking an advantage.

Now he leaned back in his chair, and gazed across the dirty

20

plates and mounds of uneaten food that still cluttered the dining-room table, at his Foreign Secretary talking into a telephone. Sspesiatkin looked tired. Not good for much longer. Give him a few more months to see if he can clear up the Israeli business. Which he can't. Then maybe a public trial; subject, the sabotage of Soviet-Israeli relationships. The other men at the table were silent, except for Marshal Ryukin who was still cracking nuts.

"What does Nikitin say?"

Sspesiatkin spoke into the telephone: "One moment." Then to his master: "It's about the Agitprop action in Britain."

"Give it to me, give it to me. Hullo, Nikitin? Well?"

He listened, grunting. Then he said:

"Good. I like it. Step it up."

He handed the telephone back to Sspesiatkin, who replaced it in its cradle and, in his turn, handed it to the footman. Kornoloff glanced round the table, and the marshal stopped cracking nuts. Kornoloff said:

"The knight's move. Pity you don't play chess, Sspesiatkin, or I could give a more elaborate metaphor, but at least you know how a knight moves. We must immediately make a really large propaganda gesture to Britain. I suggest that we dismantle our missile bases in Poland, slowly of course, and with maximum publicity. Unilateral disarmament by the Soviet Union, sounds good, eh?" He gave a brief laugh, like a cough, in which the others joined. "The knight's move. Or to take a simpler game with which you are doubtless better acquainted, Sspesiatkin, draughts." He arranged, in a straight line, a salt-cellar, the claw of a lobster and a wine glass. "Here are we. Here is Germany. Here is Britain." He removed the wine glass. "Britain is gone, disarmed." He lifted the salt-cellar over the lobster's claw. "Thus we take Germany. Marshal Ryukin, a report tomorrow on the military disadvantages, if any, of dismantling the Polish missile bases. None, I imagine, if we leave the ones here and in East Germany intact. But I want a report. Sspesiatkin, tell the British ambassador to call on me at five tomorrow. It looks promising. The knight's move, the knight's move."

He leaned across, pulled a bottle of champagne out of its ice-bucket, and gave that cough-like laugh.

In the taxi bowling along the Mall, constantly breasting the waves of light that was the stream of traffic coming the other way, Nora laid her hand on Patrick's.

"Paddy," she said, "do you feel beastly?"

"Not particularly. I just feel as though I'd been in a fight. Which I suppose in a way I have. Pugs must feel like this pretty well all the time."

"You were wonderful."

"Was I?" He leaned across and his lips brushed her cheek as the cab wheeled around Queen Victoria. "And I can tell you I'd do it again, rather than see you trampled to death by hysterical pacifists or coshed by mobile guards. Light me a cigarette, will you?"

A guardsman stamped and turned. He said:

"You must be pretty tired yourself. Would you rather skip Moyra Beaulieu's party?"

"No, not really. Besides, I want to show you off, you and your wounds. Anyhow, we can decide after supper." She paused. "But, Paddy, I do think you were wonderful, I mean not only for being so brave but just because you were there, at the right time."

"Nora, darling, I wish you'd marry me."

"Oh, Patrick, I wish I could. I love you so much, and I'd simply adore being your wife. But I can't. Because of Felix. You know that. He loves me too much for me to hurt him. And it *would* hurt him."

"And this doesn't hurt him?"

"But it does. That's why I feel so awful half the time."

"Surely if he really loved you, he'd let you go."

"You don't understand, Patrick. It's not just a question of my going. In a way I've gone. It would be the matter of his marriage going. What would they all say down in Wiltshire, all those unspeakable neighbours he attaches such importance to? And then there's the question of his priests. They bully him mercilessly and would never let him divorce me. And then there's Toddy."

"Toddy's eight. He'd have two homes instead of one and a half, that's all."

She leaned forward and called through the slit beside the driver's right ear:

"It's the second on the left."

Then she laid her hand on Patrick's once again. She said:

"Paddy, I know I'm a bitch. You'd do far better to get yourself a proper, unmarried girl. But don't you see that I can't do it to Felix? If you knew how soft and vulnerable he is beneath that rigid exterior. All that respectability he armours himself with, it's really all he's got."

The taxi slithered to a halt. Since he could not reach into his trouser pocket without elaborate contortions, she paid.

Down in Wiltshire, at his house called Broadacres, Felix Seligman laid down his book and glanced about his vast drawing-room. Balzac, he thought, is all very well, but there are a lot of things those French just don't understand. So many of their values are not the same as ours. For one thing, they over-value brains. Useful enough, like good looks, but what about loyalty, respect for tradition, honest dealing? A Rastignac or a Julien Sorel wouldn't go far in this country, at least not as far as in France, and even if he did, he'd start posing as Old Jolyon Forsyte just as soon as ever he could get away with it. He cocked an ear. Was that a sound from Toddy's nursery? No, he thought not. In any case Mademoiselle would hear. Now there was a decent French person for you. Yes, Father Crosby had found him a jewel. He wondered how much he should give her when she went back to the Berri in September? Five hundred would almost provide her with a *dot*. Well, he'd give her five hundred, perhaps even a thousand. He could certainly afford it, and this was the sort of gesture, discreet, opulent and kind, that appealed to him. It was an English gesture, he thought, English in the best sense.

He dreaded September, Toddy's first term at his boarding-school, and himself alone here. There would be the hunting, of course. And he would enjoy that, he told himself. But even with Toddy the evenings had been lonely, and now he must be alone all day. Should he, perhaps, go back to London and

23

work? But Seligman Baer ran with complete smoothness, and whenever they wanted his opinion they rang him. Would they want it more if he were in the office all day? He remembered how it had been when he did work there, in his father's lifetime. Whenever old Sir Solomon Seligman had come up from Wiltshire they had, tactfully, discreetly, found work for him to do, arranging meetings with foreign bankers after the real business had been decided. He would hate to think that younger men might now do that sort of kindness for him.

He glanced about his drawing-room. Broadacres had been built in the 1870s, and the fireplace was a huge stone Gothic edifice, like a gate house, bearing the coat of arms of the de Mauncy family from whom Sir Solomon's father had bought the property in 1903. If he were to have that removed, and a proper Adam chimney put in its place, he could hang his Velasquez over it, where it would look better than in the dining-room among the French Impressionists.

Besides, this was not de Mauncy property. Not even, he told himself, by right of tradition. They had lived at Broadacres for only half the time that his family had been here, and surely could never have loved it as he did. His love was a fierce, possessive and utterly satisfactory passion. He had been born here, had grown up here, and the whole property was absolutely and completely his, the lawns, the great rose garden that the horticultural societies came to see, the maze, the beech woods, the well-stocked lake, the rides, this was Seligman land. So why the de Mauncy arms? True, he could hardly change the name of the village pub, where he dutifully paid a call, once a year, at Christmas time. But he could remove them from his chimney. Besides, was not there something slightly bad taste, even slightly *parvenu*, in sitting beneath somebody else's escutcheon? Yes, he would have a new chimney built.

He glanced at his watch. Time for the late news on TV and then, if it were a Catholic priest or monk, the Epilogue. He got up and made his way around the Louis XV sofas and the handsome buhl tables into his library. He pressed a button and a section of books swung away from the wall. He pressed another, and after a moment the sound came from the machine. A voice was saying:

"We are now showing a film made on the spot, this afternoon, of the great demonstration in Trafalgar Square. The commentary, recorded at the time, is by John Nibbet."

The screen flickered alive, and to Felix Seligman's astonishment the first object to swim into focus was the face of his wife, Nora, turning and speaking to a youngish man seated on some sort of platform beside her.

Francesca had, as usual, prepared supper for two, had waited up to see if Mrs Seligman had any more demands to make of her, and when Nora had none, had gone. Now the meal was over, the coffee bubbling placidly in its electric percolator. Patrick said:

"Look, darling, you say that I should get married and have a wife and family. But I don't want a wife and family. I don't give a row of beans for a wife and family. I'm not a bit like your precious Felix. I just want you."

"Patrick, you've got me."

"But you say you feel awful half the time."

"I was exaggerating. I always exaggerate. You know that. I feel awful about Felix about once a day, maybe for five minutes. There. Have some coffee."

"I think it's dreadful you should feel that way, even for five seconds a day. I think it's a mess."

"Oh, Patrick, how *rude*." She laughed as she said this, and he smiled at once. "Anyhow, even if somehow I did manage to divorce poor old Felix and marry you, what difference would it make? Apart perhaps from our having children, which you maintain you don't care about and which would play havoc with my career that you always say is so important. And I might feel miserable for five seconds a day, even if I were your wife."

He stirred his coffee and then muttered:

"We could do things together."

Now she laughed aloud:

"But we do."

"I didn't mean that. I meant that we could go places together."

25

"But, my sweet, we're going to Moyra's party together this evening, and we go to the theatre, and we went to Eden Roc last year. Isn't that enough?"

"We could go to Ireland to see my aunt."

She laughed again.

"Now you really are talking like Felix. He had eight aunts, each with a huger house than the last, and when we were first married I was trotted around to be inspected by every single one of them. Paddy, I have absolutely no desire to meet your aunt. And I can't believe that you have, since you've never even mentioned her before."

"She's jolly nice. She collects seashells. Her house is full of them, and smells like the Thames at low tide."

"I'm sure she's enchanting, but I can't see that I should make poor Felix totally unhappy merely in order to smell Wapping Old Stairs."

"Well, we needn't visit her if you don't want to."

"I thought that was the whole point of going to Ireland? You're certainly not going to get me there on any other pretext. I've been over twice, on tour. All those troglodytes or leprechauns or whatever they're called gulping down that filthy whisky of theirs and making all those jokes. Catch me!"

He said, quite seriously:

"I think you are absolutely and deliberately refusing to understand what I am trying to say to you."

She was equally serious.

"Yes, my Paddy, I think I am. And now let's go to Moyra's party. Because I have a horrible suspicion that if we stay here we might quarrel, and that would be a dreadful precedent when we've never had one for three years."

"We did have one. When you were flirting with the unspeakable cad."

"My poppet, you were drunk, so it didn't count. And besides, I wasn't flirting with the unspeakable cad."

"Oh yes you were. Making great eyes at him, you were." And he mimicked her.

"Boo!" she said, and leaned across the table and kissed him on the lips.

The Prime Minister, in his room at the House of Commons, was a worried man. The Home Secretary was as imperturbable as usual. The Prime Minister said:

"It's all very well, Charles, but a thing like this could bring down the government. What are you going to reply to Braithwaite's question?"

"I shall say that since the arrested men are awaiting trial, the case is *sub judice*, and that it would therefore hardly be proper to comment on the matter at this stage."

"You always say that."

"I know I do. What else can I say? The wretched police were only doing their duty."

"I do think that you should try to persuade the commissioner to make them behave a little less brutally in future. It's not English, all this sort of thing."

"The Abbey Church of Bury St Edmund's was the largest cathedral north of the Alps, with the exception of Cologne. In the fourteenth century, I think, an infuriated peasantry pulled it to bits with their bare hands."

"What on earth has that got to do with it, my dear Charles?"

"Simply that they were English. That crowd in Trafalgar Square could have done the same thing to the American Embassy."

"Nonsense. Anyhow the point isn't the American Embassy, which in my opinion is an ugly great thing, but the behaviour of the police. They're getting out of hand."

"All right. I'll have a word with the commissioner tomorrow. But I'm not giving an inch to the Opposition this evening."

"Of course not, quite right. Now there's this other question that concerns you, about the millionaire living in the subsidized council house at Egham."

"Yes, I have my answer ready. I thought I'd comment on the millionaire's extraordinary choice of residence."

Down below, in St Margaret Street, the mounted police were pushing back a small, angry and extremely well-disciplined crowd that was attempting to enter Old Palace Yard in order to present a petition complaining of the undue violence manifested by the police in Trafalgar Square that afternoon. It was a hot, heavy night. The police were tired and cross.

Jack Beaulieu never seemed to work. He would drift into his office at noon or so, glance at a few letters, tell his highly efficient secretary how to answer them, sign those she had answered on the previous day, and with a joke or two to the girls at the switchboard, drift out to lunch. Sometimes he would look in again in the late afternoon, sometimes not. His weekends at his house near Bourne End had been known to last from Thursday till Tuesday. All the year round he had a splendid, old-fashioned tan. And though he must be getting on for sixty, he was still one of the finest players of real tennis in the country.

On the other hand, he also never stopped working. Those protracted lunches were with clients: those weekend parties were attended by sponsors or copywriters or both: it was said that he had landed the highly lucrative Deauville advertising contract while actually playing tennis with the marquis de Courterolles, not before or after the game but on the court itself.

Moyra Beaulieu's parties, which were frequent and good, formed an essential part of the pattern. To her large, luxurious flat overlooking Green Park came pretty women and amusing or famous men, and one or two, never more, of the very rich industrialists whose advertising accounts supported Jack Beaulieu Ltd. Jack never, of course, discussed business at these parties, unless one of those very rich men should wish to do so; if he did so wish, there was the terrace or the library or even a corner of the drawing-room. And Moyra, elegant, gay, with a carefully preserved girlish tendency to silliness, made the important gentleman feel that her whole party revolved around him; since her guests represented London, he was thus bang in the middle of the metropolis which, as everyone knows, is the centre of the world. This was very good for business.

Patrick was therefore not at all surprised, as he followed Nora into the drawing-room past the beautiful grey parrot on its perch, to see Moyra talking to Mr Cuthbertson. From the

28

terrace came the soft music of a Chilean quartet. They were dancing out there, while half a dozen other people, mostly known to Patrick, talked and drank in here. Almost immediately Jack and a very pretty, windswept girl came in from the terrace, hand in hand, laughing together. Like Patrick, Jack was wearing a lounge suit. In their circle it was considered faintly bad taste to wear a dinner jacket, since nowadays every commuter changed for dinner the moment he got back to his house in the suburbs. Mr Cuthbertson, however, displayed a wide expanse of starched shirt front and three huge onyx studs.

Quite quickly, in order to put an end to the conversation about his black eye and bruised arm, Patrick took Moyra Beaulieu away from Mr Cuthbertson and out on to the dance floor. Some of the guests knew the steps of this new dance, but others contented themselves with dancing a samba. Patrick, apologetically, was one of these.

"I couldn't care less, Patrick. Anything to get away from that boring American."

There was no need for Moyra to feign *naïveté* with him, nor did she do so.

"Oh, I don't know. I lunched with him today. He didn't seem so bad."

"I've met worse, far, far worse, with their endless talk about money and their total ignorance of everything else. He kept talking about Piccadilly Square."

"Well it is a square, isn't it?"

"You are being tedious, Patrick. You know perfectly well what I mean."

"Some of our own industrial wizards aren't so hot, either. Do you remember that cotton king at Bourne End?"

Moyra laughed.

"The one who kept referring to you as 'his lordship here'? Wasn't he a riot? I think I'll refer to you as his lordship here in future. Would you like that?"

"Love it."

The music had stopped, and they stood at the edge of the terrace, looking down into the darkened park, encircled in the great, pinkish aurora borealis that London cast against the warm night sky. Moyra said:

"But seriously, Patrick, don't you think that there are far too many of them, with far too much money, over here these days? I mean, they're practically running the country."

"Are they? As for their money, quite a lot of it sticks to Jack's hands, and some of it even gets into mine."

"Do you think I'd have them in my flat for any other reason?"

"Or anybody else, Moyra dear?"

"That," said Moyra with a laugh, "is one below the belt. I do have some real friends, Patrick. Of whom his lordship here is one. But seriously, what about these rocket bases? Wouldn't we be better off without them? And my friends tell me that we could double our trade with Russia and make a killing in China, if the Americans would let us. Instead of which we live on top of a bloody great heap of hydrogen rockets. Seems all wrong to me."

"It doesn't make much sense to me, either. But then politics never do. Shall we dance again? I can do a slow foxtrot."

She smiled up at him as he put his good arm about her waist. Although she must be getting on for fifty, Patrick thought, Moyra is still a very attractive woman. *Encore désirable*, as the French say. And he wondered, not for the first time, if she had lovers and if so who they were. If she did, she was certainly very discreet about it.

"I was dining at my Embassy this evening," Mr Cuthbertson said to Patrick as he absent-mindedly stroked a highly-polished piece of Esquimo sculpture, "and the ambassador was saying that he cannot understand who these people are. After all, your government is friendly, the Opposition is officially friendly, your Press with a few exceptions is friendly, we are closely allied, and yet things like this keep happening. You were in Trafalgar Square. Who are they?"

"Young people mostly. It's a cause. You know how young people love a cause. And at the moment there isn't any other. I don't think it amounts to anything more than that, Mr Cuthbertson." And he added, beneath his breath, so please don't have second thoughts about financing the British Fuelless Car Company, because if you do it will lose me, personally, approximately £2000 per annum for as far ahead as I can see."

Mr Cuthbertson nodded.

"Just kids, eh?"

"Not altogether, of course. You mustn't forget that there is a long tradition of radical pacifism in this country, dating at least from the time of the Little Englanders during the Boer War period, and the conchies of World War I. And remember how strong pacifism was between the wars. Lansbury, the Peace Pledge Union and all that. This fits into that same tradition."

"I guess I'm not as up on British history as I should be. But it smells awfully strong of Communism to me."

"Some people here maintain that you Americans see Communism in everything you dislike. The Communists here are a tiny minority, almost as small as in the United States. To ascribe all this anti-nuclear bomb feeling to them would be to make a grave mistake."

"Maybe you're right about that. But what about their bosses?"

"One of the people on the platform this afternoon was my own—my good friend Nora May, over there talking to Jack. Another, or rather another two if I'm not very much mistaken, are just coming through the hall now."

For through the open door he had seen Antonia May handing a silk cloak to the maidservant, while Rupert Page-Gorman waited.

"Why not ask them, Mr Cuthbertson?"

"Do you know, Patrick, I rather think I will."

As Antonia and Page-Gorman entered the room, Moyra Beaulieu came through the terrace windows. Patrick saw her stop, and her eyes go quickly from Antonia to the man, and the corners of her mouth drop. And then he thought he knew not only who her 'friends' were who talked to her about trade with Russia, but also, perhaps, the answer to his other question. It all took a fraction of a second, and then they had met, in the middle of the room, close to where he and Cuthbertson were standing.

"Antonia, darling! Rupert! How good of you to come,

after all you've been through today. And what a lot of black eyes for one party. Rupert, do you know Patrick Clonard? He got his shiner in Trafalgar Square, too."

"Mine isn't from Trafalgar Square," Rupert replied in a loud, almost public voice. "Mine is from Bow Street police station. Before the police realized who I was. And just what a monumental stink I can raise."

3

THE GOVERNMENT fell three weeks later over the Police (Increased Powers) Bill, though the real cause of its fall was a question of timing. The majority of the country, being law-abiding and respectable people, were truly horrified by conditions in parts of London and some of the other big cities. The higher fines imposed on the prostitutes in 1959 no longer deterred them. In this hot August they promenaded the Bayswater Road dressed only in high-heeled shoes and a light coat, which they would open to display their wares to potential customers. When a client was secured, they were as like as not simply to take him across the road, into Hyde Park, even in broad daylight, where young men were also to be seen, kissing and playing with one another on the dusty grass littered with used contraceptives. The police made arrests, of course, but in general they had far more important tasks upon their hands. There were whole areas of London into which it was becoming unsafe to go, even in daylight. Knives flashed in Soho. From King's Cross to Notting Hill it was one long race-riot, and when the police attempted to intervene, they were as likely to be shot by one side as by the other. Bank robbers no longer merely threatened the clerks, but shot them dead at once. True, the Mobile Guards were armed, and it was no unusual thing to see a running gun-fight between a carful of them and another filled with gangsters. But the metropolitan and county police forces still had nothing more lethal with which to face tommy-guns, knives and revolvers than their

32

truncheons. They might, and did, go about in pairs, but it was scarcely more difficult to shoot two policemen than one. The number of unsolved murders was frightening, and the graph was rising. For not only was it wellnigh impossible to find recruits for the various police forces, but men were resigning from them in ever-increasing numbers. The life was altogether too dangerous.

The Increased Powers Bill would have armed all police, doubled their pay, and made it impossible for any policeman to resign from the force before he had completed his time save in cases of illness or real hardship. The bulk of the country would undoubtedly have approved of this or any measure which would decrease the vice and crime wave.

Unfortunately, however, the House felt otherwise. The country was worried about the increased use of violence by the police upon the persons it arrested, but the House had seen that violence exercised upon one of its own members, Rupert Page-Gorman. Parliament is notoriously sensitive about the rights and privileges of its members. The refusal of the Home Secretary to institute an inquiry and to punish the policemen responsible caused very bad feelings, even in his own party. A score or so of Conservative MPs made it clear to the Home Secretary that they would not vote for the bill unless an addition was made to it ensuring closer parliamentary supervision of the police, and particularly of the metropolitan police, and a much tighter discipline within the force. Page-Gorman's speech in the Commons, and his brilliant interview on TV (of which medium he was a master) brought considerable support for this point of view from the country as a whole. However, the Home Secretary was informed by his senior police officers that the force, already harassed, understrength and wearied of continual insults from the public and Press, would certainly not put up with any such measure and, indeed, they themselves threatened to resign in a body.

The situation was made all the worse by the fact that a woman named Duck-Eyed Moll, known to be the mistress of a Soho crook wanted for the murder of a policeman, died in strange circumstances after being arrested for questioning. The Press were refused permission to see her body. The uproar that had followed the Page-Gorman case, and that was just beginning to die down, was revived. In these circumstances, the Prime Minister decided that it was best to dissolve Parliament and to appeal to the country for a mandate for drastic reform. In any event, there would have had to be an election in the following year. From an economic point of view, this was an ideal time to go to the country. Prosperity had never been so great, nor unemployment so low, while foreign affairs were stable. It seemed, therefore, that this election would be fought on purely domestic issues, and despite the police scandal the government believed they had a very good chance of winning it. Their slogan was FOUR IN A ROW.

But as it happened the election was not, or not primarily, fought on domestic issues.

Early in October Capri is a most beautiful place. The great swarms of noisy tourists have gone, and what few remain are engagingly eccentric. The hotels, still open, are not now crowded, the weather is usually good, and the sea still warm enough for swimming. So when Nora's play closed, Patrick took his month's annual holiday—which he had postponed in anticipation of this—and they flew to Naples. The London papers flew there too, and the air mail edition of that day's *Times* was on sale at the little kiosk in the piazza at about six o'clock each evening.

They had swum down at the Piccola Marina that afternoon, then taken the long, leisurely walk up from Gracie Fields's place to the little town, swinging the basket containing their bathing things between them. It is very seldom that a man feels conscious of good health, well-being, perhaps even of happiness.

"Nora," he said, as they stopped for breath and looked down at the Faraglioni rocks, casting long shadows across the azure ocean, "tell me something."

"Tell you what, Paddy? You know I love you. What else is there to tell?"

"Why do you never call me darling or sweetheart or . . . or angel-pie, or anything like that?"

She laughed.

34

"I call you Paddy, because you once told me nobody ever had. Isn't that right?"

"Everything's absolutely dead right," he said, as he took her in his arms, "particularly you."

And that was how Patrick still felt as he left Nora at the hotel to change, and walked on up to the elegant piazza. He bought the rice-paper *Times*, sat down outside Vuotto's, ordered himself a dry martini, and opened his paper.

First he glanced at the leading article.

"It is always a matter of regret," *The Times* leader-writer felt, "when the Police Force is dragged into the political arena. One of our most cherished traditions is that the police should remain outside, and above, politics. However, there are occasions. . . ." There are indeed, thought Patrick, as the smiling waiter placed his drink before him. He sipped it, then glanced at the opposite page, the news page. This contained two double-column heads. On the left PARLIAMENT DISSOLVED, with below A NOVEMBER ELECTION. This Patrick already knew, for an excited Englishman had spent the morning trotting about the island, apprising his compatriots, friends and strangers alike, of the news. The other major item, on the right-hand side of the page, was, however, new to Patrick. RUSSIA ANNOUNCES UNILATERAL NUCLEAR DISARMAMENT: MR KORNOLOFF SAYS: 'UP TO US AND BRITAIN NOW.'

And Patrick's immediate reaction was to say to himself: "Thank God!" He read:

Moscow, Oct. 16th.

In a speech in the Great Hall of Moscow University Mr Kornoloff addressed the political, cultural, and scientific leaders of the Soviet Union, as well as many representatives from the Eastern European countries and China, on the subject of peace. Amidst mounting applause he told his distinguished audience that the Soviet Union, wearied by the long series of fruitless Summit Conferences and by the complete lack of progress in the disarmament talks that have been going on for the last seven years, has decided to force the issue by herself disarming unilaterally. This, he said, would be done by stages, and the first stage had already

35

begun, with the dismantling of the rocket bases in the People's Republic of Poland. Journalists and others from all lands would be permitted, and indeed encouraged, to visit the rocket bases and see the work of demolition now being carried out. The next step would be the dismantling of the missile bases in the other Warsaw Pact countries, and then in the Soviet Union itself. Mr Kornoloff said that he had every reason to believe that Russia's great peace-loving ally, the People's Republic of China, was contemplating taking a similar step. However, the final scrapping of all missile bases would naturally depend on some measure of similar disarmament on the part of the United States, Britain and other NATO powers. As soon as nuclear disarmament was achieved, the Soviet Union proposed to disband its conventional armed forces. Mr Kornoloff said that never before in history had such a gesture for peace been made. Since this staged disarmament would be carried out in full view of the world Press, this should dispose once and for all of the malicious American slander that the Soviet Union had no intention of truly disarming. The Soviet Union, he said, stood now, as it had always stood, for peace. It was now up to others to prove that their past statements were more than mere lip-service paid to this great ideal which, in Soviet Russia, was a proven reality. Mr Kornoloff spoke for five hours. (The text of his speech is given on Page 4.)

And, below, under the head AMERICA TAKEN BY SURPRISE, Patrick read:

The President has so far refused to comment on the surprise Soviet move. It is known, however, that the State Department regards Mr Kornoloff's speech with a measure of scepticism. A State Department spokesman said: "We'll believe it when we see it."

Oh Lord, thought Patrick, don't say they're going to miss this chance too. Really, he thought, the immobility and pigheadedness of the State Department are truly incredible. The Russians offer peace, complete peace, and what do they say?

'They'll believe it when they see it.' God, he thought, don't they know what war is like? If they'd been in Korea they wouldn't be quite so supercilious. But then, he thought, maybe they had been in Korea. But Good God. . . .

He looked up and saw Nora coming around the corner into the piazza. And he thought, for God's sake let's have peace, real peace. Let's be done once and for all with the endless threat. It was a threat that he envisaged quite specifically. It was the threat of things being done to her wonderful, beautiful body comparable to what had been done to his, all those years ago, in Korea. This was to him an absolutely intolerable thought.

At this same hour another Englishman, even farther from home, was reading the news of Kornoloff's speech.

Summer does not linger on, after the autumnal equinox, north of the Arctic circle. It was cold and almost dark on the island of Novaia Zemlia, when Mark Vernon and the other ninety-nine men of his 'hundred' were dismissed outside their barrack hut. The senior prisoner or 'brigadier', a former German SS officer by the name of Pfeiffer, had checked their work norms. Mark had completed his, having moved the regulation six cubic metres of rocky earth where the great underground installations were to be. He would therefore get his full litre of fish soup that evening, and he still possessed a third of the kilo of bread that was handed out before the beginning of the ten-hour work-day. Other members of this 'Foreigners' Hundred' had been less lucky. The Hungarian Professor of Philosophy was already almost too weak to work: he would be lucky if he got a half-litre. And Pfeiffer always swindled the three Rumanian Zionists. He had an understandable grudge against the Jews. Had the Jews never existed Pfeiffer would not have been ordered to supervise their extermination at Auschwitz: had he not been at Auschwitz, it was unlikely that he would have spent the past seventeen years in a succession of Russian camps: therefore he plagued and persecuted the Jewish members of his 'Hundred' whenever the opportunity arose, cheating them of their rations, giving them the rockiest ground to dig, and insulting them on every possible occasion.

He used to maintain that Hitler had made one great mistake: he hadn't gassed the lot.

Having spent almost his entire adult life in concentration camps, in one capacity or the other, Pfeiffer was the obvious choice for brigadier. And he carried out his duties conscientiously and with extreme thoroughness. Despite the language problem—no less than twenty-four nationalities were represented in this barrack—their work norm was consistently higher than that of the ninety-nine Russian barracks which together formed Block C of sub-camp 17 of the Novaia Zemlia complex of camps. He saw to it that the hut was kept clean, or at least as clean as was possible when the only cleaning utensils were cold water, carbolic acid and bare hands. Woe betide any inmate of the Foreigners' Hut who failed to fold his blanket exactly as laid down in German Army regulations by exactly six am! He would soon feel the weight of Pfeiffer's fists. Talking was strictly prohibited after ten pm. And of course any criticism of the camp or of the Soviet régime was reported at once to the Russian authorities, which ensured immediate, drastic punishment (either in the form of a beating or of solitary confinement in an underground hole without food). He had even reported one of the Jews for 'not looking happy' when listening to a Kornoloff speech relayed over the camp loudspeaker. The Jew had been gone for three hours, and had returned minus three teeth.

In the Russian prisoners' huts there was filth and disorder, shouting and screaming, frequent fights over the bodies of the hundred women prisoners who cooked the fish soup for the ten thousand men. Very often the RKK guards themselves would have to intervene, with rifle butts and whips, to restore order. Not so in Pfeiffer's hut, where prevailed the perfect order of a tomb. Quietly and methodically the men of the Foreign Hundred performed their work norms: quietly and inconspicuously they grew thinner, developed the symptoms of distrophy and vitamin deficiencies, and died. The RKK men had no reason to complain of Pfeiffer, whom they treated, quite rightly, almost as an equal. Occasionally they even gave him a bottle of vodka.

Although he hated Pfeiffer with a violence that he hadn't

felt for any living human being since his father's death, Mark was in a way grateful for this iron discipline. And he had another reason for gratitude. Because Mark had blue eyes (his head and body, of course, were shaven against the lice) Pfeiffer recognized in him a fellow-Nordic. And as such he looked after him, seeing that he got the softest ground to dig and not being as meticulous about his work norm as he was with the others. Last summer he had ordered the son of the former Republican Spanish Minister for Cultural Affairs to vacate his place at the end of the top row in the barrack hut, and had given it to Mark. This meant that he was next to the door, and so got a little fresh air and a little less stench of the bodies packed side by side on the three wooden platforms. In the centre of the hut at midsummer that stench was almost intolerable. Pfeiffer slept on the other side of the door. In the winter they would move back into the middle, for warmth.

The prisoners were hobbling into their hut, to lie down for a while, or to kill lice, before falling in again with their tin mugs for the march to the cookhouse. Mark waited for them to be gone. Pfeiffer spoke to him:

"I have vodka. I shall give you some."

"Thank you," said Mark, and felt a slight flicker of pleasure. Pfeiffer pushed his way through the prisoners, into the hut.

Vodka, thought Mark. Drink. How he used to love it, and what gallons, hogsheads, cellars full, he must have drunk in his time. Beer in English country pubs, wines and ports at Cambridge, whisky and sodas in his London club, dry martinis at the Washington cocktail parties, vodka and Caucasian brandy during those first years in Moscow. And now an inch of bad vodka in a tin mug once a month was bliss.

Drink had really, in a way, got him here. The first of the scandals had been brought about because he was drunk in his office at Teheran one afternoon when the Minister sent for him. Back in London, he had been severely reprimanded for arriving at a party, at which two senior members of the FO were present, drunk and accompanied by a young Negro with whom he was living. What concern was it of theirs what he did off duty? In his mind his superiors came more and more to fill that role of stern and hateful parent that had been vacant since his father's death. It was as much to spite them as for any other reason that he had listened, usually late at night, to Raymond Buler's wild talk about a new social order, and at last had agreed to supply O'Mahony with certain classified information. Then there had been the scandal in America with the lift boy, and his quick return to the FO. Finally, when the CID man called, and asked him if he knew Buler, he had drunk a bottle of whisky, and had thought, alone in his flat, of the enormous harm he could do those parental inquisitors by simply crossing into Soviet territory. And what a welcome he would receive!

"Here," said Pfeiffer, who had come out of the hut carrying a half-full bottle. Pfeiffer took a swallow and passed it to Mark. He wiped the top of the neck with the palm of his hand and raised it to his lips.

"Enough," said Pfeiffer.

There was nothing to sit on, so they stood. While Pfeiffer drank again, Mark glanced towards the copy of *Pravda* pasted upon the wall of the barrack hut, and felt the warmth of the vodka beginning to glow within him. How dearly he would love another swallow, three more, a whole bottle, six bottles, amidst talk and music and maybe sex, and then total anaesthesia. At least in Moscow there had been plenty of vodka, too much really for his job as adviser on British foreign policy. As his knowledge became rustier, and the bottles piled up in the corner of his dingy hotel room, he had sunk to more menial tasks, principally translating. Then, with the great purge that followed the end of Khrushchev, he had simply been swept up, as were so many others, like dust, and deposited here. The first year had been awful. But he had survived, and would now survive. All he now hoped for was that Pfeiffer might give him another drink.

Pfeiffer knocked the cork back in the bottle.

"Not," he said, "comparable to our good German *schnapps*."

"No," said Mark.

"But good," said Pfeiffer, frowning at this imputation, on Mark's part, of inferiority in any Russian product.

"Indeed," said Mark, "very good."

Pfeiffer frowned again, then walked into the hut to hide his bottle. Mark moved across to the wall and began idly to glance at the copy of *Pravda*. That was how this other Englishman read the news of Kornoloff's great speech for peace. Then he collected his tin mug and fell in with his fellow-prisoners for the long march to the cookhouse.

That evening every man or woman who was a candidate, or seemed likely to be a candidate, in the forthcoming election received an identical letter. It was headed AGAINST THE BOMB COMMITTEE. On the top right-hand side were the names of the members and honorary members of this committee (no distinction being made) and these included some of the most distinguished persons, many of a very advanced age, in Britain. Also included were Leonard Braithwaite, FRSJ, MP, Canon Christian, DD, Victor Cockshore, CH, CBE, Nobel Prize-winner, Miss Antonia May, and Rupert Page-Gorman, MP, in that order, scattered among the others, for the list was alphabetical. The letters, which were typed individually, or at least appeared to be so, read:

Dear Mr ——:
We the above have reason to believe that you are standing as candidate for —— in the forthcoming election. In view of Mr Kornoloff's declaration of unilateral nuclear disarmament by the Soviet Union, we wish to know whether you favour a similar policy for this country, and if you are prepared to support such a policy if elected.
It is our belief that the present conjuncture of events offers an opportunity for ridding the world once and for all of these monstrous weapons of mass annihilation such as has never occurred before and is unlikely ever to occur again. We are therefore prepared to put the full strength of our movement, which counts over one and one half million paid-up members as well as many millions of sympathizers, behind any candidate, regardless of party, who will subscribe to the following:
(1) That this country will immediately cease from manufacturing all weapons of war with an atomic or thermo-nuclear warhead.

(2) That this country will destroy all stocks of such weapons both in this country and in the colonies and dependent territories.

(3) That all such weapons in the possession of the British Armed Forces at present stationed abroad will be brought back to Britain and destroyed.

(4) That no foreign power be henceforth permitted to operate rocket bases, heavy bombers capable of delivering nuclear attacks, or nuclear-armed submarines from British or dependent territories or in British or dependent territorial waters.

We are not a political movement and your views on all other matters are of no concern to us. In the event of rival candidates both announcing that they are 'anti-nuclear bomb' we will give our support to both in equal measure.

A mass meeting will be held, in the Albert Hall, at 8 pm on Friday, 25th October, when it will be announced which candidates have so far accepted our appeal in the name of humanity and civilization. We hope that yours will be among them. If it is, you will no doubt wish to be present at that meeting, when we shall discuss how best we can present our and your views in the present campaign. If you cannot attend, or have any questions that you wish to ask of us, please write to the Secretary, and if need be a member of the committee will call on you at your convenience.

For peace and freedom!

Signed: illegible
Secretary

That evening the Shadow Cabinet met to discuss tactics in the election. The general line had, of course, already been laid down at the party conference in September: the nationalization of sugar, steel, road transport and, in the interests of the people's health, of the cosmetics industry: the increase in old-age pensions and family allowances: a capital gains tax and a taxing of expense accounts, to cover these: school reform in the interest of increased social equality: and a long-range plan to turn the Lancashire cotton-spinners and the Welsh miners into, respectively, food-packagers (the food thus packaged to be exported to the underdeveloped countries) and oil-refiners.

It was decided, at this meeting, to make the most of the police scandals in the forthcoming campaign, and to pin the blame for these on the outgoing government, not upon the police. To win the respectable lower middle-class vote, great emphasis was to be placed in their constituencies upon the need for a 'moral re-birth' of Britain, with the re-introduction of the licensing laws partly abolished by the last government and other measures which could be referred to collectively as 'sweeping reforms'. Since the working class were now so well off, envy of the even better-off middle class was really the only constructive appeal. And finally John Maynard, the leader of the Opposition, picked up the letter he had received a few hours ago from the AGAINST THE BOMB COMMITTEE, and asked:

"Did you all get one of these?"

The Shadow Cabinet nodded or murmured that they had— all, that is, save the shadow Minister of Works, who was old and deaf.

"One of what?" he asked petulantly. "One of what?"

The letter was passed to him. He peered at it.

"But it's addressed to you," he said, glancing over the top of his spectacles at the leader of the Opposition. "Why should I get it?"

Then, while the old man read the letter, John Maynard made the sort of remark which had won him his reputation for understatement.

"It puts us," he said, "in a bit of a spot."

The Prime Minister and his colleagues also discussed the letter that evening, but far more briefly.

"Cranks," said the Prime Minister. "Always had them with us, always will. Part of the English way of life. But politically quite irrelevant. The country, thank God, is sound."

And they went on to talk about their forthcoming TV appearances.

4

FOR THE first time the election was held on a Saturday, a cold and drizzly day. Next morning one of the Sunday papers ascribed the result, at least in part, to this innovation, pointing out that while many middle-class people went away for their weekends, the working class would be at home and, since the introduction of the forty-hour week, at liberty to go to the polls at any time of the day that suited them. But this seemed a very far-fetched explanation. The last public opinion samples immediately before the balloting began had forecast, roughly, 43% Labour, 41% Conservative, 8% Liberal, and the remainder undecided. It was therefore confidently assumed, in view of the way the constituencies were laid out, that either Labour would win by a small majority, perhaps as few as ten seats, or that the Conservatives would form a new government with Liberal support. None of this came true.

Nora was at her husband's home, Broadacres, on election evening. Rehearsals were going well, Patrick was at Bourne End, and Felix had spoken of her duty to vote. So, to please him, she had come. They had driven in the Rolls to the polling booth in the morning and she had cast her vote for that nice young schoolmaster, who was standing as Liberal and Anti-Nuclear Bomb. It was, she knew, a vote wasted. Admiral Sir Guy Barnaby was bound to get in, as usual, with a thumping majority. Nor did she tell Felix that she had voted for the Liberal. It would merely have upset him, and after all she had only voted in the first place to please him. He had so clearly regarded their little expedition to the polling booth, with the maids in the back of the car, as a symbolic act, as part of what being an English country gentleman with a proper sense of responsibility entailed; the political equivalent of going to church or, in his case, to Mass. But not to have voted for Guy would have been tantamount, in his eyes, to giving the wrong responses during a religious service.

Thus, after lunch, they had been out pigeon-shooting, or rather she had walked over the grounds with him while he had banged away from time to time at the birds that rose with such a dry, card-boardy whirring from the autumnal dripping trees. Keeping down the pigeons was a duty both to himself and to his neighbours. Once, years ago, when she had said that she liked their roucoucouling in the spring, he had told her quite categorically that they were vermin—like rats. She never made that sort of remark these days.

Tomorrow they would drive over to Toddy's school, and take him out to lunch. Nora was looking forward to that. The little boy had been homesick at first, but had quickly adjusted himself to school life. There was only one very slight shadow over the school visit. In his last letter Toddy had written at some length about a truly magnificent conker that he had, apparently, purchased from a boy called Roundwood Minor. He was anxious to bring this Roundwood Minor out to lunch on Sunday. And he ended by saying: 'Roundwood Minor said I am a You. What can this mean?'

She and Felix had discussed this problem briefly, over dinner.

"What will you say, if he asks that question tomorrow, Felix?"

"I shall say that he is an Englishman and a Catholic."

"But don't you think you should explain a little more?"

"The child is too young to understand."

"If they are saying that sort of thing to him, isn't it only fair to let him know what they mean?"

"I think perhaps I had better have a word with the head-master."

"You mean get Mr Smythe to explain to him?"

There was a faint note of disapproval in her voice. Felix instantly sensed it, and looked up from his plate.

"No," he said. "But I feel he should explain to Roundwood Minor."

"Oh, no darling," she said, with sudden intensity. "You mustn't do that. It would sound as though Toddy had been telling tales."

Felix was silent for a moment.

"Very well, then," he replied. "I won't."

And for the rest of the meal they had discussed the new chimney-piece in the saloon, or eaten in silence.

Now they were seated in the library, listening to the election results. At first they had watched the television programme, which had been interrupted every time a result came in so that this might be flashed upon the screen. This had been slightly disconcerting, and the television programme had been an interminable variety turn, a sort of endless Pierrots-on-the-pier act, which had utterly bored them both. So she had asked Felix to switch to BBC sound, where they were playing music. At the moment it was Prokofieff's Fifth Symphony, played with an extreme and haunting elegance by the Leningrad Symphony Orchestra. And somehow the gentle fading out of the music, the announcement of the result in the announcer's impersonal voice, and the welling up of the music again, did not seem wrong. Nora sat in a deep leather armchair, knitting. She knew that it pleased Felix to see her knit, and indeed it was he who had first encouraged her to do so, before Toddy was born. And as she knitted she wondered vaguely about Toddy, and Patrick, and her part. Felix was seated at his huge desk, glancing through some papers. It was all most restful and soothing. The music faded out.

"Ballyrickey. P. Slattery, Liberal and Anti-Nuclear Bomb, eight thousand, six hundred and seventy-nine: Squadron-Leader H. Thomas, Conservative, seven thousand, three hundred and four. Liberal gain from Conservative." The slow movement was back again, powerful and gentle.

No, she thought, she could not destroy Felix by destroying his home, much as she loved Patrick. It would be a crime, which she and Patrick (and, who knows, perhaps Toddy as well) would have to expiate. And Felix was so good, never referring to their intimate relationship, though surely he must suspect, must have suspected something ever since that night when he had wished to come to her room. She had said then—and this was a year before she became Patrick's mistress—that she did not wish to have another baby, that indeed, in view of her commitments on the stage she could not. He had answered that, though a Catholic, there were ways of ensuring that she did not become pregnant. She had replied, it was not really that. And he had immediately understood. That night she had awoken at three and had, much to her

46

surprise, cried until half past five. Felix had never asked her again.

The music faded.

"Gloucester Central. R. Colman, Labour and Anti-Nuclear Bomb, fourteen thousand, six hundred and forty-three: Miss Margaret Ryder, Conservative, twelve thousand, three hundred and ninety-nine. Labour gain from Conservative."

The music returned. Felix looked up from his desk, and said:

"I don't like the way it's going at all." And then: "I think it might be advisable to buy more of that Canadian stock." And then: "For Toddy, you understand."

Nora said nothing, went on knitting, and wished she were with Patrick.

In New York City it was five-thirty. The very important financier whom Mr Cuthbertson called G.W. had two ticker tapes in his outer office: one was a direct line from the Stock Exchange, the other a general news tape such as are to be found in most clubs and in a very few offices. It was at this second tape that he and Mr Cuthbertson were looking. The machine was temporarily silent. Now it began to tick again, the broad band of white paper moving jerkily beneath its glass. They read: BR. ELEC. WEST WILTS ADM BARNABY CONS NO CHANGE. It stopped, as if for breath, then began again laboriously BR. ELEC. 2230 GMT STATE OF POLL LAB 98 CONS 72 LIB 2, LAB GAINS 23 LOSSES 4, CONS GAINS 3 LOSSES 24, LIB GAINS 2. The paper shot up an inch, and with a light sigh the machine fell silent.

G.W. was a very tall, very thin man in his seventies. He wore a grey suit that almost exactly matched his grey hair, and rimless spectacles. He had a hearing aid which functioned perfectly. He now turned to Cuthbertson and said:

"This is considerably more serious than you led me to expect, George."

"I don't believe anyone expected it, G.W."

G.W. glanced out of the window. They were forty floors up. Far away, beyond the other skyscrapers, the late afternoon sun caught Brooklyn Heights.

"Will you be in New York tomorrow?"

"Yes."

"Because I think we may have to reconsider the whole matter of our investment in British Fuelless."

Cuthbertson drew in his breath sharply:

"But we've already——"

"Cutting your losses, George, is also an art. Do you play poker?"

"Very occasionally."

"I don't suppose I've touched a card in thirty years. But were I to do so, I believe I'd still know when to throw my hand in. Would you mind coming to my apartment at a quarter after eleven tomorrow morning? And perhaps you could ask Willis to be there too."

"Why certainly, G.W."

The ticker tape had begun to stutter again, but neither man looked at it.

At Bourne End it was a comparatively small weekend party, just Jack and Moyra, Jack's secretary who had driven down in her little TR 7 after voting at her home in Ealing, a French commercial artist, who was doing some layouts for Jack, and Patrick. Despite the Sunday newspaper columnist, the several other guests whom Moyra had invited had declined, since it was their intention to vote. Patrick, being a baron in the peerage of the United Kingdom, did not have a vote, even though he had never taken his seat in the House of Lords.

Jack's secretary was reading a novel in the corner of the drawing-room, while the other four played bridge. The television set was on, with the sound turned down, so that they could see the election results flashed upon the board but did not have to hear the stale music and the archly indecent jokes of the comedian. Since, however, they kept glancing at the lines of kicking, top-hatted girls or at the fifteen-year-old youth clutching his microphone, while they awaited the next result, it was a disjointed game.

"Whose deal is it?" asked Jack.

"I dealt last," said the Frenchman.

"Did you? I thought Jack did," said Moyra.

48

"There's another one," said Patrick, and they all turned to look at the screen, which had momentarily gone blank. The results given on TV were more elaborate than the bald announcements on sound radio, and had indeed been modelled on Test Match scoreboards. Now this one was flashed on, and they read:

THAXSTEAD (Essex)

Leonard BRAITHWAITE, Labour and Anti-Nuclear
    Bomb: 24,657
L. T. S. Brown, Conservative: 7,542
J. Sharpe, Liberal and Anti-Nuclear Bomb: 3,154
Last Election
Braithwaite, Labour: 18,673
Brown, Conservative: 12,895
Percentage of electorate voting: 89·73
Result shows: NO CHANGE
The Liberal candidate forfeits his deposit.

The announcement remained on the screen for approximately one minute while the announcer, inaudible to the bridge-players, read it aloud—presumably in the interests of the illiterate members of the electorate or perhaps of the blind. Then it flashed off and the crooner was on again.

Patrick imitated Braithwaite's celebrated West Country drawl: "I can speak for the people because I am of the people."

Jack said:

"Or as somebody commented, *le canaille c'est moi.*"

The Frenchman smiled, perhaps to hear his native tongue mangled as only Jack Beaulieu could mangle it. Patrick said:

"They all seem to be getting in, those anti-bomb boys and girls."

Moyra said:

"I'm so sorry Antonia May couldn't be here this weekend. It would have been most interesting to hear what she had to say. But it seems she promised to go down to her brother-in-law's."

"To Broadacres?" Patrick asked, with some surprise.

Moyra looked at him sharply.

"That's right. Didn't Nora tell you?"

Jack said:

"I can't believe that the result will affect our foreign policy. Maynard has said over and over again that he'll stop making the bombs, but that he absolutely won't scrap our bases, or the American ones."

Patrick said:

"He'll have a hard time getting Honest Len the People's Friend to accept that line."

"Why should he bother? Braithwaite isn't in the Shadow Cabinet."

Moyra said:

"Whose deal is it?"

The crooner was faded out, and another announcement appeared. It proclaimed a thumping Conservative majority, even larger than last time, in a south coast seaside resort.

"God bless the landladies," said Jack. "The only really solid support the Tories still have. Takes more than a hydrogen bomb to put the wind up them."

"Perhaps they foresee massive evacuations from the cities, both winter and summer," remarked Patrick. "Whose deal is it?"

"I don't think you should joke about it," snapped Moyra, to Patrick's complete astonishment. Jack looked almost equally surprised, and said quickly:

"Neither do I. If Labour gets in with a big majority, God knows what they'll do over the next five years. Inflation, flight from the pound, import restrictions, all that stuff all over again. Already the Americans seem to be playing for time, waiting to see what the result will be. Those British Fuelless Car people——"

Moyra interrupted:

"It's difficult enough playing bridge with this election all the time. If you're planning to talk business too. . . ."

"Sorry, Moyra. But honestly I'm worried."

Patrick said:

"I haven't noticed any stalling so far as BFC go. They're on to me at least six times a day."

Jack snubbed him, gently:

"You don't deal with the financiers, Patrick. Neither do I. But Leavenport was saying——"

Again Moyra interrupted:

"For heaven's sake, let's either play bridge or chuck the whole game. It *is* my deal, isn't it?"

And without waiting for a reply, she began to deal quickly and efficiently, the cards coming from between her fingers in one unbroken stream. The Frenchman smiled at her. The two other men had swivelled in their chairs, staring at the TV screen where another result was being announced.

In the 'Foreigners' Hut' of Block C, Sub-Camp 17, Labour Camp Novaia Zemlia, all was quiet save for a little snoring and for the whimpering of Ali, the Iraqi boy. Since none could speak his language, the other foreigners did not know what misdemeanour or misunderstanding had brought this olive-skinned youth from the edge of the Arabian desert to this other desert of ice and snow. They did know that he cried himself to sleep every night, and that he could not fulfil his work norm, and that therefore he soon must die. Otherwise all was quiet in the hut, where Pfeiffer and his Nordic protégé now slept in the middle, while outside fell the muffling snow. It was two o'clock Moscow time.

Suddenly all was confusion, noise, flashing torches, and the dull glow of the 25-watt bulbs upon the ceiling. The four RKK men were stamping the snow from their boots, their shoulders and caps still white with it, the steel of their fixed bayonets gleaming harshly.

"Pfeiffer!" they shouted. "Where is the brigadier?"

Pfeiffer sat up at once, to attention as it were.

"The Englishman," they shouted at him. "We want the Englishman, Vernon."

"Oh, no!" said Vernon. "I've done nothing."

But they had found him, and were half dragging him from the boards on which he had been dreaming some vague, English, seaside dream. They pushed him and hustled him as he tried to climb into his threadbare overcoat and his wooden clogs.

"Pfeiffer," he called despairingly to his protector, "It must be a mistake! I've done nothing!"

"Discipline!" roared Pfeiffer. "*Mach schnell, mach schnell!*"

And then, before Mark Vernon could find his ragged neckerchief, they had dragged him from the hut, out into the wind and the snow, and were marching him, one each side, one in front and one behind—whither?

To his death, he must assume, for this was the time when they came for the condemned.

It happened quite frequently. In European Russia or in Siberia a *troika*, consisting of the local head of the OGPU (or NKVD or RKK, according to what the current name for the political police might be), the head of the Criminal Investigation Section of the local militia, and the local public prosecutor, would meet in secret and pass administrative sentence. Their victim would be sent to a camp perhaps two thousand miles away, while his dossier would go to Moscow. Five, ten, even twenty years later an official at the ministry might well come upon the dossier and notice, to his consternation, that the offence for which the man had been punished with imprisonment was now of a capital nature. Orders would therefore be sent to the camp to clear up this administrative irregularity, and at two or three o'clock in the morning the man would be dragged from his hut, taken to the headquarters of Department III (the RKK section within the camp), identified, and shot in the back of the neck. When Moscow received the report of this, the anomalous file could be closed, stamped FINALIZED, and placed in the archives.

So far as Mark Vernon could tell through the whirling snow, it was to Department III that he was being taken, his teeth chattering in his head not only from cold but also from fear. This must be it. This must be the end. It was for this his gentle mother had borne him to the husband whom she loathed: for this had he gone to prep school in his grey flannel suit and learned the letters of the Greek alphabet and the past subjective of *s'apercevoir* and how to prove the pleasant theorems of Euclid, and had been invariably top of his class: for this had he won scholarships and passed examinations and been awarded a first class honours degree at Cambridge: for this had he loved Mozart and understood about abstract painting and been dressed by the best tailors in London and amused the cleverest people; in order that he might be led away, in the middle of the Arctic night, and shot in the back of the neck.

He stumbled, half fell, and felt the prick of the bayonet in the hands of the man behind. He hurried on, and now, for the first time in many years, he tried to pray: 'Our Father which art in heaven, hallowed be Thy name, Thy kingdom come, Thy will be done . . .' He could remember no more. So he prayed instead to his mother, and vividly pictured the nursery fire, with the high wire screen that fitted over it to stop him burning himself. He was hustled on, between the vague outlines of the huts. He had no wish to die.

And then they were there, in a corridor pungent with coarse tobacco smoke, where other soldiers lounged on benches. And now he was being pushed into a brilliantly lighted room. Three men were seated at a table, and behind him, he knew, stood his escort. They would not shoot him here. It would make too much mess. It was a tiny reprieve.

The three men were in the uniform of the RKK. So this must be the fatal Department III. The one in the middle, a major with a pock-marked face, looked up and said:

"Mark Vernon?"

"*Da*," he said, "*Da*."

"You speak Russian?"

"*Da*."

"You were convicted, on 20th September, 1959, under Section 58, paragraph 14 of the Penal Code, of sabotage through drunkenness, in that the translations with which you were entrusted by the Ministry of External Affairs were carried out in a slipshod and inaccurate fashion calculated to cause harm to the work of the ministry and therefore to the Union of Soviet Socialist Republics. You were sentenced to twenty years' labour service. Your case has now been reviewed."

Yes, thought Vernon, reviewed and the sentence changed to death. It was extraordinary, if that was really the offence for which they had tried him, that he had not been shot at once. Sabotage was always a capital offence. But he must speak now. This was his only chance.

"I didn't mean," he began, "I had no intention of harming the great Soviet Union. . . ."

He stammered, and had difficulty with his Russian. He had spoken it so little during these last years, for with Pfeiffer it had always been German.

"Silence!" roared the major. "Your case has been reviewed, and it has been decided," he hesitated, glanced at a piece of paper on his desk, and exchanged a few whispered words with the colleague on his left. "Yes, it has been decided that the completion of your sentence will be postponed until such time as shall please the ministry. Do you understand what this means?"

"No, sir."

"It means that you will leave the camp now, but that you are still convicted of a crime. You will fly by the dawn plane to Moscow, where you will be put in the Lubianka prison. You have been in the Lubianka prison before?"

Mark nodded. It was very hot in this room, and he felt his head spinning. Were they taking him all the way to Moscow in order to shoot him there?

"In the Lubianka prison you will receive instructions concerning your further employment from a representative of the Ministry for External Affairs. Do you understand?"

Again Mark nodded. Did this mean, surely it must mean, that they were not now planning to kill him? He had heard of these cat-and-mouse games. They would put him back to translating, work him fifteen or eighteen hours a day, and with the knowledge hanging over his head that if he made a single mistake, he was already convicted of sabotage. But he would not make a mistake, he would live, for his prayer to his mother had been answered.

"And then," said the major, "when you shall have received your instructions from the representative of the Ministry of External Affairs, you will be sent to Britain."

Mark fainted.

In the library at Broadacres, the grandfather clock in the corner whirred and began, very softly and lowly, to strike the chimes of midnight. The election results now came almost without interruption from the wireless in the wall. Nora tucked her knitting away in her embroidered bag, walked across the room, and kissed Felix on the forehead.

"Don't move," she said. "Goodnight, Felix."

He smiled up at her, as she turned away towards the door, while his eyes went back to the wireless:

". . . . Labour gain from Conservative. Middlesbrough Central, S. Mackintosh, Labour and Anti-Nuclear Bomb, thirty-five thousand, eight hundred and . . ."

Quietly the clock struck ten, eleven, twelve. Nora closed the door behind her.

At Bourne End they had abandoned their game of cards, and were seated in a semi-circle facing the television set, which was now turned on for sound as well. Patrick sat next to Moyra, as they watched a well-known Cambridge don giving his impressions of the results so far received. He was saying:

". . . this is undoubtedly a great surprise for all. The electronic computer at Stafford, which, remember, is subject to a marginal error but which must decrease as it has a larger body of data to work on, now foresees a labour majority of approximately one hundred and twenty. This not only completely confounds all the pundits, including myself, but an even more surprising, er, result has been the great success of the Anti-Nuclear Bomb candidates. At the latest reckoning over seventy per cent of the Labour members elected, and all the Liberals, are pledged to nuclear disarmament. This will clearly pose considerable problems for Mr Maynard when he comes to form his government tomorrow."

The don vanished and a well-known newscaster's face, somewhat distraught, took his place. He said:

"And now we are taking you over to Dulwich South, where the result of the election in that constituency is just about to be announced."

Moyra remarked in a pleased voice:

"That's Rupert's constituency. What fun!"

And indeed there he was, on the front steps of a mock-Georgian public building, perhaps a town hall or a library or even a labour exchange. With him was an excessively pompous little man in a cocked hat, holding a piece of paper, and on the little man's other side, another man in a dark suit, presumably Rupert Page-Gorman's opponent. In the doorway behind them other figures could be seen indistinctly, Rupert looked very tired, and his expression was stern, as the official read out:

"Rupert Page-Gorman, Labour and Anti-Nuclear Bomb. seventeen thousand . . ."

His voice was drowned in a roar, and the camera now moved off Rupert's impassive face, to pan across the great crowd filling the street. They were cheering, waving handkerchiefs or perhaps banners, and here and there Patrick thought to see a clenched fist salute.

The camera left the crowd and returned to the little party on the steps. It closed on the official, whose voice was almost smothered by the crowd which was now, raggedly, beginning to sing the Red Flag. The number of votes cast for the defeated Conservative candidate was announced. Rupert had a a very large majority. Then the camera turned on him in close-up. He was smiling slightly, as he waved to the crowd. The camera drew back, and now other figures were visible, coming out of the building. Rupert turned his head, and there, immediately behind him, flushed, excited and rapt, was the unmistakable, rather plain face of Antonia May.

Patrick leaned forward to knock the ash off his cigarette. Out of the corner of his eye he saw Moyra's left hand, with the plain gold wedding ring and the large, yellow, solitaire diamond that Jack had given her on the occasion of their engagement. She was gripping the arm of her chair so hard that her knuckles were white as desert bones.

5

THE NEXT day being a Sunday there were no evening papers, and therefore not all the comings and goings of that busy morning and afternoon and evening were immediately reported, though TV did its best. It rained all morning, so that only comparatively small crowds in damp macintoshes collected in Downing Street and outside the Palace to see what is visible when one British Government replaces another.

They saw the outgoing Prime Minister, very spruce beneath a glistening top hat, give a friendly wave before stepping into his black Daimler at 11.45. He would have preferred to go to the Palace earlier so that he could get to Chequers for an early lunch, but had had to wait until the Royal Family had returned from Matins. He was, however, only with the Monarch for ten minutes, so his lunch was not delayed. At twelve o'clock the listless crowd grouped about the Queen Victoria statue gave a ragged cheer as a Ford Consul drove up to the gate, and was waved on by the policeman on duty. Although he clearly had an enormous amount of work to get through that day, this comparatively late hour suited John Maynard. He did not go to church save on official occasions of a public or private nature, such as coronations or christenings, but he did live rather a long way out in the country, at Harlow New Town, to be precise. This was something of a pose (as was the green Ford Consul, with Mrs Maynard at the wheel) but one that he felt paid political dividends. Now, of course, he would move to No 10, which would be much more convenient.

When the little green car nosed its way out through the great gates, half an hour later, John Maynard smiled and waved happily to the small, sodden crowd still standing there. A couple of Press photographers got a blurred picture, and a film camera turned briefly. The crowd cheered again, but now it had shrunk. Most of them had gone home to lunch or dinner, or to a pub. The green car moved off towards Transport House.

There had been no crowd outside the Treasury that morning to witness the unusual spectacle of high officials arriving at 9.30 am on a Sunday. Nor was there anyone to cheer the Governor of the Bank of England, when his enormous grey Rolls-Bentley deposited him there at 10.15.

Rupert Page-Gorman's flat was in an old, eighteenth-century building near Fitzroy Square. Once upon a time merchants had raised large families here, turning their children into members of the gentry and eventually of the aristocracy, thanks to the labour of coolies on plantations far away, and to the nautical skill of bearded sea-captains who sailed the great creaking clipper ships beneath their acres of sun-lit, salt-blown canvas, and to the skill, acumen and hard work of the merchants themselves. The merchants had long gone, and the square had crumbled away throughout the nineteenth century into respectable or less respectable lodging houses for clerks who kept the books for a new type of merchant, hard men who sold the pins that Birmingham made and the coal from Clydes-dale and the good broadcloth from Yorkshire, and whose children, in turn, had married into the gentry. Then the clerks had moved outwards, to Mr Pooter's London, and the artists had moved in. For a brief period these walls had re-echoed to late-night arguments about realism in the arts, and Whistler's latest spiky joke, and post-impressionism, and Roger Fry. Bearded men, earnestly Bohemian, had painted and written and talked here, had sometimes worn sandals, had pretended that their corner pub was another Nouvelles Athènes or Café Dôme. A few of their pictures still hung on the walls of the museums, more lay forgotten in the cellars of the Tate, while only scholars now read their passionate books. They themselves were forever underground. With the Second World War even the artists' epigoni left this quarter, and the merchants re-turned, but a new sort of merchant. On the ground floor of the house where lived Rupert Page-Gorman there was a firm called Calimax, Export-Import. They were very quiet. Rupert had the first floor, the *piano nobile*, while above him were Kacha-churian Carpets and, at the very top, The London Gusset Company. Occasionally, during the day, he would meet swarthy men on the stairs, sometimes carrying carpets. He never saw anybody carrying gussets, while from five o'clock on and all over the weekends the building was his alone. This suited him very well, as did the efficient charwoman who came every weekday morning, cooked his breakfast, and arranged about his laundry and the other boring trivia of a bachelor's life.

After the excitement and the shouting and the inevitable anticlimax down in South Dulwich, Rupert and Antonia had driven back to central London almost in silence, behind the windscreen wipers that flicked back and forth like Siamese-twin metronomes. Antonia could, for an essentially talkative woman, keep remarkably quiet at times. This late night drive was obviously such a time, for Rupert was exhausted. Quite apart from his own electoral campaign, had he not really been the driving force behind the whole of the Anti-Nuclear Bomb movement? Braithwaite had made many speeches, as had others of the movement, but it had ultimately been Rupert's job to co-ordinate, to arrange, in many cases to cajole. In all this Antonia had been invaluable, playing a veritable Berthier to his Bonaparte. But she had no illusions as to which role belonged to which of them. So, though she felt immensely proud and would, in a way, rather have enjoyed going to Braithwaite's little party, there to receive over cider cup or coffee the congratulations of her friends, she realized that this was a time for silence. Rupert hardly spoke at all. While crossing Waterloo Bridge he remarked, as much to himself as to her:

"And just as much to do tomorrow and the next day. If not more. This is only the beginning."

"Poor Rupert," she said softly. "You've eaten almost nothing all day."

It had been his intention, when they left Dulwich, to drive first to Chelsea and to drop Antonia at the block of service flats in which she lived. But like a tired horse heading for its stable, his car had automatically half-circled Bush House and was now moving up Aldwych.

"I'm so sorry," he said. "I'll go down Shaftesbury Avenue."

"Don't bother, Rupert. I can easily pick up a cab."

"No, no."

They drove on in silence. In Shaftesbury Avenue itself they came to a halt. As far ahead as they could see other cars were also waiting. The windscreen wipers flicked back and forth, back and forth, and the fingers of Rupert's gloved left hand beat a careful, impatient tattoo to their rhythm upon the top of his steering wheel. Antonia thought, what fine strong hands he has! She turned her head, and glanced out of the window, and her eye met a line of posters pasted to the palings that hid a building site. These portrayed, first, a huge rocket, then a mushroom-shaped cloud, then a mangled, dying child, then a city in flames, then a heap of corpses, then a blind man among ruins, then again the mushroom cloud and the rocket. Across each of these, diagonally: YOU WANT THIS? VOTE TORY. This had been one of Rupert's ideas, too.

Ahead, the cars began to toot their horns, and there was also the sound of shouting. Rupert opened his door and Antonia, imitating him, screwed down her window and poked her head out. There was clearly some sort of demonstration going on, down in Piccadilly Circus, perhaps a victory celebration, certainly not one that they had organized. And indeed such it was. They could hear distant voices chanting:

"*Down with the bomb! Down with the bomb!*"

And a hundred yards or so ahead a group, or chain, of men and women, or maybe of boys and girls, were running hand in hand, the long line snaking in and out among the frozen cars, while police blew on whistles and tried unsuccessfully to break it all up. The car immediately in front of Rupert's, which was a taxi, did a U-turn and headed back towards Cambridge Circus. Antonia said:

"If they recognize you, they'll never let you go."

The young people—it was impossible in the murk to tell whether they were the espresso bar lot or an altogether rougher crowd—were coming closer, still chanting. Antonia saw a policeman grab a girl.

"You're quite right," said Rupert, and turned to follow the taxi.

"Drive straight to your place, Rupert. I'll ring for a radio cab from there."

"Thank you, Antonia."

And so she found herself walking under the beautiful old fanlight, and climbing the wide, worn stone stairs, and even saying, as the artists had said seventy years before:

"At night this somehow seems more like Paris than London."

Rupert grunted, and put his key in the door. In the drawing-room he flicked on the lights and the mobile in the corner embarked upon its curious, convoluted circles. Rupert yawned, raised his hand to his mouth, then glanced at his fingers.

"Filthy, too," he murmured.

"Look, Rupert, let me get you something to eat. Have you any eggs?"

He nodded, smothering another yawn. Her tone was motherly, an unusual role for her and one in which she now found a delicate, delicious excitement.

"Go and take a bath. By the time you're out of it, I'll have some scrambled eggs ready for both of us. We can eat them in front of the fire, in here." And leaning down, she incisively switched on both bars of the electric fire. "You said you've got another long day tomorrow. You must eat something to-night."

"That would be lovely," he said. "You know where everything is?"

"I can find it. Go on, take your bath."

"Thank you, Antonia," little-boy like.

By the time that the electric cooker was warm, the butter, cream, salt and pepper ready to be melted in the saucepan, and the eggs to hand, she could hear, from the bathroom, the sound of gushing hot water. She placed the pan on the burner and slid the two slices of bread under the grill-toaster. Then she went into his bedroom.

He had simply stepped out of his trousers which stood, an untidy mound, upon the floor beside the great double-bed. She picked them up, extracted the underpants, folded both garments, and hung them over the back of a chair. She did likewise with the coat and tie and shirt, that had been tossed, higgledy-piggledy, across the counterpane. Finally she folded this up too, revealing a sea-green eiderdown. She could find no pyjamas. Presumably, she thought, he sleeps without them. She turned down the corner of the sheet and blankets, and lit the bedside lamp. As she did so, she noticed the photograph in the silver frame upon the bedside table. It was of Moyra Beaulieu. The soft, maternal glow quite vanished from Antonia May's eyes. But deliberately she recreated her former mood, as she switched off the overhead light and returned to the kitchen, just in time to prevent the toast from burning.

"Poor Rupert," she said to herself. "What a lonely, dedicated life he does lead."

Later, as he finished his eggs, seated in his heavy, scarlet towelling bathrobe across the fire from her, she thought again:

"How young he looks, like a sleepy little boy."

As if in answer to her thought, he said:

"That was delicious, Antonia."

"Would you like anything else? Some cheese?"

"I can hardly keep my eyes open."

"Go to bed, Rupert. I'll just finish this, and stack away, and then ring for a cab. I can let myself out."

"You're sure I can't . . ."

"No, no. Go to bed. It's nearly two."

"Do you know, Antonia, I think I will."

He got up, and leaned down to kiss her cheek. His bathrobe opened slightly as he did this, and she glimpsed, with momentary, passing revulsion, the black curly hairs upon his chest. She corrected her disloyal reaction. "Just like a little boy," she said to herself. "Just a little boy." And, aloud:

"Goodnight, Rupert. Sleep well."

Placidly she finished her eggs, then lit a cigarette and smoked it, her mind almost a complete blank. She had heard him switch off the light in his bedroom, so presumably he had not closed the door. She walked out into the passageway. Yes, the door to his bedroom was ajar, and the room in darkness save for the faint light that came from the window at the far side.

"Rupert," she said softly. "Are you asleep?"

There was no reply. So there was also no need for her to pretend to telephone for a taxi. She went back to the drawing-room, and began to undress. She did this neither with excessive haste, nor particularly slowly, but at her normal pace, methodically folding her clothes over the back of the sofa. When she was naked, she turned towards the old Spanish mirror, dark as a millpond, that hung above a book-laden table. She examined her body quite carefully.

Her breasts were small, smaller, she thought, than her sister Nora's, but firm. Perhaps because they hadn't been pulled around so by lovers and a sucking child. And the skin over her rounded belly was taut, remarkably so, she told herself, for a woman of thirty-five. With her narrow waist and the long, long curve of her hips, the body in the depths of the Spanish glass might have posed for Cranach. She loved this body of hers. And she raised her hands to her head, watching her breasts move as she did so. How unfair that she had not been given a face to match it, how terribly unfair. For she was sure that her body was in fact better than Nora's, which was too rounded, too soft, almost commonplace or chorus-girly, not at all Cranach-like. Antonia smiled at the Cranach lady in the glass, and the lady smiled back from beneath a snub nose and somewhat bulging eyes. Antonia turned away, switched out the light, and felt her way around the furniture.

In Rupert's bedroom she waited until her eyes had become accustomed to the faint light. Then she saw that he was lying, curled in the classic and embryonic position of the sleeper, on the far side of the bed. Very gently she loosened the sheet on this side, and slipped in. She lay beside him, on her back, conscious of the faint male smell mixed with soap that his body exuded. She did not close her eyes against the darkness.

She lay for a long time with her eyes open. How strange it all was, how mysterious and marvellous. She listened to the rain dripping from the eaves.

Rupert muttered incomprehensibly, in his sleep, then turned, and she felt a sudden alarm. But he was still asleep. His head was now resting against her shoulder. Again he moved in his sleep, and a heavy arm lay across her pelvis, and his head had slipped down until it was between those small, firm breasts. She lay motionless, her eyes open. Then slowly, slowly, she withdrew one hand from beneath the bedclothes and very gently touched the man's black, curly head of hair.

He nestled closer to her, his hand closing upon her flesh, and he murmured in his sleep:

"G'night, Moyra . . ."

She did not mind. Nothing mattered. This was a moment of perfection, of utter triumph. It was a long time before she fell asleep.

She awoke in a panic. A hand was closed tightly over her

left breast, a hot, rigid thing was pressing against her hip, a leg was forcing itself between her legs, thrusting them apart, a heavy body was crawling over hers, to smother and destroy her. She was instantly wide awake, in the pale dawn light.

"No, Rupert, no!"

Instantly he stopped, and she realized that he had been almost totally asleep.

"What . . .?" he asked, thickly. Then less thickly: "What on earth . . .?"

"I couldn't get a taxi, Rupert. Go back to sleep."

"I didn't . . ."

"It doesn't matter. Go back to sleep."

He turned on to his other side at once, and she too turned her back on him. Surprisingly enough, she almost immediately, and happily, slept.

Indeed, when she at last awoke it was broad daylight, and Rupert was no longer beside her. She saw by the bedside clock that it was after nine. From the kitchen came the smell of bacon frying and of coffee. Antonia felt deliriously happy. She hugged herself in bed.

"Rupert!" she called. "Rupert!"

He appeared in the doorway, in trousers and shirt.

"Breakfast is nearly ready," he said, sharply and factually.

"Can I borrow your dressing-gown, please?"

He went to the bathroom, came back and tossed the heavy red towelling bathrobe across the foot of the bed.

He had made no further reference to her unexpected presence in his bed, and indeed they had not talked over breakfast, for there were all the newspapers to be gone through, rapidly. With half a dozen results still to come from the most outlying constituencies, it was plain that Labour had a majority of between one hundred and thirty-five and one hundred and thirty-eight. It was total victory for the party and, perhaps even more, for the Anti-Nuclear Bomb movement. TOTAL VICTORY said the banner headline in *Reynolds's News*. Antonia, still in the red bathrobe, picked up the *Sunday Express*, BLACK SUNDAY, it said. And she glanced across at the man who, more she thought than anyone else, was responsible for it all. He was frowning over the leader on the inside page of the *Observer*.

She could see the headline on the front page: A PLAIN MAN-DATE AGAINST THE BOMB.

Just like husband and wife, thought Antonia, over breakfast with the Sunday papers. She smiled and picked up the *Sunday Pictorial*: WE'RE IN! it said. The telephone rang:

"Yes," said Rupert. "Yes, I was coming along anyhow. Yes, I can be there by ten-fifteen."

He immediately got up, and walked out of the room. When he came back he was knotting his tie, his jacket over one arm.

"If anyone rings before you go," he said, "you might tell them I've gone to Transport House. If it's the papers, say I don't know when I'll be free, but I'll do my best to give any interviews this evening."

He walked out into the hall, and called, as he climbed into his overcoat:

"And I imagine we'll have to have a meeting of the committee this evening. I'll know when I've seen Braithwaite. Where will you be?"

"I shall tidy up here and then go home." Her voice, in contrast to his, was sweetly domestic.

"Right." He was at his desk now, putting papers into his big yellow briefcase. "If you go out, leave a number with the answering service where you can be got hold of. I don't know what time we'll ring."

"Yes Rupert."

"Goodbye for now, then."

And with scarcely a nod he was out of the flat, and the heavy door had slammed behind him.

"Just like a husband," she thought, "just like a husband hurrying away to his office." With only this added, she told herself, that he was probably at this moment one of the most powerful men in England. But with a smile she corrected herself, or rather reminded herself that women are apt to exaggerate their men's importance.

She smiled again, stretched, and reached for a cigarette. She had no intention of leaving Rupert's flat in a precipitate hurry. After all, what was there waiting for her in *her* flat? Nothing, save the proof of next month's copy of *Minos*, a magazine of which she was sub-editor, her diary, which she had neglected during these last thrilling weeks, and her own reflection in the mirror. She picked up the *Observer* and began to read the article that had so interested Rupert. It interested her, too.

At approximately the hour when John Maynard was arriving at the Palace on that Sunday morning, and while Antonia May was slowly and voluptuously finishing the washing-up in Rupert Page-Gorman's kitchen, and while Felix Seligman with solemn care was asking that potential anti-semite, Round-wood Minor, how he did, Patrick Clonard threw down the *Sunday Times* in Jack Beaulieu's drawing-room at Bourne End, and said:

"I've got an idea."

Jack looked up.

"In the decade and more of our pleasant and profitable association, you have had many. But this, my boy, is likely to be the best yet."

Jack loved old jokes. This was a formula joke.

"Coming, Moyra?" he asked.

She was seated at a small desk, apparently doing sums.

"I don't think so, Jack."

"What about the Frenchman?" asked Patrick.

"In the first place, he's working for me, and therefore should on no account be interrupted. In the second place, even the best of Frenchmen make the most absurd faces when given a pint of bitter. We'll leave him here."

"Walk or car?" asked Patrick.

"Walk. You're overweight already." This was another formula joke.

"I suppose," said Moyra, without turning her head, "that I can expect you two masters of the dying art of repartee back some time after two."

"That," said Jack, "would be a fairly safe bet."

As they walked along the tow-path beneath a very faint and watery sun that was just beginning to get the better of the eastward-moving clouds, Patrick said:

"What do you think of it, Jack?"

"At the moment, nothing. We'll have to though—think of it, I mean, but at the moment I'm dead sick of it. Maynard's

66

all right, I suppose, but some of those others are real shockers. Whether Maynard can control them. . . . Oh, let's talk about something else. Let's talk about sex."

"I decided, only the other day, that I really don't know anything about sex, except that I'm generally for it, in a vague sort of way."

"Are you?" said Jack, looking at him sharply. "Are you? I too was thinking, only the other day, that the Almighty, or whoever it was who worked the system out, really should have tried a bit harder."

"I suppose that when he thought of the basic idea he was so impressed by the magnificence and glory and fun of it, that he didn't bother about the details."

"But he *should* have bothered about the details," said Jack. "It's the details that cause all the trouble."

Moyra gave the men ten minutes, lest one of them should have forgotten anything. Then, not really expecting an answer, she picked up the telephone and asked for Rupert's Museum number. Far away, in what she imagined to be Rupert's deserted flat, she heard the phone begin to ring.

Antonia, now fully dressed, was drying the knives and forks with an almost fleshly pleasure, when the telephone rang at the other end of the flat. Carrying the dish-cloth and the silver, she walked slowly through to the drawing-room. Three times that morning the telephone had rung; the *Daily Express*, *Time-Life* and a man called Washman had wished to speak to Rupert. She had enjoyed acting as his secretary.

"Museum 0839," she said, in a mincing voice.

Moyra had expected Rupert, or silence. This prim little voice, which sounded somehow vaguely familiar, took her by surprise.

"May I speak to Mr Page-Gorman, please?"

"Mr Page-Gorman is out. May I take a message?"

Antonia had realized that it was Moyra now. Moyra sounded slightly puzzled as she said:

"Who is that speaking?"

Antonia exaggerated the disguise in her voice:

"This is Mr Page-Gorman's secretary. May I take a

67

message?" And she could have hugged herself with the delight of it all.

"Oh, Miss Lucas, I didn't recognize your voice."

"Miss Lucas is away. I'm a temporary replacement." What a wonderful lark.

"Oh, I see. Well, I wonder if you would tell Mr Page-Gorman that Mrs Beaulieu called, and would be obliged if he would ring her at his earliest convenience."

"B-E-W-L-E-Y?" inquired Antonia with glee.

"No." Moyra spelt her name out correctly.

"Thank *you*," said Antonia, and replaced the telephone on its cradle. Then she burst out laughing. Finally she stuck out her tongue at the telephone. She certainly wouldn't write *that* message on the pad.

Down at Bourne End, Moyra stared at her white telephone, a slight frown furrowing her high and handsome forehead. Funny, she thought, very funny. She could almost have sworn she recognized that voice. And what would a temporary secretary be doing, alone in Rupert's flat, at a quarter to one on a Sunday? Still, she supposed he was very busy at this particular time. But all the same. . . . And shaking her head, she made for the kitchen to tell cook that lunch would be at half past two.

At half past two there were very few idlers still hanging about the gates of Buckingham Palace to witness John Maynard's second visit to his sovereign that day. Of those who did see the little green car drive through, fully half were American servicemen on weekend pass from the rocket and bomber bases in East Anglia and Yorkshire. They were sightseeing, in bored, gum-chewing fashion, since apart from the cinemas and the naked girlie shows, there was absolutely nothing else to do in London on a rainy November Sunday afternoon, once the pubs had closed. They did not cheer John Maynard, for the very good reason that they had no idea who he was. And even if they had cheered, he was now hardly in the mood to wave back.

In the first place he had missed his Sunday dinner, which should have been roast beef, baked potatoes and buttered swedes, of which he was inordinately fond. He had had to make do with a truly revolting ham sandwich, a great slab of fatty meat smeared with mustard and pressed between two perfect rectangles of dusty, pre-sliced bread, the whole washed down with a bottle of inferior light ale, amidst the cigarette smoke and the brimming ashtrays. In the second place, what should have been a triumphant and happy celebration of the Party's first real victory for some twenty years, had rapidly degenerated into a most unseemly and bitter row. And they had been so rude to him, too.

The climax had come when he had said, for the fifth time, and almost wringing his hands:

"But I have given my word, both personally and as the leader of the Party, that we will not dismantle the bases. I have said over and over again, that the American alliance is the cornerstone of our foreign policy. I have given my word to the American President."

Rupert Page-Gorman had replied, icily:

"Whatever you personally may have promised to any foreign government cannot take precedence over what is the clearly expressed mandate of the country, and, what is more, the pledge on which most of us, including yourself, were elected."

The shadow Minister of Works who had hitherto sat silent, with his hand behind his right ear, now said:

"I back Maynard. This is no time for internal dissension. We must stand united behind our leader." The old gentleman had been voicing such sentiments, on and off, to Lansbury and Snowden, to Morrison and Attlee, to Gaitskell and Bevan, for over thirty years. Now he felt more strongly about it than ever. Was the shadow not on the point of being transformed into the substance? He had been so happy at the ministry back in the late 'forties. To let it all slip because of some tomfoolery about atomic bases. Faugh!

"Thank you," said Maynard to the old man, and glanced at the others. No eye met his, but a beefy trade unionist, whose union officials were among the few not to have voted for nuclear disarmament at their seaside jamboree that summer, now spoke, continuing to doodle as he did so.

"Ah think we should compromise," he said.

"But how can we compromise?" Maynard almost pleaded. "We either have the bases or we don't. We can't half have them, half not. Besides, the Ministry of Defence . . ."

"The soldiers and airmen," somebody put in, "are our servants, not the other way about."

"On this, as on so much else," said Leonard Braithwaite, "I agree with my old friend, John Maynard." Maynard looked to his old friend with an expression of gratitude and surprise. He had scarcely expected to find an ally there. Nor, he soon realized, had he.

"This," Leonard Braithwaite went on, "is indeed no fit occasion for compromise. The bases must go, as the country and the Party demand. The lives of millions of children yet unborn . . ."

Testily Maynard interrupted him:

"All right, Leonard, all right. This isn't a public meeting."

And so it had gone on for three hours, while Maynard became increasingly conscious of his isolation. Finally, announcing that he must have time to think, as well as to consult the Monarch, the service chiefs, and one or two others, he prorogued the meeting until eleven o'clock that night. It was not surprising that he was in a bad temper by the time he arrived at what Jack Beaulieu invariably referred to as Buck House.

The Monarch behaved with the utmost constitutional propriety, but the Monarch's closing words had had a disagreeable sound in John Maynard's ears:

"As I understand it, you are prepared to take office and to carry out a policy which you have opposed publicly, and which you still think to be wrong and dangerous, and to do this solely because you believe that you would be a moderating force. I am by no means sure that any man's personality can carry such weight, nor that any Prime Minister should be asked to implement a policy which he believes might threaten this country's whole international position and perhaps its very existence. I must seek further advice."

Which, thought Maynard as he bowed his way out of the small study, was equivalent to telling him that he was prepared to go back on his word and to sacrifice his principles for the sake of holding office. How unfair, when all he wished to do

70

was to serve his country! Surely it was obvious that he was the only possible man. The Americans at least would see that.

The word soon got around Fleet Street that a crisis was boiling up. Rupert Page-Gorman put through four or five telephone calls to various newspapermen whom he spoke to as friends. It was thanks to his tip that the *Daily Mirror* was able to secure a fine scoop: a photograph of the man generally regarded as the next Prime Minister of Great Britain hurrying into the American Embassy in Grosvenor Square in order, as the *Mirror* was to say next morning, 'to get his orders'.

Meanwhile the Monarch received a number of distinguished persons in audience, and since the rain had stopped, there was once again quite a crowd outside the Palace to see them arrive. The outgoing Prime Minister, enjoying what he regarded as a well-earned rest at Chequers, was awakened from a heavy sleep at four that afternoon. Lord Attlee was sent for, and arrived looking the picture of health, his head well on one side, smiling on both sides of his pipe. The Liberal leader passed between the guardsmen. So, too, did Field-Marshal Montgomery, also looking extremely fit for his great age. This caused some feverish speculation among the political journalists. (One *Daily Telegraph* leader writer even began to compose a leader replete with references to Cincinnatus, Wellington, de Gaulle and Hindenburg; he had just substituted the name of Eisenhower for that of Hindenburg when he was informed that the Field-Marshal's arrival at the Palace on this particular afternoon was purely fortuitous. He had gone there to have tea with an old friend who commanded the Yeomen of the Guard.) It was a great coming and going.

The United States ambassador received Maynard with his customary courtesy but could, of course, not commit his President. He did, however, say that he knew of the very great regard in which the President held the leader of the British Labour Party. For internal American reasons, however, it was unlikely that the President could make any statement, public or private, which would imply his approval of a unilateral renunciation of nuclear weapons by Great Britain, even less so the dismantling of the US bases. However, he would naturally pass on Mr Maynard's personal request with all speed.

No, unfortunately it was not possible for Mr Maynard to talk to the President on the telephone that afternoon, as the President was out all day, bird-shooting.

The 'Against the Bomb' committee met at seven. It was a brief meeting, since they all agreed that compromise was impossible. Antonia May drafted a statement for the Press, which was unanimously approved, and which stated just this. Britain had voted overwhelmingly against the bomb: the bomb must go. Party loyalties were of the greatest importance: but loyalty to humanity must take first place.

At eleven o'clock that evening the leaders of the Labour Party met again. By now they were all tired, and tempers were on edge. Only Rupert Page-Gorman seemed his usual cool and imperturbable self. The speech he made late in the meeting was extremely short and quite devoid of oratory. He said:

"We are, in overwhelming majority, in disagreement with John Maynard's interpretation of the mandate that we have received. He speaks of partial nuclear disarmament. This is nonsense. The difference to this country between one hydrogen bomb and one thousand is non-existent. He knows this as well as we do. But what does he do? Instead of resigning his leadership of the Party, he attempts to call in American support. I believe I am correct in saying that you called at the United States Embassy this afternoon? If John Maynard were to form a government, who in fact would govern? The Labour Party? Or the Pentagon? That is all I have to say."

At one o'clock on Monday morning, John Maynard made a short, tired speech. He had, he said, devoted his entire life to the Labour Movement, and he would continue to serve the Movement in any capacity and by every means. It was, however, sadly obvious to him that he and his friends were seriously at variance over one important matter of principle—not, he hastened to add, a matter of socialist principle on which, he believed, they were all as united as they had always been. Furthermore, certain doubts as to his integrity had been raised. A perfectly normal visit to the United States ambassador had been grossly, he would almost say slanderously, misinterpreted. In view of these facts, he concluded with a choke in his voice, he saw no alternative but to offer his resignation as leader of the Party, and to wish his successor, whoever he might be, 'all the best'.

With seven abstentions and one vote against, the resignation was accepted.

At a quarter past two that same morning—which did not really imply a lengthy discussion, since they had broken off for an hour in order to drink whisky, milk, or carrot-juice, according to taste, and to munch through some more of the morning's unpalatable sandwiches, now stale as well—a new leader was elected, Leonard Braithwaite.

Precisely nine hours later Leonard Braithwaite arrived at Buckingham Palace, to kiss hands on his appointment as First Lord of the Treasury and Prime Minister. In memory of Keir Hardie, he wore a cloth cap of antiquated design.

PART TWO

6

NORA'S PLAY only ran for three weeks, and this despite the most glowing reviews, in which she herself was repeatedly praised for the extreme delicacy of her performance: she played a young mother who must choose between a husband she loves and a Mongolian-idiot child which he regards as a judgment of God. 'Brilliant', 'Unbearably true', 'I cried myself to sleep', said the critics. And, indeed, in view of the British public's passion for anything with a medical, or quasi-medical, theme, it seemed that Beaumont and Tennent had another smash hit. But yet it folded. Some said that the play was too truthful, too spiritually revealing: others that it was the political and economic crisis that kept the people at home, by their television sets. In any event it closed, though negotiations were now under way for a Broadway opening, with basically the same cast, early in the new year.

This was why Nora was able to go to the opera with Patrick. It was also why this was, in a way, a sort of farewell, for she had decided that she must spend as much of Toddy's Christmas holidays as possible down at Broadacres. And after that, she would presumably be off to New York. It was thus, inevitably, a slightly sad evening. Nor was Covent Garden full for this first performance in years of *La Forza del Destino*. Presumably even the opera fans were politically conscious. At least as the overture reached its lovely, melodramatic climax, Patrick, glancing about, saw many empty seats. As light as thistledown, Nora laid her hand on his forearm, turned to him, and smiled in the near-darkness.

"What wonderful times," she said, in the moment of silence between the end of the long overture and the raising of the curtain. "How clever you are, Patrick. *Such* a good idea."

And he laid his hand over hers as the curtain was whisked away sideways and upwards.

If only, he thought, if only it could be for always. Would they too, he wondered, ever weary of one another, ever become stale bed-fellows, nagging and bored? There was almost no married couple of his acquaintance that had not reached this state after ten years or so, often after less. Except Jack and Moyra Beaulieu. It was easy to see, from the way Jack watched Moyra move, that for him she was still the beautiful and brilliant girl whom he had married twenty-five years ago, just at the beginning of the war. "We had to regularize our union," Jack would say with a laugh: "Ration books, you understand." And yet even Jack and Moyra. . . . She was up to something, probably with this Page-Gorman fellow, of that Patrick was sure. Would he and Nora, had they been married these past three years, be that much nearer even to infidelities? It was a monstrous thought. On his part, he was quite sure, never. But what about her? Women were different. When they felt that they were growing old, that life was slipping from their grasp. . . . No, no, it was an intolerable idea, hideously disloyal. And, as though sensing his brief and painful mental betrayal, Nora withdrew her hand from beneath his. He concentrated on the opera.

Yet what of the future? If she went to America, would she ever come back? She would so long as Toddy was here, but how long would Toddy remain in England? It was hard to make out, from the little she had told him, what exactly was going through Felix Seligman's mind. Presumably she didn't know herself. Perhaps Felix didn't either. All that Patrick had heard was that on the day Braithwaite became Prime Minister, that Monday morning just five weeks ago, Felix had arrived at Seligman Baer at nine-thirty am, ostensibly to consult with his partners about the new situation, but also to arrange for the immediate transfer of a substantial part of his fortune to Canada. Many rich men were thinking as he was that morning, but few acted with such promptitude. However, even he had not been prompt enough. An Order in Council signed the previous evening had re-imposed all the currency restrictions abolished over the past ten years. As the

75

new Chancellor explained, in his first statement to the Press later that day, this was purely a temporary step, an emergency measure, to prevent, as he said, "any hysterical Tories from sabotaging the country's economy". Meanwhile the bank rate had been raised to six per cent. Now, five weeks later, the emergency restrictions were still in force, and the bank rate stood at seven and a half.

Felix Seligman, however, was not the senior partner of a great banking house for nothing. Never before had he used his position for his own, personal purposes. Indeed, he would have regarded it as wrong, unethical, un-English to do so. But, he told himself, this was not for him: this was for Toddy. And so he had twice flown to Canada, and making use of all the loopholes available, had moved a sizeable portion of his capital overseas. By the time the government plugged the last of these holes, Felix Seligman had about three-quarters of a million pounds very well invested on the far side of the Atlantic.

Patrick did not, of course, know the sum involved, but Nora had quoted her husband as saying that if the worst came to the worst, they and Toddy would 'always be all right' in Canada. So Patrick guessed that it was a very substantial amount.

But, he wondered as Plinio Clabassi launched into his first big aria, *Buona notte, mia figlia*, could Felix ever bring himself to leave Broadacres, to turn his back upon this England that he loved with such an intense and conscious passion? For obvious reasons of delicacy, he and Felix almost never met these days, yet there had been a time when they had been, if not friends (for Felix really had no friends), at least fairly close acquaintances, and he recalled a conversation he had had with that proud, reserved and usually silent man, in the bow window of Boodle's. It was a conversation that had stuck in Patrick's mind, because it was the only occasion on which he had ever heard Felix refer to his Jewishness.

"You must realize," Felix had then said, "that we Jews are not at all nomads, far less, I think, than the Greeks or even the Irish. If we have wandered all these centuries, it is not through choice but from compulsion. We have nothing whatever in common with the Gypsies, save that Hitler gassed both races at Auschwitz. We long to settle, to have a home, to put down thick, strong roots. That is why the Israelis would fight to the last drop of their blood for the home that they have finally won for themselves. And that is why we English Jews are so grateful to this country, which has allowed us to live here unmolested for so long. That is why some of us—myself, I suppose—seem to others to be almost exaggeratedly English, to exaggerate our patriotism. Take Disraeli, for example . . ."

Could this man be seriously contemplating abandoning his country? But, Patrick told himself, there were other forces at work, deeper loyalties of which Felix had perhaps been unaware, that afternoon long ago at Boodle's; there was his feeling for his son, that dumb and dangerous love which Abraham had felt for Isaac and David for Absalom. Patrick knew that his own life was intimately and inextricably bound up in his love for Nora. If she went, all went. Could it be that his future might yet be decided by the outcome of a tug-of-war between two deep emotional strains in the soul of Felix Seligman? But no, he told himself, he was now exaggerating in his turn. It was the fault of Verdi's galloping music. Felix was only doing what any sensible rich man would do, he was only re-insuring. And yet, the very moving of the money to Canada, the very fact that he had morally, if not of course technically, broken his country's laws by so doing, was in itself an ominous indication of what must be passing through his mind. There was a German expression, how did it go— something about finger-tip feeling? What was it that Felix Seligman was feeling in the tips of his long, tapering fingers? What had led him already to act in a way that was patently out of character? But no, it was Verdi who was inspiring these silly fears. Things hadn't reached that point. Nor were they likely to.

Maria Meneghini Callas's lovely notes flooded forth, filling the theatre with liquid, silver song. The critics, thought Patrick, say that she is past her prime, that she is going off. They've been saying it for years, but she still sounds all right to me.

But what point had things reached? So much had happened in the past month and, he suspected, a great deal more that

77

he and the rest of the public didn't know about. Did Felix Seligman?

To the great British public the formation of the Braithwaite government had had some of the excitement of the picking of a cricket team to tour Australia. Apart from certain obvious candidates, such as the Minister of Works, Braithwaite himself, and Maynard, there was little that the forecasters could go on. It was so long since Labour had held office that, apart from these three, there was no one left who had held any but very junior cabinet rank under Attlee. Nor did membership of Maynard's Shadow Cabinet count for much, now that Braithwaite was in control. Braithwaite on his first television appearance as Prime Minister had announced his intention of forming a 'young' Cabinet.

"Too long," he said, "has this country lived under the paralysing conditions of age, old men, old methods, and old prejudices. It is youth that has turned them out, and put us in, and it is in the spirit of youth that we shall give this England of ours a renaissance, a rebirth. We shall sweep the cobwebs from our minds, just as we plan to sweep the refuse of vice and crime from our streets. To do this, I shall want lieutenants who are themselves young enough to understand the noble aspirations of youth. We shall build a new, clean world, a world without fear and without the bad old inequalities of class and income that have for too long blighted our fair land. It is therefore to the youth of Britain that I now appeal, whether you be watching me in your homes, perhaps glancing up from your studies, or in your coffee bars where our great Anti-Nuclear Bomb movement first flourished, or in your youth clubs that must be encouraged to multiply. The youth of England is a youth of sportslovers. . . ."

And much more of the same. And, indeed one appointment was remarkably youthful: Rupert Page-Gorman got the Foreign Office, the youngest man to hold that important post since Anthony Eden in the middle 'thirties. The Chancellor of the Exchequer, too, was quite young, and had also never before been a member of the Cabinet. Indeed, he had only been an MP for five years, but then he was a very famous Cambridge economist. So his appointment was not really so startling.

John Maynard, after displaying a certain coy reluctance, was eventually persuaded to take the Home Office. Here he would be able to tackle the question of the police and other related problems, without being in any way involved in the disarmament programme with which he was known to disagree. As he explained to his friends, he had accepted the Home Office in order not to split the party. Braithwaite, besides the premiership, reserved the Ministry of Defence for himself, thus reviving a custom that had lapsed since Churchill's wartime ministry. His motive in so doing was, however, quite different from Churchill's. As he explained to his friends: "If those bloody-minded air marshals get up to any of their tricks, they'll have *me* to deal with." The rest of the Cabinet consisted of rather undistinguished politicians of whom a high proportion had come to Parliament by way of the trade unions. *The Times,* in its leading article on the new Cabinet, although expressing reservations about both Page-Gorman and the Chancellor of the Exchequer was, in general, satisfied. This leader was headed: 'A Steady Team'.

Maynard almost immediately presented Parliament with his Police (Increased Powers) Bill. It did not, in fact, differ greatly from the Conservative Bill that had brought down the last government, but the essential demand for tighter control was met by the appointment of an official within the Home Office to be in charge of all the various police forces throughout the country. These county and urban forces lost a considerable amount of their previous autonomy. It would be possible, now, for the Home Office to move bodies of police from one part of the country to another. Furthermore, although the ordinary police would not be automatically supplied with arms, the Home Secretary was given wide discretionary powers to arm such bodies of police as he saw fit, to meet conditions as they arose. The special force known as the Mobile Guards was also increased in strength, and was now directly subordinated to the Home Office, and not to the metropolitan commissioner as hitherto. All this was described by Maynard as 'streamlining the force', and was apparently popular both with the public and with the police themselves. An immediate drive was begun to clean up the gangster-controlled areas in London, Manchester, and Glasgow. Once this was done, it was intended to tackle the nasty problem of race-riots, and also to cope with public vice.

The nationalization, or re-nationalization, of certain industries was a lengthier business, but was proceeding. In order that this be not impeded, nor the country confused, by the advertisements against such measures with which the industries concerned had long flooded the newspapers, a brief act was passed that prevented most such advertisements. This was called the Control of Industrial Propaganda Act.

A Royal Commission was appointed to inquire into how the grammar schools and so-called public schools could best be incorporated into the national educational system. It was not expected to report until some time in the spring, when it was believed that its recommendations would be drastic.

But of course it was foreign affairs that really hit the headlines. For weeks the papers had been filled with reports and photographs of the dismantling of the Russian rocket bases in Poland. The last government had followed the line of the United States government in treating this Soviet gesture as suspect, and had even declined the Russian invitation that official inspecting teams be sent to Poland to watch the operation in progress. Braithwaite immediately reversed his predecessor's policy, and had dispatched a mixed team of scientists and soldiers to Warsaw, where they were royally entertained by Russians and Poles alike. Tactfully enough, Braithwaite announced that the purpose of their visit was not to verify that the Russians were in fact doing what they said they were doing (the newspapermen had already shown that this was so) but to collect experience against the day 'now soon approaching, when we shall do likewise here'. It had already been announced that the manufacture of these weapons in Britain had been discontinued, and forever.

But the snag, of course, lay with the Americans. Complicated diplomatic negotiations of a very delicate nature were in progress in Washington. These were supposedly secret, but needless to say rumours circulated, and these rumours—which said that the Americans were taking a very tough line, and were insisting that Britain should fulfil all her commitments as laid down by the various alliances and in the North Atlantic Treaty Organization, while the British were equally adamant concerning bases in the United Kingdom—were to a certain extent confirmed by public announcements in the two capitals. In an address to the nation, Braithwaite stated that while Britain was prepared, and indeed anxious, to preserve the traditional very close links that bound the two great English-speaking nations together, it was essential that the rocket bases go: these, he said, were now a cause of disunity rather than unity. Freed of this threat and burden, Britain could look America straight in the face and say: 'Old friend, we've chosen our way, which is not yours. But that does not mean that we cannot march forward together, arm in arm, to greet the dawn.' The American President, at a Press conference, spoke in rather less emotional terms. "As I see it," he said, "the British government is anxious to opt out of the solemn promises and agreements freely entered into by its predecessors. Our global defensive strategy is predicated on certain assumptions, one of which is that Britain would never break her word to us. If that assumption is no longer viable, there are various courses open to us. Since the matter is now under urgent consideration, and since negotiations are going on, I can say no more about this at present." A journalist: "Mr President, do you regard the proposed action of expelling the American rocketeers from Britain as a potentially hostile act?" President: "No comment."

Next morning the *Daily Express* had as its main headline: US THREAT TO BRITAIN, with below: PRESIDENT CLAIMS RIGHT TO BASES. The left-wing Press was even more outspoken, and that evening a crowd collected outside the American Embassy, chanting in unison: 'No bases here! Go home, go home!' The police did not intervene, though present in force. Next day, in order to forestall the danger of incidents, the American military authorities forbade all American service personnel to leave their posts until further notice. This caused considerable annoyance to the owners of various public houses and to certain teen-age girls, but was generally regarded as a tactful and sensible measure.

The Russians now decided to take a hand in the game. Without warning and giving no reason, they sealed off West Berlin.

Immediately the Americans, but not this time the British, began an airlift, though it was known that this could not now solve the problem of supporting the beleaguered city. Red fighters buzzed the heavy transports, but did not shoot. American and German armoured formations moved to their assembly areas on the zonal border. For forty-eight hours it looked as though there would be war. Once again crowds collected in Grosvenor Square, this time chanting: 'Hiroshima! Hiroshima! We won't die for Berlin!' Then, again without giving a reason and with equal suddenness, the Russians lifted the Berlin blockade. Braithwaite implied that a series of messages from himself to Kornoloff had played its part in securing this happy ending to a momentarily terrifying situation. The Americans said that they had called the Russians' bluff. The Russians continued to say nothing at all. But it had, indeed, been a frightening forty-eight hours. All this had happened a week before Patrick's and Nora's visit to the opera.

The first act curtain came down to steady but unenthusiastic clapping. Nora applauded with redoubled vigour, as if to shame the rest of the audience, and remarked to Patrick:

"Look at all those stuffed shirts. What does Callas have to do to get a cheer out of them? Swing from the chandeliers?"

"They'd regard that as vulgar," said Patrick. "A speech about how Britain has regained the moral leadership of the world would probably raise the roof, though. Come on, let's get a drink."

They made their way along the narrow, curving passage-way behind the stalls circle, amidst repeated murmurs of 'Sorry!' and up the broad stairs, and into the Crush Bar. There was not much crush tonight, and Patrick had no difficulty in ordering a half bottle of champagne, but as usual all the tables were occupied, so they drank standing at the bar. Nora said in a low voice:

"Paddy, there's a man behind you who keeps staring at me."

"Aren't you used to that by now? What do you want me to do, knock him down?"

"Paddy, you *are* in a rough mood tonight."

"I'm worried about politics."

"But the thing is I think I know him. Do look. He's got a sort of sandy crew cut."

Patrick turned, casually, then said to Nora:

"I think I know him, too. He looks familiar, anyhow."

"Oh dear, he's coming over. What are we going to say?"

The man, who was wearing a rather ill-cut, foreign-looking suit and an Old Etonian tie, was between them.

"Excuse me," he said, "but I'm sure we have met before, haven't we?"

"I . . . I think so," said Nora. "My name is Nora May. And this is Lord Clonard."

The stranger with the lined, sad face now looked truly embarrassed.

"Of course, that's why I know your face. Forgive me. You must think me very rude. But I have been out of England for such a long time."

Nora seldom missed an opportunity for putting anyone, man, woman or child, friend or stranger, at his or her ease. Now she said, with a smile:

"But the funny thing is I think I know your face, too. What is your name?"

"Mark Vernon," the man replied.

For perhaps half a second Nora appeared bewildered. Then she giggled, and said:

"Do you know what I was about to say? I was about to say: 'Not *the* Mark Vernon?' Oh dear me, well, now we all know each other."

Mark Vernon's portrait-photograph, smiling, posed, and youthfully self-confident, had been plastered over the papers at the time of his celebrated disappearance, a dozen or so years ago. But this was recognizably and obviously he. Patrick glanced at him, his attitude one of interest mingled with distaste. Then he saw that Nora was, as he might have expected, enjoying this surprising encounter with the mythical Vernon, and so, overcoming his strong disapproval of the man, he said:

"Perhaps you would care to join us in a glass of, er . . ."

And he pointed vaguely towards the bottle.

"Why, thank you, that's very kind."

And indeed the man did seem to be almost humbly grateful.

"What a wonderful performance," said Vernon. "Do you know, I've never heard Callas before."

"But didn't she go to Moscow last year? Or perhaps you weren't in Russia then."

"I was in Russia, but not in Moscow."

"Where were you?" Nora went on, "I mean, if it's not a secret?"

"I was in the north."

Vernon spoke slowly, almost wearily. Nora was clearly becoming rattled by his manner and relapsed into a sort of parody of cocktail-party conversation, such as she might have learned in her repertory days from the plays of Lonsdale or Coward:

"The north? But how frightfully interesting."

Vernon said nothing, sipping his champagne. At this moment the first bell rang to announce that the intermission was ending. Patrick took advantage of this to say:

"I think we'd better be getting back, Nora."

"Goodbye, Mr Vernon," she prattled, "it's been such a pleasure meeting you."

And the moment they were out of earshot, to Patrick:

"Well, blow me down."

Patrick glanced back. Vernon was still standing by the bar, the champagne glass in his hand, his eyes following them, his expression one of unutterable sadness. And as they made their way down the stairs, Nora said:

"The people one runs into at Covent Garden."

As soon as they had vanished around the bend on the stairs, Mark Vernon made his way to his own seat. The house lights were going down as he reached it. The melancholy-looking, long-jawed Irishman in the next seat said:

"Well?"

"Yes."

"You will talk to them again in the next interval. This way is better."

The alternative way, as Mark Vernon knew, had been a direct introduction to Antonia May, and thus to Rupert Page-Gorman. Indeed, a direct introduction to Page-Gorman could have been easily arranged. But the people he worked for preferred the roundabout approach.

As it happened, however, Mark Vernon did not get another chance to talk to Nora May that evening, Patrick had no desire to meet the returned renegade again, and Nora, too, had seen enough of him. So during the other two intervals they went out to the Nag's Head.

For London lovers the city is dotted with places that are identified with their love. In such and such a street did first they meet; after dancing here, they first did kiss; it was to this restaurant that they went when first they had made love. And so long as the love remains happy, the lovers will return to those places, which seem to contain and reflect and flatter their affections. For Patrick and Nora the restaurant called *L'Escargot Bienvenu,* in Greek Street, Soho, was such a one, though it was by now old-fashioned and unfashionable.

"Ours is a snaily love," Nora remarked cheerfully, as they stepped into the taxi after the opera.

But when they reached the corner of Old Compton Street and the Charing Cross Road, they found the entrance into Soho sealed off by a wire barricade guarded by police. A crowd was being ordered, in forceful tones, to keep moving, and from behind the barricade came distant shouts and the pounding of running feet. They heard the taxi driver call out:

"What's up?"

And a man on the pavement called back:

"You can't get in there. They're rounding up all the Soho 'ores."

Patrick called through the window:

"Try going round by Soho Square."

"Right," said the driver, and they moved off. A little farther along the Charing Cross Road they saw half a dozen women being bundled, quite roughly, into a Black Maria.

But the entrance from Oxford Street was also blocked and barricaded, as was Berwick Street and Dean Street.

"Don't think we'll get in there," said the driver, laconically.

"All right," said Patrick, "put us down here, and we'll see if we can do it on foot."

It had not as yet occurred to either of them that the police could simply seal off the whole area bounded by the Charing

85

Cross Road, Oxford Street, Regent Street, and Shaftesbury Avenue. Patrick and Nora walked up to the nearest barrier. A policeman said, sharply:

"Go on, move along there."

"We want to get through," said Patrick politely.

"Well yer can't," said the policeman, rudely. "Haven't you got eyes in yer 'ead? This street's cordoned off."

"But——"

"Do what you're told. Get moving."

At this moment, just beyond the barricade, two policemen appeared from a nearby house, half carrying, half dragging a screaming, yellow-haired woman, past her first youth.

"Lemme go, you bloody bastards, lemme go, you bloody rozzers. It ain't my turn."

The two men with the woman had reached the barricade, which the policeman who had urged Patrick and Nora to move on was now opening. The woman twisted away from one of her captors, and kicked him on the shin. Patrick saw the man wince, then, with his free hand, punch the woman hard in the stomach. With a nauseating retch and gurgle, the woman doubled up. They dragged her through the barrier.

Patrick limped forward.

"What on earth do you think you are doing?" he said, his voice clipped and angry.

"Who the hell are you?" said the policeman at the barrier. "Didn't I tell you to move on?"

"I'm Lord Clonard, and I want to know by what authority you men have assaulted that woman."

As was customary with the police, when they realized that they had a gentleman to deal with—and even more, a nobleman —their manner changed. Almost wheedling, the original policeman now said:

"Now look here, sir, this is none of your business. We're just carrying out our orders. And these are horrible people, sir, not at all the sort what a gentleman like you should intervene on behalf of. Please be so good as to move along, sir, otherwise I'll have no choice but to charge you with obstructing the police in the performance of their duties."

Patrick was furious.

"I'm not obstructing anybody. As a member of the public I wish to know by what right——"

The other two coppers had disappeared with the woman. There was really nothing that Patrick could do. And now a police officer had appeared upon the scene.

"What's all this?" he asked.

The policeman explained briefly. The officer, who had a small, black moustache, said:

"My advice to you, sir, is to get out of this in double-quick time."

Patrick said:

"I should like to know your name and number, as I intend to report you for failing to keep discipline among your men."

An angry gleam came into the police officer's eye.

"Very well," he said. "My name is Prendergast. Your name, I gather, is Lord Clonard. I shall also see that your name is circulated throughout the force. And the next time you require the help or protection of the police, I can only say that I shall be surprised if you get it."

"That remark will also be reported. And your number?"

The police officer gave it to him.

By the time they reached Rules, where they had decided to dine, Patrick was no longer trembling with fury. They had walked there in silence, Nora holding his arm. She said, as they entered the restaurant:

"Don't let it upset you too much, Patrick."

He grunted, as he handed his overcoat to a waiter.

At the top of the stairs they saw, to their surprise, Jack Beaulieu dining with, of all people, Antonia May. Antonia was leaning forward, talking earnestly. Jack, whose back was to the door, sat with bowed head. Antonia glanced up as the couple entered the room; recognizing Nora and Patrick, she waved and stopped talking.

Air Chief Marshal Sir Hector Boreham took the sheet of paper from his typewriter, noted with irritation that he had, as usual, made two typing errors, corrected these, and signed the letter. It was addressed to the Secretary of State for Air, and in it the air marshal requested that he be relieved of his appointment as Chief of Air Staff, and placed on the retired list. He then re-read the other letter that he had written since returning from No 10 Downing Street, an hour ago. Because he had felt that it would be more respectful, Boreham had written this one by hand. It read:

Your Majesty:

Though I have doubts concerning the propriety of my writing direct to you, I believe that in view of the extreme gravity of the situation, it is my duty to do so. In the final analysis my loyalty as a serving officer is to yourself, as the symbol of the nation. I therefore consider it my responsibility to give you the reasons which make it impossible for me henceforth to serve this present government as Chief of Air Staff.

For the past fifteen years our air policy has been based on the assumption that we had only one enemy to fear, namely, the Soviet Union and, to a lesser extent, China. Our very considerable air defences have been built with the main, really with the sole, purpose of allowing us as best we can to parry that threat should it ever materialize. In close collaboration with the Royal Navy, NATO, and the United States Air Force we have, at great expense, built a defensive system which, though by the nature of modern warfare it cannot of itself ensure the defeat of the enemy should he ever attack us, does ensure that such an attack would cost him very dearly indeed.

For the past five weeks I have been arguing against the government's expressed policy of weakening, or rather destroying, this country's defensive–offensive air shield, and in this I have had the full support both of my Staff and, I believe, of the Admiralty as well. Tonight, however, I was finally overruled by my minister, in the presence of and with the backing of the Prime Minister and the Secretary of State for Foreign Affairs. Specifically, I have been instructed to issue orders for the immediate dismantling of our rocket and bomber bases designed to close the exits from the Baltic and the Denmark Strait to Russian surface and underwater craft.

Since I believe that even this first step towards disarmament would dangerously weaken our defences (and, incidentally, the defences of our American ally) and since I regard it as my duty to safeguard, not to destroy, this country's defensive capabilities, this is an order that I cannot pass on. I have therefore no choice but to resign.

I have the honour to remain Your Majesty's obedient and devoted servant,

Hector Boreham, Air Chief Marshal.

Clumsily expressed, he thought, as he re-read the letter. Yet what else could he say: 'In the name of God, turn out this government'? It was not possible. Sir Hector was by no means an expert on constitutional procedure in this country, but that at least he knew. However, he also believed that the Palace could, and occasionally did, bring pressure to bear on governments, discreetly, quietly, and behind the scenes. But would Braithwaite and Page-Gorman listen to the Palace any more attentively than they had listened to him and to the admirals? Those endless speeches about Humanity and Youth and Peace from old Braithwaite, those cold and cutting remarks of Page-Gorman's.

That very evening old Admiral Cornwallis had growled:

"But, Prime Minister, the Navy does not regard it as its duty to worry about generations yet unborn. Our duty is to defend the lives and interests of generations that have been born already."

"That," said Braithwaite, "is precisely why the formulation of policy is not entrusted to admirals and air marshals."

And Boreham had said, later:

"Opening the Denmark Strait will affect the continental defence of the United States. Have you consulted with them?"

To which Page-Gorman had replied, icily:

"Foreign policy is my concern, not yours."

No, thought the air marshal alone in his rather bleak flat, his letter to his sovereign was not strong enough. If only his wife, Mary, were still alive! She had had a marvellous ability for self-expression. He had been the man of action, the bomber pilot turned administrator, and even that change had been hard enough. Mary would have helped him with this most difficult of letters. But Mary had been dead these many years, killed, paradoxically enough, by the forerunner of these very rockets for the maintenance of which he was now fighting. Killed by a V-2 that had hit their street in South Kensington, one October day of 1944, while he was commanding a bomber wing in Burma.

What else would Mary advise him to do, were she still here? Once he was on the retired list, he could, he supposed, write a book or at least a series of articles for the papers. But it would take so long, and be so difficult, and then, of course, there would be the question of the Official Secrets Act. Still, it would be something to do in his retirement. Since Mary's death he had buried himself in his work, for twelve, fourteen, sixteen hours a day. Writing would at least be a semblance of activity, a substitute. However, it would surely be too late, any book that he might write. The time for action was now, while the bases were still in being. Boreham pulled at his grey, clipped moustache. What about the Americans?

He got up and took a few turns between door and window. The idea of going to foreigners in order to complain about his government was, to Boreham, repugnant. Yet perhaps pressure from that source might be effective? Besides, was it not his moral duty to see that General Studebaker was informed with all speed? There was no telling what sort of double-dealing Braithwaite and those others were capable of. He filled his pipe, then picked up his telephone and asked for a Ruislip number. The duty officer quickly gave him the Commanding General's home number.

Mrs Studebaker answered the phone.

"Hullo, Mrs Studebaker? Hector Boreham here. Can I have a word with Dick?"

"Why yes, air marshal. He's right here."

"Dick? Bad news. I've resigned as Chief of Air Staff. Can't stomach their policy, or for that matter their insults. Braithwaite called me a bloody-minded air marshal."

"This *is* bad news, Hector."

"No, that's not the bad news. Listen carefully. Tomorrow orders go out for dismantling Batteries 16, 18, 22, 24, and 68. Got that?"

"That's the Skaggerat, Kattegat, and Denmark Strait, isn't it?"

"It is."

"Hell!"

"Quite. You see why I resigned."

"I do. Hector, I appreciate your telling me this. We'd heard rumours, of course, but nothing definite."

"So I imagined. See if you can bring some pressure to bear."

"I'll get on to people who can. And fast."

"Goodnight, Dick." He suddenly felt intensely tired, and had no wish to continue a conversation which he still regarded, with a part of his mind, as an act of disloyalty.

"Say, Hector, one minute. Who's taking over?"

"I've no idea. But doubtless they'll find some air marshal who isn't so bloody-minded."

"Look, let's meet soon."

Boreham gave a bitter laugh.

"Whenever you say. I'll have plenty of time from now on. Goodnight, Dick, and ring me one of these days."

The flat seemed extraordinarily empty and silent, once he had replaced the receiver. What would he do with all his leisure? He looked at the photograph of Mary on his desk. smiling at him across twenty years from beneath her WAAF's cap. Oh, Mary, Mary, he thought, why did it have to be?

A strange idea came to him. There was perhaps just one way in which he could draw the attention of the country to its danger; one way in which he could ensure that the papers were filled with news of him; one way of circumventing the Official Secrets Act and perhaps confounding Braithwaite and Page-Gorman. He opened the drawer of his desk, and took out his revolver. After all, he had always been prepared to die for his country in the air. Why not on the ground, now that his career was over? He weighed the revolver on the palm of his hand. Then his eye travelled to the photograph once again, and he replaced the revolver in the drawer. Mary would certainly not have approved of *that* idea.

At Rules, meanwhile, Nora and Patrick were finishing their meal, seated at the same table as Jack and Antonia. None of the four had particularly wanted to sit together, but it had proved inevitable. Since there was only one other table free, and that one next to Jack Beaulieu's, there was really no alternative for Patrick and Nora, apart from walking out of the restaurant. And since Antonia had seen them, this was clearly out of the question. So there the four of them had sat, for an hour now. Patrick had told the others about what was happening in Soho.

". . . and so," he ended, "I think that that police officer should be reported."

"So do I," said Nora. "Too beastly."

Jack, who had apparently been listening with only half his attention, turning his brandy glass round and round, now looked up.

"How do you propose to do it?"

"I don't know. Write to the commissioner, I suppose."

"And do you think they'll take any notice?"

"I've no idea. But I think I should do something. Don't you?"

Antonia now spoke:

"Why don't you write to Rupert? He can pass it on to the Home Office. Or, better still, meet him and tell him exactly what it was you saw."

Jack's eyes returned to his brandy glass, and his fingers to its stem. Patrick said:

"But I don't know him."

"I do. I can easily introduce you."

"He's so busy."

"Yes, he is busy. But, well, I can easily arrange a meeting. Over a drink or something. Would you like that?"

Patrick would have preferred to avoid it. He had no desire to be indebted in any way to Rupert Page-Gorman or, for that matter, to be involved in Antonia's complicated schemes. But, as with the matter of where to sit, he saw no way of politely refusing her offer. Besides, he was afraid that to do so might in some way offend Nora.

"Thank you."

"Good," said Antonia, the practical woman of affairs. "Will you be in your office tomorrow?" He nodded. "I'll ring you there when I've spoken to Rupert. And now I must spend a penny before we go. Coming, Nora?"

Almost the only criticism Patrick had ever heard Nora utter of her sister was her habit of forever making her go to the lavatory with her. "I suppose it dates from our nursery days, her being a year older, I mean. And the funny thing is, I always go. Even if I don't want to at all." And she had laughed. Now, however, she once again dutifully followed her sister out of the room.

Jack had half risen, then relapsed into his chair and moody silence. What on earth, Patrick wondered, had happened to him since this morning? He remembered how they had joked over naming a new detergent. Patrick had proposed YETUNU-THAH WHITAH! and Jack had replied that if anyone wanted a fancy name for a soap powder, he had long ago copyrighted ETERO. And now here he sat, like an old man, turning his brandy glass between his fingers, his eyes on the tablecloth.

Patrick said:

"I didn't realize Antonia was a friend of yours."

Jack looked up, and his eyes were vague.

"A friend? No, she's not a friend. She rang me up and asked me to dine with her, and since Moyra has had to go . . ." He fell silent for a moment, then went on, painfully, ". . . to go to Bognor, to see her mother, I agreed, and . . ."

Patrick held out his cigarette case, and the older man took one, almost with the gesture of a sleepwalker. He said:

"She told me that Moyra is having an affair with that horrible Page-Gorman fellow, and that I should break it up, as Page-Gorman belongs to her. Patrick, do you think it can be true?"

Patrick looked him straight in the eye. He talked fast.

"No, Jack, I don't. I daresay Antonia is up to something with Page-Gorman, but, well, she's a *fantaisiste*, you know. All novelists are, to a certain extent. They invent situations."

"Moyra and I, we talk as though we were great gadabouts. Always have. Everybody does. But in fact, never. . . . Not Moyra. I don't know."

"Listen, Jack, Antonia is not to be relied upon as a source of information about anything."

"But then why should she say all this? She told me that Moyra is in his flat, now."

"The man probably didn't want *her* in his flat, so she imagined this. A woman scorned. Making a nasty, feminine drama out of it all."

Jack looked up again, and his face was haggard.

"I telephoned her mother. She's not there. And wasn't expected. And she's not at home, either."

At this moment the sisters came back. The men paid their bills and they all left.

7

OUTSIDE, IN the hall of Broadacres, the waits stood huddled together, peering over one another's shoulders at the words, singing about a Bohemian king of long ago. Their average age was perhaps ten, their voices thin and ragged. No curate or schoolmaster had taught them their Christmas carols: rather was their incentive tradition strongly reinforced by the hope of gain, specifically gain from the hand of Felix Seligman who, in years past, had been known to give as much as two pounds. Calculating quite correctly, they left this most important of their visits until Christmas Eve and the full flowering of the season of goodwill. Indeed they had even left it so late on Christmas Eve that Toddy had had to be put to bed before they arrived.

Competing with their childish voices there came, through the open door that led to the saloon, the sturdier tones of Rupert Page-Gorman. One shoulder leaning against the Adam mantelpiece, a glass of Felix's Tio Pepe in his other hand, he was haranguing a small audience consisting of Nora, Antonia, Mark Vernon and Felix himself. He was saying:

"At the root of it all there is this Jewish eschatological hope-myth. We get it three ways, through Christianity, through Marxism and even, though to a lesser extent, through the theories of Freud and the other psychologists. I am referring,

94

of course, to the ridiculous belief that history will somehow and at some time stop. And the even more absurd prejudice that such an ending to history would be a good thing."

"I suppose," said Antonia, "that the masses need hope, a simple sort of hope, a belief in a possible golden age."

"Exactly," said Page-Gorman. "All myths are to a greater or lesser extent tranquillizers in one way or another. But a government can't function on Milltown. Or at least not for long, or very well."

Felix glanced somewhat anxiously towards the open door. Although it was not his custom to be in the hall throughout the whole of the carol-singing, he and his guests (when he had had any) had always listened to the singing with a certain reverence. On the other hand it would surely be impolite to silence Page-Gorman, or even to imply disapproval. He therefore said:

"I thought you were a Marxist yourself."

"I am not any sort of -ist," Page-Gorman replied loftily. "Except a pragmatist and perhaps an empiricist. There are aspects of Marxism that still seem to me valid, just as there are aspects of the Christian ethic that seem to me useful——"

He was interrupted by the bullet-like arrival on the scene of little Toddy, skidding around the edge of the door in his striped flannel pyjamas, his hair tousled and his face flushed with sleep.

"Daddy, daddy, *do* come out!"

Felix smiled apologetically at his guests and got to his feet. Neither Page-Gorman nor Antonia moved. Mark Vernon also got up, but hesitated. Felix, noticing this, said:

"Don't move, the rest of you. Are you coming, Nora?"

"Of course."

Mark Vernon now sat down again, fearing, quite correctly, that he had nearly intruded on a private ceremony. He reached for his gin and tonic, as, outside, the waits began their next carol. Rupert was silent for a moment, then joined in with the prep school version of the third and fourth lines:

> ". . . a bar of Sunlight soap came down,
>   And they began to scrub."

He laughed briefly, and Mark Vernon politely did the same. Antonia glanced from the man leaning against the mantel to the portrait above him, the great, dark Velasquez called 'The Man with the Helmet'. And she thought that though they were physically so utterly dissimilar, there was perhaps yet some link between the two men, something in the hold of the head or the power and lucidity of the dark eyes. What a pity that there were no decent portrait painters nowadays! Or perhaps in centuries to come a similar portrait of Rupert Page-Gorman might hang over a similar fireplace, and a woman not unlike herself might wonder and admire. . . .

From the hall now came alto voices, in which the voice of Toddy, slightly off key, predominated, singing:

"I'm dreaming of a white Christmas . . ."

"Is *that* a carol these days?" Mark Vernon asked, in surprised tones.

"My dear Vernon," Rupert replied, "there is no more an absolute in carols than in any other field of human endeavour. Perhaps even less. Call a stale dance tune a carol, and it becomes a carol. And eventually any man who dares maintain that it is not is likely to be shot as a heretic or deviationist. You should know that better than anyone."

How clever he is, thought Antonia, what a really superlative mind!

What a fool he is, thought Mark Vernon, to imagine that his paradoxes are amusing and, even more so, that his mind can control events, that his decisions will count in any but the shortest run. Can he not see that he and all his sort are but accidental phenomena of no intrinsic value, that their actions are but pointless episodes which can in no way affect the ultimate unfolding of the great world-historical drama?

From the hall came a high-pitched chorus of thanks, as Felix distributed his largess. But Mark Vernon hardly heard it, for he had had a sudden and very clear mental image of his last instructor, in the Lubianka. What true and lucid sense had lain behind those rimless pince-nez, what nobility, what ultimate wisdom! Compared to the professor, these clever gabblers were as undergraduates or as thistledown in the wind of true thought. To think that once upon a time he had been just such a one himself! And Mark Vernon felt a gratitude to the professor even more profound than that being expressed so shrilly by the waits as they clambered into their little overcoats. Felix Seligman had given them ten shillings each, a sum almost double their expectations: but the professor had given poor, battered Mark Vernon an insight into absolute truth, the existence of which he had not hitherto even suspected.

Christmas Eve at Novaia Zemlia. A day like any other. Six cubic metres of earth moved in exchange for one kilo of dark bread and one litre of fish soup. And Christmas Day would be the same. However, Pfeiffer, though an atheist, had a sentimental streak to him. He had ordered those members of his Hundred who knew a little German to learn the words of 'Stille Nacht, Heilige Nacht'. Shortly before lights-out he ordered them to sing it. Those who knew no German simply hummed the tune.

Christmas Eve in Praed Street, Paddington. When the pubs closed there was a scuffle between a half dozen Irish labourers, who were drunk, and eight or so Barbadians, also drunk. Another Irishman, passing by on his way to midnight Mass, was accidentally knifed, and had to be taken to the Middlesex Hospital. It was believed he would recover.

Christmas Eve at Bourne End. They had played four rubbers of bridge, for rather high stakes—Jack Beaulieu always maintained that it was pointless to play low—and Mr Cuthbertson and Patrick had each won close on twenty-five pounds. (They had not cut for partners: Jack also maintained that there was no purpose in his wife and himself exchanging cheques.) Moyra stretched, and said:

"The arms of Murphy for me."

Jack said:

"Nightcap, Cuthbertson? Patrick?"

Jack wished his wife a distant goodnight over his shoulder, as the soda water hissed into the Scotch. Patrick passed Mr Cuthbertson his drink, then went and sat down on the sofa with his own. He wondered, briefly, how Nora was getting on with all those terrible people down at Broadacres. He had been slightly annoyed when she told him that Mark Vernon had rung up, and that out of pity she had agreed to lunch with him. But to ask him down to Broadacres for Christmas just because the little horror was simultaneously 'lonely' and pursued by journalists seemed to be overdoing it. Still, he told himself, it was really no concern of his. And, indeed, in a way he loved this renewed display of her generous nature, because it was her nature that he loved as much as he loved her body and her mind. But it must really be terrible down there. As if Page-Gorman and Antonia weren't enough! However, this was no time for that sort of speculation. Mr Cuthbertson was saying:

"There is one point, Mr Beaulieu, about which I think it best that I be quite frank with you and Patrick."

Neither of the Englishmen answered. After a moment, Cuthbertson said:

"As you know, it is at the moment unlikely that we shall go into production within the foreseeable future. Or if we do it'll only be on a very small scale. Not at all what we originally had in mind. G.W. feels that we must put the whole project into cold storage till we see which way the ball bounces. But . . ." He hesitated, then took a cigar from his case and, as he lit it, said: "As I told you, we plan to go ahead with this excellent advertising campaign of yours. While waiting to see how the political angle jells. It will also give us and our associates a good periscope here. Do you follow me?"

His cigar was well alight now.

"Yes," said Jack, "I think so."

"So that there will be people coming to see you who will be more interested, or more immediately interested, in the political set-up here than in the actual production or selling of British Fuelless Cars. Can I take it that you two will give them your full co-operation?"

"Why, yes," said Jack, in a somewhat surprised tone. "We shall naturally do what we can."

"Fine," said Mr Cuthbertson. "Fine. The deal's on."

Christmas Eve in the Kremlin. Outside, the snow was falling on the great city and on the small congregations, mostly women or men of more than sixty years, who were making their way to the occasional dilapidated, musty churches. Inside, a comfortable office was the scene of an informal conference attended by Mr Kornoloff, General Nikitin, Sspesiatkin, Marshal Ryukov, and one or two others. They stood about a table on which lay spread a map of Europe.

Kornoloff's forefinger was orange with cigarette stain, as he pointed, first, at the Denmark Strait and then at the exits from the Baltic.

"Clear?" he asked.

"So far as the British batteries go, yes," replied Ryukov.

"And the British bomber bases?"

Nikitin now answered:

"Our information shows that they are in fact doing what they say they're doing, and destroying their atomic warheads."

"How?" asked Kornoloff.

A scientist present answered this one:

"An article by a certain Cockshore in a British daily paper says that they are feeding the fissionable material into their atomic power stations. It doesn't make sense to us. But of course Cockshore is a metallurgist, not a physicist or an engineer."

"It is unimportant, but may give us a card to play some time. I want, not later than tomorrow afternoon, a paper on how we would dispose of our bombs, should we wish to do so. Something technical, but in language I can understand."

"Right," said the scientist.

"And the American bases?" Kornoloff now asked.

Sspesiatkin spoke:

"We have nothing definite. Page-Gorman has informed our ambassador that the Americans will be asked to go."

"When?"

Sspesiatkin looked helplessly from one cold face to the next.

"Soon, I believe."

"Soon, what does soon mean?"

Nikitin now spoke:

"We have certain indications. The most important is probably the crash programme started by the Americans last week. This is secret, of course, but a good source reports that it involves intensified building of rocket bases in Greenland, Newfoundland, and along the Eastern seaboard of Canada and the

99

US. It is logical to assume that these bases are intended to replace the British ones. The very high priority given to these bases implies that Washington does not believe the British bases will be available for long."

"How soon can we expect the Americans to have these new bases operational?"

Nikitin shrugged his shoulders.

"Between four and six months? But of course that is largely guesswork."

Kornoloff said:

"So there is likely to be a hiatus between the closing down of the bases in Britain and the coming into operation of these new ones. Good. That will be the moment to move on to phase two. Meanwhile, I believe we should do nothing to worry the British or the Americans in any way. Indeed, quite the contrary."

Sspesiatkin, anxious to win a good mark, now said:

"You had the very brilliant idea of inviting the British Prime Minister to visit Moscow."

Kornoloff looked at him sharply.

"When the proper time comes, I suppose I shall have to have the old windbag here. Meanwhile, something more dramatic is needed. The Polish bases have gone. We can't dismantle the Czech ones. I know—the Rumanian bases."

"But," said Ryukov, with bewilderment, "there aren't any Rumanian bases."

Kornoloff gave a low chuckle.

"Exactly. Run up some dummy ones, fast, and then pull them down with maximum publicity Starting the demolitions next week."

"But . . ." said Ryukov, three times a Hero of the Soviet Union.

Kornoloff turned and frowned at him, and the triple Hero of the Soviet Union turned quite white.

Christmas Eve in the White House. The tree outside, facing Pennsylvania Avenue, was bigger even than last year's, carrying more coloured lights, in more colours, than ever before. The passengers in the cars which flowed past it, a steady double stream, commented, according to taste, on its beauty, or its vulgarity, or not at all. Inside the White House, at the foot of the main staircase, was an almost equally pretentious fir, with almost as many electric bulbs nestling in its branches. From the big drawing-room, where the First Lady was entertaining her guests, there came the sound of music: a small chamber orchestra was playing the Third Brandenburg Concerto, the one in G major, and playing it extremely well. Both the President and his wife were very fond of music, but had rather hackneyed, old-fashioned tastes. "I like the three Bs," the President had been quoted as saying. "Bach, Beethoven, and Brahms never lower their sights."

But the President was not there to hear the Bach this evening, or at least he could only hear it very faintly, a ghostly melody. There were several more women than men in the big drawing-room (many of them, it must be admitted, utterly bored by the music). The missing men were talking in the small library that the President had had built above the drawing-room, to hold his private collection of rare books. Those present included the Secretary of State, the President's special adviser on defence, the head of the Central Intelligence Agency, and the financier to whom Mr Cuthbertson referred as G.W.

"I shall have to hold a special Press Conference tomorrow," the President was saying. "And I honestly don't know what line to take. After all, this thing"—and he tapped a piece of paper that he held in his left hand—"is almost equivalent to an ultimatum, at least in tone."

"Is there any reason," the Secretary of State asked, "why we should publish it?"

"I guess not, unless the British do. But Braithwaite's letter to me is so very different in tone, that I imagine the official communication is drafted for the purpose of publication."

"Can't we go on playing for time?" asked the head of the CIA.

"No, I don't believe we can. The whole gist of this, I don't know what you'd call it, this demand, is that we move the combat elements of the Strategic Air Command out by 15th January, dismantle the rocket bases by 1st February, and evacuate our military, air, and naval personnel by 15th

February. And then, in his private letter to me, Braithwaite talks of cementing the close ties of friendship that have always united our two great peace-loving democracies. What the heck does he mean?"

The head of the CIA said:

"He probably thinks he means what he says. After all, it's what he's been saying all along. You know, like those wives who say to their husbands: 'I want a divorce and a fat alimony, and then we can be good friends.' Sometimes they really believe it, too."

"That brings up another point," said the President. "What about alimony? As you know, we've been falling over backwards making it easy for them. But in view of this"—and he tapped the paper again—"shouldn't we bring a little financial pressure to bear? Robner over at Treasury tells me the till must be getting pretty empty over there. There's a whacking amortization payment due next month. We could offer to waive this, in exchange for time. Because, hell, they're bound to come to their senses before long."

The President glanced at G.W., who replied slowly:

"I naturally don't have the information available to Robner, but maybe I have other sources. There are some pretty wild men in this Braithwaite government, Mr President, who are quite capable of either repudiating the debt or, worse, of going to the Russians for gold. And the Russians have plenty."

The head of the CIA now spoke again:

"So far as influencing British public opinion goes, any attempt to bring financial pressure would be interpreted as blackmail, and would be a gift to our enemies over there. Look at the way even the Conservatives reacted to that sort of thing at Suez."

"But they reacted."

"Which doesn't mean these ones will. I'm with G.W. I think anything on those lines would be playing straight into the hands of the Russians."

The President shrugged his shoulders almost helplessly.

"So what do we do? Pack up like good little boys, say thank you for the lovely party, and come home?"

The Secretary of State said:

"I don't see that we have an alternative at present. As you know, I'm one hundred per cent with you in your belief that the British aren't really like this. But I'm quite sure that anything that could be construed as an unfriendly gesture on our part would only harden them in their present attitude. As I see it, we must hold our horses and wait for Kornoloff to put his foot in it. He's bound to sooner or later. They always do."

The President said:

"I wish I felt as confident about that as you do, George. But I guess you're right. Only what do we do till we get the new bases operational?"

The special adviser on defence said:

"The Navy and SAC can do something about the Denmark Strait and the Baltic. We're back where we were five years ago, that's all."

"Five years ago the Russians didn't have two hundred nuclear subs."

"When will the bases be ready?" the President added.

"Fifty per cent operational by 1st June, the remainder by 1st October."

"Which means spreading the navy and air jam very, very thin for six months and more. During which time we *hope* that the Russians won't start anything, and we *hope* that the British will see sense."

"That's right," said the Secretary of State. "What else can we do?"

"Meanwhile," said the President, "what about my Press Conference?"

A young man who had been silent hitherto, now said:

"As a former Press man, Mr President, I should advise you against holding a conference on Christmas Day. That sounds like a real crisis."

"This is a real crisis. But I get you, we don't want to play it up."

"Anyhow there are no papers in Britain tomorrow."

"Don't they have another holiday the day after Christmas?"

"That's right," said the Secretary of State. "They call it Boxing Day."

"Why?" asked the President.

"God knows. Maybe they all go to prize fights."

"Not that it matters," said the President. "But do they have papers that day?"

Nobody knew. The President turned to the former newspaperman:

"Will you please find out if the British papers publish on the twenty-sixth? If they do, I'll hold a Press Conference that morning, in plenty of time for their evening papers. If they don't, then the twenty-seventh. That'll give us time for two full Cabinets, which I guess we'll need. And now let's go down and listen to some music."

Christmas Eve in Hampstead. Leonard Braithwaite and his wife had driven back to their old home from No 10. This was to perform an annual ceremony, and though the Prime Minister was excessively busy, it was the one part of Christmas that he was determined not to miss.

They let themselves in, and he switched on the hall light of their little house. Signed photographs lined the walls and the stairs. Ramsay MacDonald had gone in 1931, never to be rehung, and a youthful, thin Aneurin Bevan now hung in his place. Otherwise this was the steady accumulation of half a century. 'My portrait gallery', Mr Braithwaite liked to call it. And when he had lived here he had frequently stopped, while showing a guest out, in front of the photograph of Bertrand Russell, or the Webbs, or Kingsley Martin or Harold Laski, almost at random, it seemed. For he always made the same remark: "There was a man for you, a real man."

He now hesitated outside the drawing-room door.

"Shall we go in here for a moment?" he asked. "Or shall we go straight up?"

Mrs Braithwaite did not reply; so, as usual, he answered for her. "Straight up, I think."

On the first landing he stopped, for he was tired and short of breath. Then they went up to the top floor, and opened the door, and turned the switch.

The room was exactly as the boy had left it, that September day in 1936 when, to his father's great pride, he had decided to go to Spain instead of returning to the London School of

Economics. Only, of course, all had faded with the years. The orange spines of the Left Book Club publications in the shelves had turned to saffron: the chintz bedspread was now an almost colourless pattern of geometrical shapes. Only the Medici print of Van Gogh's 'Chair' that hung above the writing table was as brilliant as ever. On the table, the sheets of paper, which he would have covered with his bold, sprawling hand had he ever returned from Spain, had darkened. On Christmas Eve, 1936, a Moorish soldier had seen something move in the rubble of the University City outside Madrid, and the sights on his rifle had been true. So the white paper was now grey, and blank.

Mrs Braithwaite knelt beside the narrow bed with the curved white iron ends and buried her face in her hands. Each year Leonard Braithwaite wished that she would not kneel; he had never liked to ask her to whom it was she prayed. He himself stood with clasped hands and head bowed, and forced himself to remember his son. It became more difficult with every passing year. Yet there was one image that he could always conjure up. They were walking across the Heath, on a blustery autumn day, and the boy, aged ten, had looked up at his father and had said:

"When I grow up, I want to be exactly like you."

At this memory Braithwaite felt, at last and with gratitude, the tears welling up behind his eyes. But he did not weep: the boy would not have liked him to weep.

Mrs Braithwaite got to her feet, opened the cupboard, for a moment fingered the two suits and the grey flannel trousers and the brown tweed jacket hanging there, then turned towards the door. They walked down the stairs in silence, and in silence they stepped into the waiting car. Only when they had reached the Marylebone High Street did Braithwaite speak. He said:

"It gives me new strength to carry out my task."

And Mrs Braithwaite had replied:

"Poor Leonard. You are so tired."

Down at Broadacres, Rupert Page-Gorman had gone through some papers after dinner. These had taken rather longer than he expected. In particular there was an excessively long dispatch from the ambassador in Bonn, who had apparently been closeted for hours or even days together with the German Chancellor and the Foreign Minister. These two worthy Teutons had advanced every logical argument, and some not so logical, against the policy of withdrawing what still remained of the British Army of the Rhine. They even, Page-Gorman noticed with a frown, saw fit to criticize British policy as a whole. And the ambassador had reproduced this rhodomontade, apparently *in toto*, and in their own heavy style. Sir Charles Duncan had clearly been in Bonn for far too long, Rupert thought, and needed a complete change of scene. Reading between the lines, he thought to detect that the British ambassador almost seemed to agree with these Germans of his. A complete change of scene: maybe Rio, or Cairo, for Sir Charles.

It was thus nearly midnight by the time Rupert Page-Gorman re-entered the saloon. Only Antonia and Mark Vernon were still there. She looked up and smiled as he came in, and he said:

"Where is everyone?"

"Felix has gone to midnight Mass, and Nora to bed," Antonia replied. And then, softly, "You must be tired, Rupert."

"Tired? No, not particularly. Tell me, Vernon, what are you planning to do, now you're back?"

Mark Vernon tried his little-boy look on Rupert, but visibly without effect.

"I don't really know. First I must wait for the newspapers to have had enough of me, I suppose. After that—well, the only thing I know anything about is the Foreign Office. And I don't imagine that they would want to have me back."

Rupert replied, dryly:

"I don't either. In fact I had a hard time persuading them to drop the charges they'd prepared against you. If the Russian ambassador hadn't asked it as a personal favour, and hadn't explained what it was you actually did in Moscow, you'd probably be inside now. On the other hand, there are other jobs, not unconnected with foreign affairs, in which I imagine you could find a niche."

"You mean Chatham House, that sort of thing?"

"Not quite. After all, you're not a historian. But there are times when a man like me might want advice on Russian questions, no, not advice, explanations rather, from sources other than purely official ones. But this is probably all very premature. Meanwhile, there's always journalism."

"Yes," said Mark Vernon sadly and without a flicker of interest. "There's always journalism. A Sunday paper has already offered me five thousand for my life story. Ghost written."

"Take it, Vernon, take it."

"But what can I say?"

"Why bother about that? The ghost will know what to say."

Felix had, in fact, left for midnight Mass half an hour earlier than was really necessary. This had taken the Italian maids by surprise, and had led to considerable scurrying and *Mamma mia*-ing in their wing of the house, lest they keep the good *signore* waiting. But Felix had felt that he could not put up with any more of Antonia and that traitor Vernon. It would have been rude to go and sit somewhere alone in the big house, and, besides, there was always the danger that Page-Gorman might find him, and come and talk at him. Better, far better, to go to the church and wait.

He had taken the Jaguar, driving it himself, with the three maids seated side-by-side in the back, occasionally whispering together, their cotton-gloved hands clutching their missals upon their knees. It was quite a long drive, since the nearest Catholic church was fifteen miles away. But the car was warm and smooth, and Felix enjoyed driving in the dark, enjoyed the sweep of the headlights as he cornered, the occasional, startling illumination of a tree-trunk, or the eyes of a cat brilliantly yellow. It was almost all side-roads and he met very little traffic coming the other way. The rain had stopped, but the road still glistened blackly.

It was inevitable, he supposed, that Nora should invite Antonia for Christmas: after all, it was traditionally a family gathering. And since Antonia was apparently involved with this Page-Gorman fellow both politically and, he guessed, emotionally, no doubt they had to have him too. Besides, he had thought that it would be interesting to meet the famous, he might almost say notorious, Foreign Secretary, and possibly even useful to get some inkling of what was going through those people's minds. Furthermore, was it not in the truest English tradition that men and women who were violently inimical politically could yet meet with perfect social ease in one another's country houses? So, at least, he had always been led to believe. But this Vernon fellow was something else again. Nora had simply told him that she was asking 'a rather sad and lonely queer' who, she believed, would amuse Antonia. Why had she not told him who it was? Why, indeed, had he not asked? She had not exactly lied to him, but it had been, he thought, a lie of omission.

Had it not been Christmas Eve he might even have turned the man out of his house, when he realized, over tea, exactly who it was that he was entertaining. But he was glad now, in a way, that he had not done so. After all this *was* the season of goodwill: and Nora had been quite right, the man *was* pathetic, a dingy sort of husk. Furthermore, he supposed that we ought to forgive our political enemies along with the other sort. One of these days he must ask Father Crosby about that. Meanwhile it was logical to assume that we should forgive them as individuals, even pray for them, while opposing their atheistical machinations with all our might. One thing, though, he was determined about: he would not take Vernon, no, nor Page-Gorman for that matter, to the Barnabys' on Boxing Day. Christmas Day was one thing, Boxing Day another. Anyhow, Page-Gorman had already said he must be back in London on Christmas afternoon. He'd just have to drive Vernon—who had come down by train—up with him. Felix was certainly not taking him to Guy's to meet the county. Nora would have to make that quite plain. But he did so wish that she had not told him that lie by omission.

They had reached the village where was the church. It was not yet half past eleven. He drew up outside the small, unpretentious building, more like a village hall or a Nonconformist chapel, which was where he came to worship. The girls got out, murmuring thanks. They would get a seat, he explained, that was one advantage of being so early. He would go and park the car.

It was quiet in the village, though the row of petrol pumps outside the garage was brilliantly illuminated. One of these days, Felix thought, all these garages will be as useless and antiquated as blacksmiths' shops, and even less decorative. That, however, would not be for a long time. His broker had urged him to buy a substantial block of British Fuelless, when the shares were first put on the market. He had done so, at twenty-five shillings, and had watched them rise very quickly to forty. Then, much to his broker's horror, he had sold. And where were they now? Twelve and six. True, the whole stock market had slumped heavily since the election. But British Fuelless had taken an outsize header. Presumably because of the rumour that the American backers had cold feet. No, Felix told himself as he edged the long, black car into a convenient space off the main road beside the war memorial, it was not just that. There were huge fortunes to be made in atomic power, obviously, but it was still a risky business, besides being a natural for nationalization. And oil would always be wanted, both in his lifetime and in Toddy's too. He had been very wise to sell British Fuelless and buy Socanada Pref.

But this, he told himself as he switched off the engine and sat for a moment in silence, was no time to be thinking about investments. This was Christmas Eve. Where would he be the next time Christmas came around? Surely he would be here, would he not? And by next year he thought that Toddy might even be old enough to come to midnight Mass with him. But he could not help this gnawing, nagging feeling that somehow he would not. Would it be some French-Canadian priest whom he would see elevate the Host a year from now? It seemed incredible. And yet, and yet. . . . Few people in the City, he knew, shared his apprehension. Closehaven, for whom Felix had a great respect, had pooh-poohed his fears, remarking, quite truthfully, that they had weathered the '45 administration with very little trouble, and if they could deal with Cripps they could deal with anything. Socialism had been red-hot in those days: now it was an almost extinct volcano. And to judge by the way this fellow Page-Gorman had talked over dinner, he hardly seemed likely to go around confiscating people's capital. "Socialism," Page-Gorman had remarked, "in the 1950s was steered by a bunch of unimaginative, doctrinaire politicians on to a sandbank of fundamentally parochial issues. Nationalization, then old-age pensions, then colonial matters—can you wonder the electorate was apathetic? What we have done is to set Radicalism afloat again by raising real and important issues: first of all the issue of peace and war, secondly the issue, which is really an educational one, of producing an egalitarian society, and thirdly the issue of public morality." And with a laugh, Page-Gorman had added: "Our predecessors in the Movement fought to abolish poverty, and to a large extent they were successful. We are fighting for a far more ambitious programme: for the abolition of death, the inferiority complex, and sin." A man who could dismiss his Party's vote-catching slogans as cynically as that was hardly the sort to turn the country upside down. And as for this precious foreign policy of his, maybe there was something in it. Maybe the Russians were being genuine, and an age of perfect peace was about to be ushered in. May be. And yet, and yet. . . .

Were it not a question of Toddy's schooling, Felix told himself as he got out and locked the car (such a nuisance the way one had to lock everything up these days), he would almost be inclined to go to Canada now, for a couple of years, and see what the life was like over there. And why not? After all, he wouldn't be spending any time with Toddy, except in the holidays, and then the boy could fly across in a few hours. And with Nora acting in New York, he would see something of her. In fact, why Canada? Why not a house outside New York, one of those many pleasant houses to which he had been invited in Connecticut or on Long Island? Nora could come there for weekends, perhaps even every night after the theatre, if it wasn't too far away.

He was walking along the village street now, which was also the main road, on his way to the church. He passed the open door of a pub and heard the landlord calling out in singsong tones: "Come along now, please, long past time please." Felix caught a glimpse of the clock over the bar. Five to twelve. He was about to lengthen his stride when he remembered that they always keep the clocks fast in pubs. "Goodnight, Charlie," he heard. "Goodnight, Bill. Merry Christmas. Merry Christmas, Gertie." Good, friendly voices, warmed by beer and Christmas, he thought, without arrogance and without a cringe. English voices. Why should he leave this, his country, to try and live in America?

To be with Nora? Would she want him over there? She was always friendly here, always came down to Broadacres or met him in London when he asked her to, almost never suggested a meeting herself. Would she want him over there? He assumed she had a lover in London, and from a couple of remarks that he had heard, he guessed that the man was Patrick Clonard. A pleasant-enough fellow, so far as Felix remembered, with warmth as well as breeding, the sort of man whom a woman like Nora might well fall for. It had always astonished Felix that she had ever agreed to marry him: she was so brilliant, and beautiful, and sought after. And he was really nothing, except rich. And she had certainly not married him for his money. That she liked him he knew, and always had known. That she might come to love him had seemed to him, before their marriage, impossible. Then for a while she had, or she thought she had, and she had given him those four, wonderful years. But he had never believed that he could own her completely; her career alone had prevented that. So when, with gentleness and what was almost an unspoken apology, she had withdrawn her love, he had quite simply accepted, grateful for the years that were gone. Then, when Patrick, who had occasionally come down and had often been mentioned, ceased to be a visitor and dropped out of the conversation, he suspected that perhaps they were lovers. And now he had another cause to be grateful to her: her discretion and the care that she took not to hurt his feelings or insult his modest pride. And if she had to have a lover, as he supposed she did, then in a way Felix was glad that it should be Patrick, who would certainly neither damage her nor disgrace him.

A hundred yards ahead the church doors were open, and he could see people entering the welcoming, yellow light. Felix already felt that mellowness stealing over him which, for him, was perhaps the first emotion connected with divine worship, the loving warmth that he almost always felt when he communed with his God. Before surrendering altogether to that marvellous *caritas*, however, he had one last thought about his wife.

Was she, he wondered, really happy living this double life? Once, very delicately, a year ago, she had touched on the subject of divorce. He had immediately explained that for him divorce was, in all circumstances, unthinkable, first because of his faith, and secondly because of Toddy, who must have a mother and a proper home, and thirdly because of his position. Had this been unkind? His position, well, that he could sacrifice, if indeed it would be in any way affected. Oh, some of the more old-fashioned people whom he saw down here such as Lady Barnaby would disapprove, would look at him strangely, would probably be reminded (if they ever forgot it) that he was not *really* one of them. But that should not and could not be allowed to stand in the way of Nora's happiness. His faith? He could see that in certain circumstances—which he did not believe had arisen as yet, and, he hoped, never would—he might conceivably have to act against the letter of his faith in order to follow its profoundest teachings. It would be an awful decision to have to face, should the choice ever be between disobedience to his Church and unhappiness for Nora. But, he suspected, he would decide for Nora. On the other hand the question of Toddy was something else again. And here there could be no compromise. Toddy's home life must be perfect, at least until the boy was old enough to understand, which would certainly not be for another seven years. Yet he sincerely hoped that during these next seven years Nora would not be unhappy. He would certainly do everything in his power to ensure this. For he loved her.

And it was with this thought that he entered the bright little church, where the smell of woollen clothing mingled with the smell of old incense and that of the candles upon the altar. He made a deep genuflexion, then found a seat off to one side and near the back, and his mind became filled with thoughts of God.

8

THE ORDERS were out, the stores packed, the inventories completed, the barracks cleaned. Day after tomorrow, that is to say Monday, 21st January, the 1403rd Heavy Transportation Company, United States Army, would get into their ten-ton trucks, drive from Essex to Liverpool, and there embark for the journey home. The company had originally been stationed in south-east London, and had carried out a shuttle service between the Surrey Commercial Docks and various bases in East Anglia. Six weeks ago it had been moved to one of the major USAF bases, where for a while it had had nothing much to do. Lately it had been transporting the movable equipment from the base to the ports. Now the base was deserted: the big bombers had flown away, to the Continent or back to America: the maintenance staff had followed: the base administration, the hospital, the cooks, and so on had left in their turn: apart from a skeleton staff of RAF with whom they had no contact, there were no soldiers left on and about the huge, deserted airfield, save only the 1403rd Heavy Transportation Company, and they were ready to roll.

The barrack was an old, World War II Nissen hut, with rounded corrugated-steel roof and cracked concrete floor. A dozen soldiers were whiling away their last Saturday afternoon in England. Seven of them, three white and four coloured, were shooting dice, without much enthusiasm, in the corner by the stove: two were asleep: two were reading comic-books, lying on their beds: Pfc Lincoln Lee was writing a letter, slowly and awkwardly, for the pen seemed as fragile as a matchstick in his huge, black hand as he pushed it laboriously along the lined, blue paper, frowning.

'. . . well, sugar,' he wrote. 'I guess there's not much more to say cept . . .' He hesitated, crossed out *cept*, wrote *exept*. One of the soldiers who had apparently been asleep rolled over, sat up, and said:

"Next week, Times Square. Boy, oh boy, oh boy." And he whistled loudly. A comic-book reader replied by singing the first line of 'California here I come'. The crap game took no notice. Linc went on writing.

'. . . exept that I will always love my sugar and maybe one day the clouds will roll away and . . .'

He looked up at the dusty window, against which an occasional scurry of rain was blowing. He weighed two hundred and sixty-eight pounds, stood six foot four and a half, and his skin was so black that it had blue lights in it. Carleen, the girl to whom he was writing, weighed seven stone three, and her hair was dyed yellow, and her face very thin. She had once said to him, trying to talk American: "We sure must look funny together, me and you," and had giggled. He had given his deep rumbling laugh, walking hand-in-hand along the edge of the Serpentine in Hyde Park. That had been last summer.

I don't care if I *never* see Times Square again, Linc thought. All I want to see is my sugar, my Carleen, like a little doll she is, so fragile and small, my little doll.

People had been good to him, here in England. Oh, they had funny ways and it was hard at first to understand what it was they were trying to say, and their warm beer had seemed terrible to begin with, but they had been kind to him down in Bermondsey. It was Carleen's father who had first talked to him. He was a docker and when he learned that Linc's father had also been a longshoreman, on the East River, till a roll of swinging newsprint broke loose from a crane and landed on him, and that Linc had also worked the docks as a boy, there was a bond, a subject of talk. One Sunday, seeing the big, coloured man lounging about the streets alone, the English docker had, on an impulse, invited him to his back-to-back home for tea. Carleen had been visiting her parents: she lived on the other side of London, where she worked in a laundry. They had left together, and when he had asked her if she would like to have a drink, she had said:

"I don't mind if I do."

That was how it had begun, she aged eighteen, he twenty-two. His Carleen, his little doll, his sugar. Once, when they were lying together, she had leaned over him and said:

"Linc, why are the insides of your hands pink when the rest of you is so black?"

And he had answered, lazily:

"I don't know, sugar. I guess that's just the way the good Lord made us folk."

And she had said:

"Oh, Linc, I *love* it the way you are!"

Then he had laughed and taken her in his arms. And now he had been locked up here for six weeks, without one single pass to go to London and see Carleen. And Monday they were leaving England for ever. He returned to his writing paper.

At the far end of the hut the door flew open, and with a burst of wind from off the North Sea and a flurry of raindrops, M/Sgt Floyd Mills was there, in shining helmet-liner and waterproof cape. From down the room came cries of: "Close the door! For Chrissake close the door!" The master sergeant did so, then announced:

"See here, men. Captain Lewison says as we're leaving Monday, he'll give six-hour passes for Bishop's Stortford for tonight. Transportation leaves from outside the mess-hall at eighteen hundred. OK, who wants to go?"

There were cries of: "Yippee!" groans, questions:

"What's this place?" "Can we go to London?" answered by "No!" but eventually they all put their names down. With a fresh gust of wet east wind, the door of the hut closed behind M/Sgt Mills. Those of the men who had not sent their civilian clothes on ahead dug them out of their kitbags or valises. The crap game was resumed. Linc did not continue his letter, for he had decided what he was going to do.

Jack Beaulieu had also decided what he was going to do that evening.

He and Moyra had motored down to Bourne End the evening before. This was to be the first weekend that they had spent alone together for a very long time and might, for all Jack knew, be their last. For he had decided that the time had come to sort this tangle out. He dreaded doing so; on the other hand he dreaded even more the thought of having to go on watching his wife play-acting in front of himself and others, and relapsing into dumb misery whenever she thought she was unobserved. What was she miserable about? Her infidelity to him? The way Page-Gorman was treating her? He must find out, the situation must be clarified. Nor was there anyone he had to ask down, for business was slack these days.

He had let Friday evening come and go, in the big house by the river. They had played backgammon, and Moyra had smiled whenever she thought she should, and then they had watched the television, and gone to bed. Next morning, too, nothing had been said. Only after lunch, after the coffee things had been taken away, had Jack tackled the subject, head-on.

"Moyra," he said, "you must tell me the truth. What is the matter?"

She had replied, quickly and nervously:

"The matter, Jack? What do you mean?"

"We've been together too long for me not to . . . well, not to sense your moods. What is it you're so unhappy about?"

She had given a false little laugh.

"Unhappy, Jack? Why should I be unhappy? Perhaps I've been a bit worried. Everybody's worried these days. About politics and so on——"

He interrupted her:

"Really, Moyra."

She went on, almost desperately:

"And then your business. You told me yourself things were bad. People closing down accounts all over the place, and not opening new ones, and——"

"Darling, when we were *broke* you didn't act like this. And we're far from broke now. Or likely to be. Do be honest with me, please."

He went across and sat on the sofa beside her. She looked at him, and suddenly she burst into tears, burying her head on his shoulder.

"Oh, Jack, I feel so awful. I hate myself so. I've made such a mess of everything. Jack, I'm such a dreadful person these days." He took his silk handkerchief from his breast pocket, and passed it to her, and she went on, dabbing her eyes, with her tears now more or less under control. "You shouldn't be nice to me like this, Jack. I don't deserve it any more. And you've always been so sweet."

"Is that what it is? Or has he been treating you badly?"

She drew away from him slightly, and looked up, her eyes red-rimmed. She said:

"He?"

"Rupert Page-Gorman."

She said, very softly:

"You knew? How did you know?"

"Antonia told me, six weeks ago."

"The bitch!" Moyra said, loudly now. "The dirty, low-down bitch! Oh, Jack, she didn't tell you, did she?"

"Yes. She wanted me to intervene. She said he belonged to her."

"But, but why didn't you say anything?"

"What could I say?" There was a note of bitterness in his voice. "Tell you that you must stop seeing your lover because that popeyed pacifist wanted him? Besides . . ."

"Besides what?"

"I didn't believe it could last. Not with a self-centred bastard like Page-Gorman. And particularly if he was two-timing you at that. But I thought you'd better find that out for yourself."

"Why did I have to go and fall for such a heel as that one? Why, Jack?"

She had quite stopped crying, but she held on to his handkerchief, screwing it up into a ball, her fingers twisting about it.

"We don't have an awful lot of choice in these matters, darling. At least not always. Half the time it's glands or something. You know. Like me with that French girl at Juan. She was awful, too."

"Oh, Jack, you are so sweet to me."

"But, Moyra, tell me this. And think hard before you answer. It is all over between you and him, isn't it?"

She looked down, hesitated, then said:

"Jack, I hate him."

"So do I. But if you do, then it isn't all over."

"Yes it is, Jack, I promise you it is. It's not just that he lied to me and cheated me and treated me like a tart. I suppose he had a right to do that. I behaved like one. But he's so, I don't know, so horribly cynical. I mean about his politics."

"What about his politics?"

"All this talk about Britain for the British, and turning out the Americans and hurrah for the flag. And all the time he knows that the Russians are coming."

"What are you talking about, Moyra?"

"It's the truth. We dined at that big new hotel at the top of Hertford Street night before last and he said it would make a lovely headquarters for the Russians. I thought he was joking, but later that evening at his flat. . . . Oh, I'm so sorry, Jack. But then we had this terrible row, about that bitch. And I couldn't sleep. And I went into his drawing-room to smoke a cigarette, and there on his desk was this piece of paper. I read it. And it said about the Russians coming. And they are to have that hotel. He wasn't joking at all."

"What exactly did it say?"

"I can't really remember. I was in such a state. But it was marked Top Secret, and it was headed RUSSIAN INSPECTORATE, and it said about that hotel. I thought it was all so awful that I dressed, oh, forgive me, Jack, and left. He's a crook, a dirty, low-down crook."

When Jack now spoke, after a pause, his manner was quite changed, and extremely calm.

"Moyra, do you promise me you'll never see him again? At least not without telling me?"

"Yes, Jack, I do, I do. I never want to see him again."

"You may have to. I hope not. Meanwhile, where is this flat of his?"

She told him.

"Are there any servants? I imagine not, if he took you there."

"Just a char."

"Does he normally keep papers there?"

"I—I don't know."

"Have you got a key to it?"

She nodded, and turned her head away.

"You've still got it?"

Again she nodded, and said:

"He, he wanted me to give it back to him. For Antonia, I suppose. That's what started the row."

"Give it to me."

"It's in my bag, upstairs."

"Get it, please."

She left the room. While she was gone, Jack walked across to the telephone on her desk, looked up Page-Gorman's number in the leather address book, and asked for it. There was no reply. Then he put through a call to the Foreign Office.

"Mr Page-Gorman's private secretary, please."

Moyra re-entered the room, the two keys, a heavy, old-fashioned iron one for the front door, and the Yale that opened the flat, in her hand. He took them from her, smiled, and put them in his pocket, as he said into the telephone:

"I should like to speak to Mr Page-Gorman please. No, it's private business. My name is Beaulieu, Jack Beaulieu. Yes, he knows me well enough."

There was a moment's silence, then the watching woman heard her husband say:

"Hello, yes, Beaulieu here. There is something I must discuss with you. This evening. I daresay you are busy. I hardly expected you not to be. No, it won't wait. It's about Moyra. What's that?" Page-Gorman said something at the other end, and then Jack spoke in a voice of icy crispness such as Moyra had never before heard. "If you are suggesting that I am attempting to blackmail you, I suggest you think twice before you make such insinuations. I see. Good. I imagine you are as anxious to avoid a scandal as I am. No, it will not take up much of your precious time. Yes, I can be at the Travellers' at six. Goodbye."

He jiggled the telephone rest, then asked for Patrick Clonard's number. To him he simply said that he would be round at five, and to cancel any appointments he might have before eight o'clock.

Finally he telephoned his admirable secretary, who was also fortunately at home, and told her to go at once to his office, and to arrange for the photographic room to be made ready. There were some lay-outs that he wished to photograph that evening. No, he didn't need any technicians. He knew how to use the cameras himself.

General Nikitin was the only man left who made Mr Kornoloff nervous. Not that he had any reason to suspect Nikitin of disloyalty, he thought, as he glanced across the table at the heavily-built man with the shrewd and kindly eyes; but Nikitin was clearly not frightened of *him*. Therefore it was likely, indeed logical, that Nikitin must have at his disposal reserves of strength of which Kornoloff was not aware. The trouble was that these people always did. True, when it came to the point the successive heads of the OGPU, NKVD, and so on had been eliminated by his predecessors without a great deal of trouble. But one never knew, until they were dead, quite what they were up to. And Nikitin undoubtedly had foreign contacts in Peking and elsewhere which he kept to himself. Kornoloff glanced up at Nikitin from under his bushy eyebrows, and met Nikitin's steady gaze. Kornoloff had become unaccustomed to being looked straight in the eye. It made him feel uncomfortable. He said:

"Will you be going to London yourself?"

"I have a good man there, but I think I should."

"Who is your good man there?"

"The name would mean nothing to you. He is an Irishman."

There you are, thought Kornoloff. And this Irishman would presumably treat the Russian ambassador just as Nikitin was treating him, *fobbing him off*.

"This Irishman, does he speak good English?"

"Of course."

"Why, of course?"

"They all do. They all speak English."

"That is incorrect. They used to speak English. Now it is compulsory that they speak Irish, since the Irish Revolution. It has all been changed in the past forty years. You should know that, Nikitin."

Nikitin said nothing, and Kornoloff was pleased to have won his point. He went on:

"Therefore I think it advisable that you should go to London yourself. The inspectorate is fully prepared?"

"The first wave can leave at six hours' notice. The Special Battalion RKK can follow within twenty-four hours. The six airborne divisions have been alerted."

"And when will you go yourself?"

"Probably with the RKK battalion. Do you believe that the

Chinese will in fact start the Formosa operation on the date fixed?"

Kornoloff was instantly wary. Did Nikitin perhaps know more about this than he did? He said:

"Have you any reason for believing that they won't?"

Nikitin shrugged.

"No, none. Except that they are Chinese."

"They have promised—Monday. Therefore the first wave of the inspectorate must be ready to leave on Tuesday."

"I have told you, it is ready."

"And it is my opinion that you should go with it."

"I have various matters to attend to here, and in Prague."

Various matters, Kornoloff thought, there you are again!

"What matters?"

"Administrative problems."

And so the conversation went on.

"That," said Jack Beaulieu, "is what I want you to do. And now, though it is only five o'clock, I should be much obliged if you would give me a smallish whisky and soda."

Patrick walked across to the cupboard in the corner of his drawing-room.

"And what," he asked, "do you propose to do with these precious papers once you have photographed them?"

"Once *you* have photographed them, Patrick. While I keep him busy at his club. Why, first I shall read them. Thank you." He took a swallow of his whisky and soda. "And then, if they are what I suspect they are, I shall make it my business to see that they get into the right hands. I hope and believe this will make certain that the bugger is kicked out of public life once and for all."

"You're asking me to commit a fairly serious crime."

"That's right," said Jack.

"Suppose I'm caught, ransacking his desk?"

"You were there on my behalf, looking for compromising letters from my wife."

"That'll look sweet in the papers."

"Don't be silly. Page-Gorman would never let it reach the papers."

"Jack, you're telling me to do this as if you were ordering me to take a client out to lunch. But you engaged me as an advertising man, not as an international spy."

Beaulieu dropped his deliberately flippant, hard-boiled manner which, as Patrick realized, he had only adopted as self-protection while talking about his wife's infidelity.

"Listen, Patrick, this may be very, very serious. A man came to see me last Friday, from Cuthbertson. He wanted to know, as a matter of supreme urgency, whether I had heard any rumours about Russian military experts visiting this country. I naturally said I hadn't. And now I have. Don't you see what it could mean?"

"No, Jack, I don't. After all we sent an inspectorate to Poland. Why shouldn't they do the same here?"

"Because their motives are not the same as ours."

"I think it's all a lot of hoo-ha."

"Do you, Patrick?"

"No, not really. But I'd like to." He paused. "OK. I'll do it."

"There's a good fellow. Now just ring Antonia, to make sure she's at home, and stays at home. And I'll see you at the office at seven."

The ten-ton truck dropped Linc, and twenty-five other men of the 1403rd Heavy Transportation Company, in the middle of Bishop's Stortford, in the darkness and the rain. Though they knew it not, they were the only men of the United States forces in Britain who were legally out of barracks not on duty. At least they thought that they were out of barracks legally, for they certainly all had a pass, signed by Captain Lewison, their company commander: they could hardly know that their presence in this somewhat uninviting little country town was yet another proof of the power of the printed word.

For Captain Lewison, as bored as his men by forcible incarceration in the deserted air force base, had lately been reading. He had only just finished a book, which last summer had topped the non-fiction best-seller list in the *New York Sunday Times*, called *Irresponsibility*. It was a brilliant and pungent attack on the spinelessness of the American male, his conformism, and his growing inability to assert himself, show initiative, or question the orders he received. It had all made a lot of sense to Lewison, particularly the part that dealt with the sex-life of the American male. He examined his own attitudes, and sex-life, and found that in many respects he was just such a man as the author of *Irresponsibility* described, and by God! he was going to do something about it. Why should his men be confined to barracks for absolutely no offence, because the politicians had frigged up relations with Britain? The natives of Essex were perfectly friendly, and, when on duty outside the base, he had more than once heard the civilians express regrets that the soldiers were no longer about. Here was a clear opportunity to show initiative: he would let his men, or those who wanted, out for the evening, to Bishop's Stortford of course, not to London. The captain felt a braver and more manly male as he signed their passes and ordered the truck.

So the little group of soldiers made their way down Hill Street, looking vaguely for a pub called the Goat and Compasses which, rumour had it, was frequented by girls of the flashier sort. When at last they found it, there were no flashy girls in sight (they had ceased coming up on the afternoon train from London when the soldiers were confined to their bases), but the landlord gave them a warm welcome. They ordered their drinks, and switched on the juke box, and ordered another drink, and then one or two of the local *vivandières* did drift into the saloon bar, for rumours travel fast in small country towns. It was half an hour before anyone noticed that Linc Lee was not with them. By then he was seated in a train bound for Liverpool Street, wiping the rainwater from his blue-black face with a large khaki-coloured handkerchief.

Jack Beaulieu entered the Travellers' Club at two minutes past six, and asked for Mr Page-Gorman. The porter replied that he would see if Mr Page-Gorman was in the club, and Jack was about to turn away when he heard a friendly voice behind him say:

"The most extraordinary political appointment since Caligula made his horse consul."

It was his old friend, Sir Charles Duncan.

"Hullo, Charles," said Jack. "What are you doing here? Why aren't you in Bonn?"

"I'm not in Bonn because your charming friend, Rupert Page-Gorman, saw fit to sack me last week."

"No friend of mine, Charles, old boy. Are you getting another embassy? Washington, Paris, Moscow?"

Charles made a face.

"The boy-wonder has offered me Rio. I may take it. Ah, here's my guest. Do you know Air Marshal Boreham? Mr Beaulieu. Join us for a drink in the bar, Jack, if you feel like getting the taste of horse-manure out of your mouth later on."

The two elderly knights moved away together, Jack was still puzzling over the violence of the language used by Charles Duncan, usually the most urbane of men, when a page arrived to lead him to the Foreign Secretary.

Patrick parked his car on the far side of the square from the house in which Page-Gorman had his flat, having first driven slowly past it in order to identify the number. Then he got out of his car, locked it, and had a good look at the house that he must burgle. There was no light anywhere. The drawing-room, as he knew, faced the front, with long windows opening on to a narrow, wrought-iron balcony. Even with the curtains drawn, a chink of light would surely have been visible were there anyone in. Page-Gorman, he knew, was with Jack. Antonia had told him, when he rang her twenty minutes ago, that she was having her Russian lesson, but would love to see him between a quarter past and half past six. Why should there be anyone in Page-Gorman's flat? Nor was there a policeman outside, as there was outside some of these cabinet ministers' London homes. But then this was not Page-Gorman's official home. For as long as he was Foreign Secretary, his country gave him a house in Carlton House Gardens. It was there that he lived. This flat he kept for his unofficial activities, amorous and, if Jack was right, of another sort as well.

With his empty briefcase in his left hand he made his way, limping slightly more than usual for this wet weather was bad for his leg, past all the other parked cars. The old square was deserted under the brilliant orange street lights; from behind the buildings came the grinding of traffic and the huge hum of London.

Beneath the lovely, eighteenth-century fanlight he stopped, glanced both ways, then put the iron key in the lock. The big door creaked open, and he slipped in, closing it quietly behind him. It was not pitch dark in the stone-flagged hallway, for a beam of orange light poured down on the stairs, but it was too dark for him to find the switch. He stood motionless for a moment, testing the silence of the old house, and conscious of his heart-beats. He had not felt such tenseness, such acuteness of perception since . . . since when? And then he remembered Hill 405, and the patrol that he had led to within a hundred yards of the Chinese positions, which had taken them so long to find. Again and again they had stopped, and he had listened, just as he was listening now. Only then he had not been alone.

In the darkness he shrugged his shoulders. Here at least there was unlikely to be a machine-gun pointing at him down the stairs, and time was short. He took his lighter from his pocket and flicked it. The inch-long gas jet made the whole stone hallway and stairs jump forward, and the banisters cast strange, moving shadows as he made his way up. He had no trouble in opening the door of the flat. He switched on the lights, went into the drawing-room, and switched on in there. Then he drew the curtains. A practised burglar, he thought as he did so, would have drawn the curtains first instead of revealing himself full-length to anybody who might be passing in the square below.

He had been in this room once before, when Antonia had taken him there, dragged him he might almost say, to make his complaint about the police officer Prendergast. Page-Gorman had then sat in that armchair, he and Antonia on the sofa, and Page-Gorman had listened to his tale with the weary tolerance of a house-master when a boy is making a complaint which, understandably serious to him in his little world of school, can only appear trivial to a grown man. Patrick had stumbled through to the end, whereupon Page-Gorman had made a few remarks about the police doing their duty, but had agreed that in this case it had been somewhat over-done. He would see to it that the man was reprimanded. Page-Gorman had then made it unmistakably plain that Clonard was dismissed, the audience over, and with relief Patrick had made his way out into the square, leaving Antonia behind him. Nor had he ever heard any more about his complaint. With a grim smile Patrick hoped that Prendergast would not walk in here now.

He walked across to the big, flat-topped desk that stood between the windows, and switched on the desk light. It was very tidy. In the far right-hand corner stood a portable typewriter, balancing the telephone on the other side. Beneath the desk lamp stood one of those little pieces of furniture that hold writing paper, envelopes of various size, with, in front, inkwells and a small tray for pens, indiarubbers, and paper clips. There was also a blotter, fairly clean, perhaps a hundred sheets of good foolscap paper, and a clean ashtray. This desk looked as though it had not been used for months. There were four drawers, two on each side.

He opened the top left-hand drawer. It contained nothing save a small dictaphone. Page-Gorman, he thought, was certainly fully equipped to give permanent shape to any thought that might cross his mind. He closed that drawer, and opened the one below. Here were three cardboard folders, and he felt for the first time something of the excitement of a treasure hunt, as he laid them on the desk. But they were quite uninteresting. The top one was marked INCOME TAX. He glanced through the papers it contained, and they were, indeed, just what they purported to be, Page-Gorman's income tax returns for the last ten years and his correspondence with his tax accountant. Patrick noted that his income for the previous year had been £6548. The realization that he found this fact momentarily interesting, and even wondered how Page-Gorman could have made as much from his occasional journalism, suddenly disgusted Patrick. What on earth was he doing, prying about in such matters? The second folder was marked BANK AND SECURITIES, and again was just that: bank statements, and security transfers and correspondence with his broker. The third, too, FLAT, RATES, &c., was not worth the attention of an international spy or even of a jealous husband. He replaced the folders, and closed the drawer. At that moment the telephone rang on the desk.

Automatically he reached for it, and only just withdrew his hand in time. It was as though he had been about to pick up a stick which he had recognized at the last possible moment to be a poisonous snake. And his heart began to beat again, ferociously, almost to the rhythm of the telephone buzzer that seemed to go on and on and on.

Funny, Antonia thought, as the telephone that she was holding to her ear gave its fifth, sixth, seventh ring in the distant flat. Rupert had said he would be back just after six. She glanced at the small pile of socks that she had been mending during her Russian lesson. It would have been such fun to tell him that his socks were ready, and perhaps he would have liked to come round, and have a drink, and pick them up. Then they might have dined together, and maybe gone back to his flat, and she could have done those things, those quasi-maternal things, to him that he appreciated so and that gave her such exquisite pleasure. Funny that there was no answer, she thought, her eyes resting on the back of Mark Vernon's head as he gazed out of the window. He might be in the bathroom. She would let it ring a little longer.

Was she, she wondered, making a mistake in refusing to allow him to have sexual intercourse with her in the normal way? But had he not said himself, when she had explained to him about her revulsion ever since her brief and ghastly marriage:

"Such a relief, Antonia. Most of these women just want to squeeze a man like a tube of toothpaste. All they care about is their own orgasms."

That was what he had said, and in different words repeated more than once. As for the other, he could get that anywhere. From Moyra Beaulieu, for instance, or any casual pick-up. But should she perhaps see a doctor, just in case?

No, he was certainly not at home. She replaced the receiver.

In Page-Gorman's flat Patrick felt an enormous surge of relief as the telephone stopped ringing. Quickly he opened the right-hand drawers. Here, too, were folders. The first was of Press clippings. The second was entitled GEN. ELECTION. A rapid glance showed that it was out-of-date material. But the other two, marked respectively FO and O'REILLY were clearly what he had been sent here to find. Indeed the first paper in the O'REILLY folder must be the one that Moyra had seen, for it was a Foreign Office document, classified TOP SECRET, headed USSR INSPECTORATE and was annotated in a small, neat hand that, judging by the titles on the folders, was not Page-Gorman's.

Patrick put the two folders in his briefcase. The bottom drawer contained nothing save tins of tobacco and tapes for the tape recorder. These were new, still cellophane-wrapped, and could be of no interest. Patrick switched off the lights, but did not draw back the curtains. He would have to come back, to replace the folders. This was a job that he did not relish at all.

It was nearly eight o'clock by the time Linc's taxi dropped him at Carleen's address, off Copenhagen Street, which is behind King's Cross Station. Linc gave the driver a pound note.

"Keep it," he said.

"This is a quid mister, this isn't a ten-bob note."

"Keep it," Linc repeated.

The taxi driver glanced at him, then shrugged. Why not? These Yanks had money to burn. He put his taxi into gear, as Linc turned towards the shabby brown house, and began to climb the steps to the peeling front door. It was all new to him. Carleen had moved here since he had gone to Essex. He rang the bell.

After a longish pause the door opened, and he was confronted by an elderly woman in carpet slippers, her stringy grey hair in curlers. She said, at once:

"Nothing to let here," and closed the door.

He rang again. This time the door opened only a crack, and the woman said:

"Can't you read the notice? No coloureds."

Linc explained that he wasn't in search of lodgings, that he wished to see Carleen. The woman now opened the door a little wider and looked at him with the greatest distrust. Then, without a word, she turned away, and shuffled up the stairs. Linc stood motionless in the brownish hall, amidst the smell of drains and cabbages and stale tobacco.

Then, suddenly, Carleen was there, running down the stairs and into his arms.

"Oh, Linc, Linc, I never thought I'd see you again. Oh, Linc, Linc."

"My baby," he said, "my sugar doll," as his great arms closed about her thin, vibrating body, and his pink lips met her scarlet ones.

"Stop that at once!" The woman in carpet slippers was half way down the stairs. "Stop it! This is a respectable house."

They both turned to face her, he with one arm still about his girl's shoulders.

"Disgusting!" said the woman.

"This is my fee-ong-say," said Carleen.

"I've heard that one before," snapped the old woman, who was now standing beside them. "What will the neighbours say, standing there in the hall with the door open. . . ."

Carleen said:

"Come on up to my room, Linc."

"Oh no you don't," said the landlady, with mounting fury. "What sort of a house do you think this is? You ought to be ashamed of yourself."

Linc was bewildered. Why was this old woman interfering between Carleen and himself? What did it all mean? Carleen's voice was almost equally shrewish when she replied:

"I know what sort of a house this is. You're nothing but a bloody old, bloody old . . ."

"Don't you dare talk to me like that. You'll pack your bags and get out tomorrow. Bringing niggers in here. Disgusting!"

Linc moved forward when he heard the insulting word, then stopped. Carleen said:

"Wait here a minute, Linc, while I get my coat."

"He can wait outside," said the landlady in a stony voice.

And so Linc waited outside, in the pouring January rain. When Carleen joined him, she led him first into a doorway a few yards up the street that gave a little protection, and there they kissed for a long, long time.

Patrick replaced the folders in the drawer which he then closed. Outside a clock was chiming eight. He glanced quickly around the room, to ensure that there was no sign of his two visits. So far as he could see, there was none. Then he walked across to the windows, thought better of it, and switched off the overhead light and the desk light before drawing back the curtains. From behind him came the faint light in the hallway: in front, beyond the knitting needles of winter rain, the lighted square. For perhaps five seconds he stood there, looking out.

He was aware of a car turning into the square. It turned again, and was now coming this way. It stopped almost immediately outside the house, and Patrick was suddenly, once again, entirely tense. He walked quickly across the drawing-room. Had the door into the hall been open or closed? He could no longer remember. He switched off the hall light, opened the front door, and closed it, as quietly as he could, behind him. At that moment he heard a key turning in the big, iron lock downstairs.

Three steps at a time he bounded up the stairs, and had just reached the corner when the lights went on. He heard the street door bang, as he flattened himself in an angle of the staircase. Footsteps echoed up the well.

It was Antonia's voice he heard first.

". . . and then rang up at seven and said he was sorry, he couldn't make it. I wonder what he wanted."

"He's Nora's lover, isn't he?"

"That's probably what it was. Though he's never rung me before."

Now he could hear them slowly climbing the stairs, and he shrank back even farther into his corner. Rupert asked:

"Have your Russian lesson?"

"It's awfully difficult, but Mark's very sweet and patient."

He heard Rupert grunt, then say:

"You may need it sooner than you think."

"Oh, Rupert, you don't mean you're thinking of taking me——"

He could just see the crown of Page-Gorman's brown hat, as they stopped outside the flat door. He heard the clink of keys, as Rupert replied:

"Taking you? Taking you to Moscow? Good God, no."

Then the door had opened and closed behind them. After a

few seconds the light in the hall went out, and Patrick made his way, as quietly as possible, down the dark stairs and out into the street.

Linc's voice was hoarse and urgent:

"Let's find some place, sugar. There must be some place."

He loosened his grip on her slightly, and ran his huge hand over her wet, yellow hair. He could almost crush her little skull in that one hand. "Don't you know anywhere?"

She shivered, and looked up in the pale light.

"I'm so cold, Linc. I'll think of somewhere. But let's go and have a drink first. I'm so cold."

They moved out of the doorway.

Patrick was suffering from the usual reaction to strain when he entered Jack Beaulieu's office ten minutes later: he felt tired, and the slight ache in his wounded leg was worse. Jack, seated on the desk, talking into the telephone, waved to him. Patrick looked across at Jack's superlative secretary, who smiled back. She was engaged in putting the result of their evening's work, a sizeable pile of black-and-white positives on shiny paper, into two sets of brown manilla envelopes. The negatives formed a neat, curved mound on the far corner of her desk.

Jack was saying:

". . . no, Charles, I can't possibly discuss it over the telephone. What's that? Then bring the air marshal along. Good idea. Of course this isn't a joke. When have I ever played a joke on you?" There was a pause, and he laughed. "But my dear Charles, we were undergraduates at that time." Charles said something, and again Jack laughed. "In that case, all I can say is you're a permanent third secretary. Do you know the joke about the diplomatist and the French tart? *Il entra simple attaché* . . . Oh, you told it to me, did you? Yes, at my flat, at nine. And by all means bring the air marshal. Be seeing you."

He hung up, and swung around to face Patrick.

"My boy, if you think your day's work is over, I'm afraid you're making a big mistake. Is your passport in order?"

131

Patrick nodded.

"I have, with the greatest difficulty, got you a seat on the Super-Comet that leaves at midnight. You will be taking material concerning our advertising campaign for British Fuel-less to Cuthbertson. I assume you have no objection to going to New York?"

Nora was in New York.

"I haven't got an American visa," Patrick said.

"A good point. I've put through a personal call, what they call a person-to-person call over there, to Cuthbertson. At the moment he's playing golf at Piping Rock. They're fetching him in from the fourteenth green, furious no doubt. I don't imagine he'll have much trouble in seeing that the immigration authorities let you through."

"How long do I stay in New York?" Patrick asked, with a happy smile. Nora, he thought, Nora.

Jack Beaulieu had seen his smile and understood it.

"During the Peninsula War a subaltern asked Wellington for a week's leave, to meet his wife who was arriving in Lisbon from England. The Iron Duke replied that forty-eight hours was the longest time that any normal man could possibly want to stay in bed with the same woman, and gave him two days."

The secretary, pretending shock, said:

"Really, Mr Beaulieu!"

Jack ignored this, and went on:

"But I'll be more generous. Come back Wednesday or Thursday."

The telephone rang. Jack picked it up, listened, then said:

"This is my call to Cuthbertson."

The pub was at the corner of Copenhagen Street. In the summer its exterior was stonily, dingily forbidding, with its frosted glass windows, its brown stonework, and its general air of belonging more to Mayhew's London than to the city that now existed. The ghosts of women in shawls with pinched-faced children clutching at their skirts still seemed to wait on the kerb while their drunken husbands spent the week's earnings within. The smell of a century's slops and sweat seeped out to greet the passer-by.

In wintertime, and particularly on a raw, wet night such as this, it presented a better face to the world. Light streamed through the frosted glass, the sound of voices and occasionally of music was audible as the swing-doors opened and closed, a promise of warmth and companionship and human fug, the immemorial attraction of the cave.

Carleen pushed the door marked SALOON and they went in. Momentarily the light, which was very bright, blinded them. Then they saw that the bar was fairly full. At the table in the corner sat half a dozen youngish men of the type who would have been called Teddy boys ten years ago, bootlace ties, black leather windcheaters, sideburns. With them were three girls. Four men were playing darts in the other corner, one of them in the blue uniform of British Railways, perhaps a ticket-collector from the station. Three men of more affluent appearance, two in raincoats, one in a camel-hair coat, stood at the bar. Behind the bar the landlord was in his shirtsleeves, a heavy gold watch chain across his paunch, his nose broken, an obvious ex-prizefighter. There were many bottles behind the bar, row upon row, reflected in the huge mirror with a gold-letter advertisement for a defunct distillery that backed them.

Linc and Carleen walked towards the bar, as conversation died away among the Teddy boys and their girls.

"What do you want, sugar?" Linc asked, looking down at her.

"I'm that cold. Cherry brandy please."

Linc Lee was not a drinking man. He said:

"What's that, sugar?"

"It's ever so good."

They had reached the bar. Linc said:

"A cherry brandy, and I guess I'll have a beer."

"Sorry," said the landlord.

There was now silence in the bar, except for the sound of the darts entering the plasticine board. Linc did not understand, or rather assumed that the landlord had not understood. He raised his voice:

"A cherry brandy, and a small beer."

Three of the youths had got up, and were sauntering across

the room. Two of the girls with them looked excited, the third frightened. The landlord said:

"I'm not serving you."

Linc looked around, at the ring of faces that now encircled him. The other youths had got to their feet. The darts game stopped.

"That's right," said one of the men. "We don't want no spades in here."

"I don't——" Linc began.

Carleen interrupted him.

"Come on, Linc, let's get out of here."

"That's right," said a spotty-faced man, his face close to Linc's. "Get out of here, nigger, and take your whore with you."

He had an Irish accent, and pronounced the word 'hoor', but Linc had not listened as long as that. It was the second time in an hour that he had had the prime insult directed at him, and between lay the frustration in the gateway, the inability in this great city to find any bed where he and the girl he loved might lie down together on this, their last, stolen evening.

His great left hand shot out and closed about the spotty man's throat. What happened then was extremely confused.

The landlord vaulted over the bar, as Linc caught another youth on the point of the chin and sent him sprawling over the bar in the opposite direction. He released his grip on the spotty one's throat, as another came at him with a knife, and he knocked this one out cold, but his arm was quite badly cut. The man in the camel-hair coat backed away, saying: "Now, now, now," while the darts players simply watched. The landlord, who had had commando training in the Second World War, brought the back of his hand down, fingers extended, against Linc's neck, the rabbit punch. But it was not enough for that thick neck, though Linc lurched forward Then, turning, he threw his arms about the landlord, picked him up, and hurled him into the tiers of bottles, which crashed and broke. As he did so another knife was struck into his back, between the shoulder-blades, but again he turned and caught this enemy a blow that, as was discovered next day, broke his jaw. Now they all backed away from him, as he stood there grunting, the knife still in his back, blood pouring from his sleeve. There was a moment's silence. The landlord, only momentarily stunned, got up from among the broken bottles, and crawled towards the telephone, to dial 999. Carleen said:

"Come on, Linc. Come on."

She was pulling him towards the door. He walked slowly, his eyes rolling, glancing continually over his shoulder. The dart players backed away.

Outside in the darkness he took three steps and collapsed.

"I'm hurt, sugar," he said. "I'm hurt real bad."

He was half sitting, half lying on the kerb. Carleen appealed to the passers-by, but they hurried on. Just another drunken coloured man. Then three of the youths came running out of the pub. One saw him.

"There he is," he shouted. "There's the dirty——"

They ran at him, and one of them kicked him on the side of the head. But suddenly, mysteriously, half a dozen West Indians were there, and they were fighting all around him, while Carleen crouched beside him, repeating over and over again:

"Are you all right, Linc? Linc, say you're all right."

With a roar and a warbling scream, the Mobile Guards arrived. As mysteriously as they had come, the West Indians vanished. Nor was there any sign of the white youths, save only the spotty-faced one, who was dead.

Three hours later Linc Lee died in the St Pancras Hospital, asking for Carleen till the end. But she was not there to hold his hand, for she was in the cells. It was the only arrest that the police made this evening in the district, and the charge against her was 'conduct likely to cause a breach of the peace'.

At exactly the same hour that Linc Lee breathed his last, a trim and pretty air hostess asked Patrick, Lord Clonard, whether he would care for a drink His plane was then over Gloucester and had not yet really warmed up. He asked for a small cherry brandy.

9

ONLY ONE Sunday paper carried news of the King's Cross murders next morning. This was the *Sunday Pictorial*, which reported it on an inside page, beneath the head: YANK SOLDIER STARTS N.E. RACE RIOT. (The opposite page was fully occupied with MY SOHO DIARY: MORE REVELATIONS OF A FORMER PIMP, while the front page only had room for a picture of a young woman and the headline, ROYAL SCANDAL: SHOCKING ROMANCE?) The more serious papers were occupied with more serious matters: the increasing strain of the Formosa crisis ('Premier urges moderation'), the forthcoming visit of Mr Braithwaite to Moscow, which visit this same Premier had also and already described as 'a meeting of minds along the road to peace', the further heavy drain on the country's gold and dollar reserves, for which the 'Ruhr industrialists' were somehow held responsible in one paper, and finally the news that a huge international 'Against the Bomb Youth Congress' was to be held in London in the near future.

O'Mahony, in his hotel room off Tavistock Square, was pleased that the King's Cross affray had not so far been properly reported. The angle in the *Pictorial* was obviously the correct one, but was capable of considerable amplification. He looked up a number in his little brown address book, then dialled it. The man he wished to speak to was secretary of a newly formed organization The White British Loyalists.

"O'Reilly here," said O'Mahony. "This King's Cross business. Not your doing? All the better. Get on to the Press and stress the fact that it was an *American* soldier. American army aggravating race problems in north London. Got that? More money? You had five hundred only last week. I daresay they are expensive, but there's precious little to show for it so far. All right. Come and see me tomorrow morning, and I shall want a close accounting of how the last was spent. 'To entertaining' just won't wash. Right."

He replaced the telephone, which rang almost at once.

"Yes?" he said. "Oh, yes?" coldly. It was Mark Vernon at

the far end. O'Mahony had a low opinion of Mark Vernon, had indeed been against his coming to England at all, but had been overruled by higher authority, who attached an almost mystical importance to what they believed were Vernon's social connexions, and quite failed to see that he was totally discredited in Britain. It was O'Mahony who had arranged this job for him, tailing Page-Gorman, though he didn't believe that anything would come of it. Still, it might, and meanwhile it kept Vernon out of harm. Mark was saying:

"I'm afraid I've very little for you." O'Mahony grunted. "I spent yesterday evening with the girl. She still doesn't know whether or not he's going with his boss."

O'Mahony said:

"Please don't waste my time. Whether or not he goes is of no importance to us, and in any case our friends will be informed officially. Have you nothing for me?"

Mark spoke more quickly now:

"Nothing definite. I talked to her about the Far East crisis. She doesn't believe that the people here will intervene in any way, but that they will offer to mediate. I asked, what about if Australia and New Zealand get involved and ask for help? She is in favour of acting as mediator in that case too."

"She is? What does he say?"

"That's what I tried to find out, but it's not easy. On the one hand, I think she gets almost all her ideas from him, but on the other I don't believe he tells her nearly as much as she pretends. What I mean is, I think she guesses what is going through his mind a lot of the time, and she can't distinguish between what he has actually told her and what she has guessed. Do you understand me?"

"I'm afraid I'm not very good at these *bourgeois* subtleties," said O'Mahony, with heavy sarcasm. "I want facts."

"But that's exactly what I'm trying to get you. Only it's so difficult."

O'Mahony grunted again. What a useless fellow! They should have left him up in Novaia Zemlia. Moving earth was about all he was fit for. Still, he asked:

"What about Mr B?"

"His boss?"

"Of course."

"Nothing, really. She referred to him and Maynard——"

O'Mahony spoke sharply:

"How many times must I tell you not to use names over the phone?"

"Sorry. Anyhow, she referred to them both as a couple of old has-beens, ready for the scrapheap."

"That I already knew."

"I mean that's what she thinks, and I imagine that's what her friend thinks too."

"Your powers of deduction astound me. Why do you not talk to the man yourself?"

"I've tried, honestly I have. He was supposed to come round last night. Then at the last minute he couldn't, or something."

"What about this job he spoke to you about?"

"There's been nothing more."

"Then make something more. Get it."

Mark Vernon sounded close to tears.

"But how?"

"Why should I care how? *Get it*. That's all."

And he hung up. Mark Vernon, too, carefully replaced his receiver, and suddenly had a perfect and clear memory of what it felt like to march to work, when there was snow deep on the ground, and the terrible, suffocating Arctic blizzard called the *purga* blew for days on end, so snow-filled that a man could scarcely breathe. He shivered.

It was midnight when Patrick Clonard's plane took off from London airport, but it was only twelve-fifteen when they touched down at Idlewild, 00.15 EST that is, for the flight had taken just over five hours. New York was still brilliantly lit as they circled the city, and as far as the eye could see the lighted suburbs spread away, north and west and south.

All most confusing, Patrick thought, dreamlike, as improbable as the dream from which the pretty air hostess had aroused him, to tell him about his safety belt.

And dreamlike, too, was his departure from the airfield. Mr Cuthbertson had been there, with another man, and they had led him through a side door, where his passport had been quickly stamped, and immediately out to the large waiting car. They had driven very fast into New York, hardly talking, except to exchange a few banalities about the crossing and the weather, and then they were in an apartment high above the city, and another man was there.

Patrick took the brown manilla folder from his briefcase, and placed it upon a low coffee table. The man who had been waiting—the other man who had been with Cuthbertson at the airport had gone—was dressed like an Englishman, even to a Guards' tie. Only a certain heaviness about the jowl, and the ring that he wore, and a faint Boston accent revealed his nationality. He said:

"Would you be so good, Lord Clonard, as to tell me how you came into possession of these papers?" and he tapped the envelope.

Patrick told him.

"And how did you happen to possess the keys to Mr Page-Gorman's flat?"

"Does that really matter?"

"I'm sorry. You must be very tired. But I'm afraid every fact is relevant."

Well, thought Patrick, it was all Jack's idea, so I suppose I'd better tell this stranger about Jack's private life. He did so. The man said nothing, and opened the envelope. Then he asked:

"Have you read these yourself?"

"Some of them. They don't mean much to me. Except that Page-Gorman is obviously playing a double game of some sort."

"Have you any idea who this man O'Reilly might be?"

"None."

"You can't cast any light, in fact, on the contents of these documents?"

"No," Patrick replied. "I'm just . . . just the thief."

"Lord Clonard, I won't keep you up any longer. You will be in New York for a few days?"

"Yes."

"Would you be good enough to ensure that Mr Cuthbertson knows your whereabouts at all times? I may have to see you urgently."

Patrick made a wry face.

"If you insist."

Then he was gone. And Patrick was led, by Cuthbertson, into a most luxurious bedroom, with bath. He was so tired, that his eyes ached. Yet when he was in bed he could not immediately go to sleep.

He thought: a spy, spying against my own country.

The night air was very cold and crisp, for he had opened the window. Out of his line of vision a sky sign must be winking on and off, for regularly, every ten seconds or so, the window frame turned pink, then white again. Patrick closed his eyes and tried to envisage Nora and their meeting tomorrow. But he could not.

He thought: a spy, a traitor, why have I come to this? Why have they made me do this? What concern is it of mine? Why am I here, instead of encouraging starlets to go to Deauville, which is, after all, what Jack pays me for?

He turned over and opened his eyes. Behind him he heard the faintest sound, like a hand touching velvet. Quickly he turned again. Outside it had begun to snow, and the snow was brushing against the window panes.

He thought: a traitor to my country. Like Mark Vernon.

And then he fell asleep.

Patrick was not the only man on this Sunday morning to feel that he was acting out of character, that circumstances had forced him to behave in a way alien to his traditions. A half dozen men, mostly elderly, who would normally have been getting ready for church, or eating a late breakfast, or reading the Sunday papers, were assembled at the improbable hour of half past ten in Jack Beaulieu's drawing-room overlooking Green Park. They had been assembled over the telephone, and with considerable difficulty late last night, by Sir Charles and Air Marshal Boreham.

Some would have described them as a typical cross-section of the 'Establishment', the editor of a great newspaper, the former Conservative Foreign Minister (the former Conservative Premier was holidaying in Cuba), an elderly peer who was said to have great power in ill-defined fields, a most important industrialist (who happened to be a friend of Jack's), Admiral Cornwallis the ex-First Sea Lord, and a very senior Civil Servant whose name never appeared in the newspapers but who was undoubtedly the most powerful man present. Eight or so men, all aged sixty or more, the elders in whom the wisdom of the tribe is supposed to reside.

The former Conservative Foreign Minister said:

"The country will never stand for it. All we have to do is to give Braithwaite and his friends enough rope, and they'll hang themselves."

"If they don't hang us first," remarked the elderly peer, glancing with distaste at an action painting that Moyra Beaulieu had bought only last month.

"You say you got on to Maynard last night?" asked the industrialist. "Personally I have quite a high opinion of John Maynard."

"I did," said Boreham. "I even motored out to Harlow New Town to see him. He wrung his hands as usual, began by saying he didn't believe it, and ended by maintaining that he couldn't split the Party."

The former Foreign Secretary nodded; that was a reaction he both understood and respected. The editor of the great newspaper said:

"On the face of it, it seems shocking enough, but if one takes the longest possible view there may be some sense, considerable sense, in what Page-Gorman is doing. After all, the Americans would have gone soon enough, even if he hadn't pushed them out. They don't really need bases in Europe any more. By taking the initiative, and even more so by this latest development of inviting Russian inspection teams here, we are proving our goodwill to the Soviets beyond a shadow of doubt. And remember, Russia doesn't want a war any more than we do. Kornoloff is no fool. But if they attempt to take advantage of this gesture, then we shall know exactly where we stand."

"And what do we do, what does the government do, in that case?" asked Sir Charles.

The industrialist said:

"Don't forget that we remain the banker for the sterling bloc, head of the Commonwealth, and in many respects the moral leaders of the free world. We're not the sort of country that can be pushed around, like Tibet or . . . or Latvia."

"Even if we are for all intents and purposes disarmed, without allies, and with Russian troops actually in London?" asked Admiral Cornwallis.

The elderly peer said:

"So far as I can make out from these papers that you have shown us, this Russian inspectorate can hardly be described as 'troops'. At most, a token force: at the least, a group similar to our inspectorate in Warsaw. No, that doesn't seem to me the crux of the matter. What is extraordinary and, in my opinion, sinister, is that Page-Gorman has apparently been carrying on underground negotiations with a foreign power without the authority either of his Cabinet—to judge by what Maynard said to you, Boreham—or of the Foreign Office."

The former Foreign Secretary said, not without glee:

"Yes, I think he's taken enough rope to hang himself already."

The senior Civil Servant had a dry voice.

"The Civil Servants have been kept in the dark before now. Suez . . ."

"That was an entirely different matter."

Boreham now intervened.

"The reason that Charles and I invited you gentlemen to come here, at such short notice, is that it looks to us as though Page-Gorman is implementing a policy which is certain to be disastrous and which smells of something very like treason."

"Oh, come, come," said the editor of the very important newspaper.

"I think that's a bit hard, too," said the industrialist. "Though mind you, I disapprove of these people at least as much as you do. If for different reasons."

Jack Beaulieu had said nothing. Now his eyes went from face to face. These are good men, he thought, and they and their like are supposed to have immense power in this country. In time of war they would work—they did work—eighteen hours a day, sacrifice their fortunes, never weaken even when their children were killed. Yet now they do not know what to do. They are, in fact, going to do nothing.

As one of them remarked to another, on the steps of the Athenaeum later that morning, what *could* they do?

John Maynard was in a considerable state of agitation, as he strode the carpet at No 10.

"What is going on, Braithwaite? What does it all mean? Who is O'Reilly? Why has the Cabinet not been informed?"

Braithwaite had a heavy cold in the head, and was seated close to the fire, an old camel-hair dressing gown that resembled a Capuchin's habit over his trousers and waistcoat.

"You said all along that our disarmament programme was no concern of yours. Do you expect Page-Gorman to require a report from you every time someone calls at the Home Office?"

"But so far as I can make out, he's planning to give the Russians the Hertford Hotel. It's a very large hotel."

"Well?"

"It's in the area marked off by the police for the big anti-vice operation. I should have been told."

"It'll have to be adjusted."

Braithwaite sniffed at a small bottle, and a pungent smell of eucalyptus filled the room. Maynard said:

"Who'll be in charge of all this . . . this inspectorate business, while you're in Moscow with the trade unionists?"

"Page-Gorman."

"But you said that I was to act as Prime Minister in your absence. How can I, when I'm not even told what's going on?"

"We've agreed all along that disarmament was not your field."

"Why did this air marshal have to come and see me? Why not you?"

"I suppose because you have the reputation for being right-wing. I expect he was trying to split the Party."

Maynard nodded sagely:

"That is something I would never do. But I really do think I should be kept a little more in the picture."

"If you wish. I'll ask Page-Gorman to make a statement at tomorrow's cabinet. Will that satisfy you?"

"I suppose so. Meanwhile there's this race riot problem."

"After this latest outrage by the American soldiers, it is certainly high time drastic action was taken," said Braithwaite.

"Next week all the Mobile Guards will be busy rounding up the vice gangs in Mayfair. It's all so difficult."

"Why not a dual operation, against Mayfair and the Notting Hill–Paddington area? And Hyde Park too, while you're about it?"

"I just haven't got enough police."

"Then bring them in from the provinces After all, that's what you were given special powers for."

"You think so? It'll be a full-time job, and with you away in Moscow . . ."

"Nothing would make me happier than to come back from Russia to find that here, as there, the virus of race-hatred has been eliminated from the body politic."

"Very well. That's a nasty cold you've got, Braithwaite. You should try hot whisky and lemon, last thing at night."

"You know I'm a teetotaller, Maynard."

"But surely, as medicine . . .?"

On the far side of the world, in the maritime province of Fu-Kien, it was still the middle of the night. Not that this made much difference to Corporal Hsu, in his blue, padded uniform, for the corporal and his company lived permanently underground. Long and twisting corridors connected the command post in which he worked with the actual rockets, themselves buried at the bottom of shaft-like pits. The rockets were fuelled, only the thermo-nuclear warheads had to be added, and a lever pulled, in order to ensure that every living thing, human and animal, was immediately destroyed on the island of Formosa.

Corporal Hsu was standing a yard from the lever, which he had reason to believe that his captain would be pulling in twenty-four hours' time It was a shiny steel lever, somewhat crudely finished, and it bore Russian lettering which had long fascinated Hsu.

Corporal Hsu gave a sidelong glance at his captain, who was seated at a table, reading a book by Mao Tse-tung, his eyes going rhythmically up and down the page. The captain, Hsu thought, is God.

Hsu could read and write, which was why he had acquired this marvellous job as clerk. And he therefore knew that the Gods had been abolished in all China. That was why the captain was now God, as were Mao and Ho, and all the other new Gods. But if the Gods had been abolished, Hsu wondered, how come that there were still Gods? During the last three months, in which time Hsu had not once seen the sky, he had worried a great deal about this problem of the Gods and their non-existence.

When he had been a boy, for instance, among the brown hills a thousand miles away, the Gods had still existed, and the Devils too. They had lived overhead, not very far overhead, no higher than a kite could reach, in a confusing and confused world of their own where they could occasionally be heard moaning or chattering together. They were forever interfering in human affairs, usually for the worse, and they were known to be intensely touchy. It had therefore been a good thing when the soldiers had come and abolished them in all China.

Hsu had been eight years old then, and since the soldiers had also abolished his mother and father, he was taken off to the children's camp, and then put in the army. And during all those years he hadn't thought about the old Gods and Devils at all. Now, suddenly, for these last three months he had thought about almost nothing else.

And he had reached certain conclusions. One was that these old Gods had not all been abolished, but that some had escaped across the sea, gliding just above the waves, to Taiwan. It was to liquidate them once and for all, along with their worshippers, the Fascist hyenas and the long-nosed barbarians, that these rockets had been built and buried here. He, Corporal Hsu, had thus a role of paramount importance to play in the spiritual history of the world.

This conclusion had filled him with pride.

But then another thought had occurred to him, first as a mere theoretical supposition, then as a fear, and finally almost as a certainty. *There was no time to be lost.*

If they could glide across the seas to Taiwan, then they could glide back. They would hang about overhead, the foul-faced fiends, over the shaft entrances. When they were ready, they would come sneaking down the shafts, and fiddle with the mechanism of the rockets, and break them. They might even make their way along the corridors, and come in here.

Hsu felt intensely frightened. He looked at his captain again, but the captain was still reading. And then Hsu knew with a perfect certainty that the captain was not what he seemed to be: that the captain was a traitor, a fiend in human shape, in league with all the Gods and Devils who even now were creeping down the rocket shafts on their way to punish him, Corporal Hsu, for the terrible crime of blasphemy. His ears became filled with a strange ringing sound. It was them, it was them!

Hsu reached out his right hand and pulled the shiny lever. The captain jumped up, but too late. The fuel in the base of the four rockets was already beginning to burn, incidentally frying to death a dozen mechanics who were working on one of them. Within seconds the noses of three of them emerged above the surface of Fu-Kien province, slowly, then faster and faster. (The fourth burned out deep in its shaft.) And now they were clear of the ground, passing through the layers infested by Demons and Gods, vanishing upwards and in the direction of Formosa.

The three rockets landed on the island a few minutes later. Since they had no warheads, they did very little damage, killing only two children, one woman, and a sheep.

The news that three rockets had been launched against Formosa reached the C-in-C, US Seventh Fleet, simultaneously with the exact radar pin-point of the launching sites. He therefore ordered that Plan K (Operation Corncob) be implemented at once. The guns of his heavy cruisers, patrolling seven miles offshore, opened up, firing HE.

The shells descended on the rocket sites with an ear-splitting screech, audible even below ground. Hsu, his captain, and the rest of the unit were buried alive. The screeching shells continued to fall for twenty minutes. The Devils were back with a vengeance.

Patrick waited until half past ten before ringing Nora. To his considerable surprise, and momentary embarrassment, it was Felix who answered. But Felix was clearly so much more embarrassed than he, that Patrick had to be almost unnaturally natural. After this brief conversation, he was put through to Nora.

"But, Patrick, what a marvellous surprise. You must come round at once, I mean almost at once, just as soon as I've had a bath and got dressed. Where are you? But that's no distance at all. Come round at a quarter to twelve, not a moment later."

She replaced the telephone, threw aside the heavy Sunday papers, and jumped out of bed. She was just putting on her bedroom slippers, when Felix called from beyond the door:

"May I come in?"

She tried and failed to persuade him that he get out of the luncheon engagement (which she was sure he had invented two minutes before) but on the other hand he showed no disinclination to be in the apartment when Patrick arrived, and to have a drink with him. This, she realized, was not because Felix had the slightest wish to see Patrick, but because he feared that to refuse to do so would almost amount to a 'scene', and might well distress her.

And as she ran her bath she thought, not for the first time, how lucky she was to have two such men in her life, and how really impossible it would be if either of them were a stinker. Then she looked at her unmade-up face in the glass and said, aloud:

"The only stinker is me."

But she didn't really believe this, or indeed let it worry her for long, because her thoughts immediately went to Antonia and Rupert Page-Gorman.

"Now there's a real stinker," she said to herself, again aloud, and laughed. She shouldn't laugh, she knew. Poor Antonia, what a one for her to get involved with. And to think of all the charming, intelligent, sensitive, kindly men whom she had thrown Antonia's way, only to see them dismissed as boring, bourgeois, philistine, or just plain stupid. Heigh-ho, she thought, I must do something about Antonia. However, she could not succeed in making herself feel sad about Antonia this morning, because, as she lathered her arms, she was so happy to think that in one hour Patrick would be there.

"A most extraordinary city," Felix was saying, as with a tiny glass pestle he crushed the sugar in the bottom of the old-fashioned glasses. "I never cease to be surprised and, in a way, horrified. At Mass this morning, for instance . . ." He added the slices of orange, while Patrick wondered why they always said 'Mahss'. ". . . there was a woman with a rosary made, apparently, of solitaire diamonds strung together." He now poured the bourbon over the ice. "Each one the size of a sparrow's egg. Quite blinding it was." He handed the drinks to Nora and Patrick, then added with a self-deprecatory laugh: "It almost put me off my devotions."

Patrick laughed politely. Nora smiled, and said:

"Does this city horrify you, Patrick?"

"No, I don't think so. I always find New York so exciting. But then of course I haven't been here very much or very often."

"How long are you staying now?" Felix asked, with the utmost casualness.

"I'm not quite sure. Not long. Three or four days. It depends on the people I've come to see." Then, in order that he make his meaning perfectly clear, he added, "I'm here on business, with the Fuelless Car people."

"Fuelless Cars?" Felix asked with evident interest. "I've got some money in that. I've even got a fuelless car."

"Really?" said Patrick. "I'm handling the advertising for their English company, but I haven't ever seen one of their products."

"They're just like ordinary cars, except that the engine's all wrapped in lead and they cost nothing to run. I thought the English company was being wound up."

"No, they're postponing production, that's all. They're waiting to see what the Socialist government is going to do."

"What is the Socialist government going to do?"

"You know more about that than I do, Felix."

"There's a great deal of anti-British feeling in this country. You can hardly blame them. The way they've turned the Americans out, and this perpetual flirtation with the Russians."

"Quite," said Patrick.

"If I were an American financier I'd think twice about making a heavy investment in Britain just now. Indeed, I've been thinking of moving over to this side altogether."

Now Nora spoke:

"But you'd hate that, darling."

"I can't say that I've enjoyed this visit. I find myself constantly having to defend the policies of a government that is anathema to me. They say that England is finished, and I tell them that that's a lot of rot, and then they say: 'Well, look at the government you've chosen', and so I have to try and explain about the English passion for security, and they shrug their shoulders and say: 'Venice spent what Venice earned'. It's all extremely awkward. You'll see."

He had spoken with a quite unusual vehemence, and Patrick realized, for the first time, that beneath Felix's diffident appearance and exceptionally gentle manner there was a very steely personality indeed. And Patrick remembered a man who had served with Felix in the Coldstream saying that Felix had had the reputation of being one of the toughest officers in the Guards Armoured Division.

Patrick said:

"Do you like it here, Nora?"

"Well, they make the most tremendous fuss of me, which is nice. And the play's a smash hit, which helps. And of course they don't talk politics to me. But sometimes I feel desperately homesick."

"Your play will run for ever?"

"It looks like it. But I may get out of it. I've been asked to play Cordelia in Gielgud's *Lear*. I'd adore that."

And so they talked about the theatre until it was time for Felix's luncheon appointment (if he had one) at the Racquet Club. He dropped Patrick and Nora at a restaurant of her choice, on 62nd Street, driving them there in his new fuelless car. He was quite right, it was exactly like an ordinary car, only slightly bigger.

"Too big," said Felix. "Everything here's too big."

The restaurant called the Amalienburg was not too big, its three rooms only slightly larger than the original, Cuvilles's perfect pavilion at Nymphenburg, and the blue and silver décor was an almost exact reproduction, even to dummy windows which appeared to look out upon a Mozartian park bathed in autumnal, eighteenth-century sunlight. The food was as good as the decorations, for the chef had learned his art under the great Walterspiel. While the service, aged men who had once waited at Sacher's and Horcher's and the Vierjahreszeiten, was considered, by those who know, to be the nearest thing to perfection in the United States.

Therefore it was all the more surprising, when Patrick and Nora entered this paragon of restaurants, to find the place in a state of chaos, though deserted chaos. There was no porter, no *maître d'hôtel*, no bartender. The bar was littered with half-finished drinks. They walked through into the blue-and-silver room. Some of the tables were scattered with plates of uneaten food: kidneys in a chafing dish were giving out a cloud of oily, black smoke: at one table a waiter, his head buried on his arms, was sobbing loudly. And from behind a service door a powerful voice was talking incomprehensibly. Patrick and Nora were dumbfounded.

Patrick laid a hand on the weeping waiter's shoulder, and the old man looked up.

"What's happened?" he asked.

The old man's chin was trembling, and he had difficulty in speaking. Pointing vaguely towards the service door, whence came the voice, he said at last:

"*Es ist Krieg. Ach, die arme Menschheit!*"

"What does he say?" Nora asked.

"He says it's war. Come on!"

And he led her through the service door, through the gleaming kitchens into a small office, where were crowded staff and customers alike, white-faced, watching a television set.

The newscaster was a somewhat rumpled-looking man in his fifties, with a deliberately laconic manner who, in contrast to the feverish excitement of his colleagues, had cultivated his quiet, Texas drawl as a trademark. Even he, however, could not play down the intensely dramatic nature of the moment. He was saying:

". . . while the Chiang Kai-shek government reports wide-scale destruction as a result of the Red attack, American sources on the island do not as yet confirm this. We are taking you now to Tainan, where our correspondent, Joe McManus, is waiting. Hello, McManus, are you there?"

The television camera closed on a map of Formosa behind the newscaster's head, as McManus's voice came in, now fainter now louder, like the surf breaking on some distant, Pacific beach.

"Hello, SBC, hello, SBC, this is Joe McManus speaking from Formosa where World War Three may have begun just four hours ago. What has happened here is not entirely clear however. One fact is certain: the Chinese Reds have fired medium range rockets at the island, and the US Seventh Fleet has retaliated by shelling, and apparently destroying, the Red rocket sites. What damage was done by the Red rockets is far from clear. The Chinese authorities here speak of damage on a massive scale, with hundreds or even thousands killed. This is not confirmed by American sources, and it certainly seems unlikely that the Chinese have used atomic weapons, or if they have they must have been of an extremely low yield. Nor has the original bombardment been repeated as yet, possibly because of the immediate counter-action taken by the Seventh Fleet, which, incidentally, was also apparently not made with atomic weapons. Meanwhile the Chinese government here has declared a state of war emergency, and all American forces have been alerted. There is no sign of panic, though the skies are black with planes. I return you now to New York City."

The newscaster was back on the screen.

"Los Angeles. As the news broke of the Formosa bombardment, thousands poured out of the city, blocking highroads and creating traffic problems on a hitherto unknown scale." The picture now showed an endless double line of cars, crawling through the suburbs of a great city. "A similar exodus, though on a lesser scale, is taking place from San Francisco and Seattle.

"Flash. Washington. The State Department has just issued the following statement: 'At approximately seven hundred hours this morning, Eastern Standard Time, the so-called Chinese People's government launched an unprovoked attack

151

on the Island of Formosa, which was subjected to a severe rocket bombardment. In accordance with our treaty obligations to the Chinese government of Marshal Chiang Kai-shek, the United States Seventh Fleet immediately shelled and destroyed the launching sites from which the attack was made. The Seventh Fleet did not employ atomic shells. The United States will not engage in atomic warfare against the mainland of China unless and until the Chinese Communists inaugurate warfare of this sort. In which case our retaliatory measures will be massive and immediate.'"

The newscaster glanced at a piece of paper that had been placed before him while he was reading this announcement, then began again:

"Moscow. There has been no comment either official or unofficial from any Russian source on the events in the Far East. However, *Pravda* this morning launched a bitter, and obviously inspired, attack on the British government of Leonard Braithwaite. In an unsigned article which almost certainly emanates from the Kremlin, the British government is accused of having failed to carry out the agreed destruction of atomic weapons in the British Isles. It is also maintained that the American troops have not in fact left Britain, but have simply been put into civilian clothes and moved to new sites. The article ends with a very strongly worded demand for Russian inspection of the former rocket sites.

"Flash. Washington. The Defence Department in a statement just issued says that the bombardment of Formosa earlier today was not made with atomic weapons, and that the damage caused was slight. It is not clear whether this was a range-finding test attack or not. The United States forces in the area have been fully alerted and are ready for any emergency."

Another piece of paper was laid before him. He looked at it and said:

"We are now taking you over to City Hall, where the Mayor of New York has a special announcement to make."

For perhaps five seconds the screen was blank, then the mayor was there, seated at his desk, fingering his spectacles. He glanced inquiringly at somebody off-shot before he spoke.

"New Yorkers. You have heard the news. We do not know

what the future will bring. But *please do not panic*. There is no need for you to leave your homes. Those of you who have already done so are urged to *get off the main roads*. If this is war, those roads *must be kept clear*. Those of you still at home, please stay at home. You will be safer in your own homes. If it is considered necessary to evacuate the children from New York, this will be done in an orderly way. *Do not panic*. Wait until you are told what to do. Don't block the roads. By doing so you are endangering your own lives as well as those of your fellow citizens. God bless America."

Patrick said in a low voice to Nora:

"That should make 'em panic all right."

In this little room, however, the atmosphere had already changed. Looking almost shamefaced, the diners, followed by the waiters, began to drift back into the restaurant. And in a surprisingly short time they were all seated at their tables, almost as though nothing had happened. Patrick noticed, though, that eyes kept moving towards the service door and the kitchens. But perhaps, as he remarked to Nora, this was merely evidence of hunger.

"Nothing like fear for making you hungry," he said.

Nora said:

"I wish I could be all British and stiff-upper-lipped and imperturbable like you. But I can't. I'm frightened sick too."

Patrick grinned at her.

"So, my darling heart, am I. That's why I can hardly wait for my *Leberknödelsuppe* and my *Backhendl mit Nockerln und Gurkensalat*."

She hesitated, then said:

"Patrick, if there's really going to be a war, I want to be at home. I mean I want to be with my own people. And Toddy. I've made up my mind. I'll break my contract somehow, and take that job in London."

"Of course I wish you would, but . . ."

"But what?"

"How about Felix?"

"If there were a war can you imagine Felix being anywhere else except in England? In fact I bet you he flies back tonight.

153

Besides, what would be the point in bringing Toddy over here, if America is going to be atom-bombed?"

"England might be bombed too."

"I thought the whole point of this beastly government was to keep us neutral. And, do you know, after this morning, I'm beginning to think maybe they're not so stupid, at that."

Looking into her wide-open, gold-flecked brown eyes, a sudden, awful abyss of doubt opened before Patrick. Surely all that mattered was to see that Nora was safe, unhurt? Beside that, nothing counted, nothing at all. So why was he here? Why was he trying to bring about the overthrow of a man who, unattractive and probably dishonest as he was, at least advocated peace on any terms?

"Patrick, what is it? You suddenly look so miserable."

For a moment he could not look at her, and twisted his napkin in his lap. Then he said:

"It's all so bloody, isn't it? I mean, this endless crisis, and this Page-Gorman man, and not knowing what one should do."

He looked up at her now and saw the worry in her eyes, worry for him, and he forced himself to smile. It was a lame smile. She said, almost briskly:

"I remember reading about the London blitz, and how badly the girls all behaved, I mean being terribly brave but going to bed with people all the time. Well, you're going to think me awfully forward and immodest, but I feel just like that now, not the bravery bit, but the rest. So I do wish the waiters would stop telling each other jokes in German or whatever it is they're all doing over there, and after lunch . . ."

Patrick said:

"Darling, you are marvellous. But don't they arrest people for going to bed with each other in America?"

"Oh dear, you *do* think I'm forward and immoral. I don't care. And I don't care if they do arrest us. And I'll tell you something more while I'm about it. It's not the war or the blitz or anything else. It's just you."

It worked, exactly as she had intended and known it would. And then the waiter was there, pouring out the rich, brown soup. He was the same old waiter who had been crying when they entered the restaurant: now he seemed entirely composed.

Kornoloff and Nikitin had finished their discussion. Nikitin's assistant was putting away the various papers that had lain upon the conference table, as Kornoloff said:

"I am sorry that you cannot be here for the Braithwaite visit." Nikitin said nothing, and Kornoloff went on, "But still. We've arranged a most interesting trip for him." Kornoloff laughed. "Eighteen factories, two Sovkhozes, an industrial fair, a WFTU conference, and five banquets, beside a visit to the atomic power station at Irkutsk and to the workers' winter-sport holiday camp in the Carpathians." Kornoloff laughed again. "He will have plenty of opportunities for making his speeches."

It was at this moment that Sspesiatkin entered the room. Kornoloff looked up, frowned, and Sspesiatkin almost dropped the single sheet of paper he was carrying. His peptic ulcer reacted with its usual speed, a knife turning in his ageing belly. And it was bad news, terrible news, that he brought.

"Yes?" said Kornoloff.

To be the bearer of bad news is at all times unpleasant. Bearing it to Kornoloff, particularly if one were Sspesiatkin, was highly dangerous as well. The peptic ulcer gave him another vicious jab in the gut. Rather than speak the evil news, Sspesiatkin handed his dictator the sheet of paper. It was a cable from the Russian Embassy in Washington, and told of what had happened in the Formosa Strait.

Kornoloff read it, frowned, read it again, and then, to his Foreign Minister's extreme alarm, burst out laughing, peal upon peal of deep-chested mirth.

For a moment Sspesiatkin was more frightened than ever. Had Kornoloff gone mad? His brilliant and complicated plan was in danger of miscarrying because of human error or even perhaps of sabotage on the part of the Chinese, and here he was, roaring his head off.

"Perfect," said Kornoloff. "Perfect. An unprovoked American attack on the Chinese mainland! On no account must the Chinese retaliate. We announce that we shall take what measures we see fit, after a full inquiry into the American atrocity. Meanwhile we send up the big new sputniks. One of them must be visible from at least one of the major American cities at every hour of the day and night. That should keep their eyes off England."

Kornoloff, who had got to his feet, gave Sspesiatkin a huge slap on the back, so that he almost pitched forward, and said:

"Don't you see, Sspesiatkin, that this is a vast improvement on your original, rather crude plan?"

Sspesiatkin forced himself to give a very insincere smile.

Rupert Page-Gorman leaned back in his armchair, his slippered feet stretched towards his electric fire. Antonia knelt on the floor beside him, her fingers dextrously, gently, and smoothly massaging the back of his neck where the nerves in their column, exasperated by one of the most exhausting days that Page-Gorman had ever lived, were taut and knotted. Her firm fingers, she thought, were compelling those naughty, recalcitrant, male nerves to relax, to give the man the rest and peace he needed. Firm and gentle, firm and gentle, she kneaded away at the top of his back-bone. The television screen was blank, for Rupert had said:

"I see enough of his goatish old face all day."

Only the Prime Minister's voice came from the box, and it too was softly persuasive, with its West Country burr, gentle but firm, recalling a farmer who must restore order among a flock of sheep frightened by a motor car on their way to market.

". . . to give you a reckoning of our stewardship to date. But now, today, two more events have occurred which make me all the more happy that I had arranged to talk to you to-night. In the first place there is the dangerous, I would even say criminal, outbreak of shooting—what sort of shooting we do not yet know for sure—in the Far East. There was a moment this afternoon when you feared, yes, and when we the government feared too, that perhaps the Third World War had begun. It may yet be so, though as you have heard just now on the nine o'clock news, it seems likely that the Chinese fired their rocket by mistake, and that the American bombardment of the

Chinese mainland was therefore carried out in error. But no matter what the developments of this terrifying crisis may be, there is for us in Britain today one small measure of compensation: it no longer concerns us. Ten years ago, five years ago, even last year, we would tonight have been on the very brink of war. For the sake of Marshal Chiang Kai-shek and his army of ageing brigands, the youth of this country would have been faced with the imminent danger of total annihilation. Tonight that is no longer so. With no enemies, and with friends everywhere, our policy is one of total, of unconditional, neutrality. And we have told our friends, everywhere, that if they wish to play power politics, then they must play it without us, and not on our British soil. For I repeat, our policy is one of total, of unconditional, neutrality. And we can all sleep the safer tonight in consequence. When I was a boy on a Somerset farm, we had a saying . . ."

"I'll bet they did," said Page-Gorman. "Very soothing, Antonia, don't stop."

Round and round her fingers went, pressing and smoothing the hard flesh above the nearby bone, and round and round her thoughts. There was so much she could and should do for this man-child of hers, this wonderful father-son, this great man who was yet in some ways such a *little* boy. So much. She was Gretchen to his Faust, Ophelia to his Hamlet, Walewska to his Bonaparte, even, though not of course in the Freudian sense, Jocasta to his Oedipus. So much. And all so gratifying.

"And now," Braithwaite was saying, his long and untruthful reminiscence about Somersetshire farm life over, "I come to the second of today's developments. The Russians have asked that we allow inspection teams to come here, in order to survey our rocket-disarmament programme. It may seem to you strange that the Russians should doubt our word. But I can only remind you that international politics are a tough business. And it is not our word that they are doubting, but the word of the British government as they have seen it in action over this past half century. We must never forget that it was a British government that sent troops—yes, British troops—to Archangel in the early years of the Russian revolution, in an attempt to strangle that great revolution at birth: it was a British government that attempted to make peace with the Nazi criminals before the Second World War, and that was responsible for the shameful betrayal of Munich: it was a British government that, after the war, helped rearm Western Germany and gave the Americans nuclear bases in this country, two actions pointed directly at the Soviet Union. Is it surprising that they distrust us? Were the Conservatives still in office here, I believe that I should distrust them myself. Thank God that in this period of crisis they are not. But we have nothing to conceal, and therefore I welcome, yes welcome, the forthcoming visit of this Russian team of scientists and technicians. We can learn from them, even as they can learn from us, how best these horrible machines of mass-destruction can be destroyed."

"Quite well put," said Page-Gorman.

"You'd have put it better," said Antonia.

Page-Gorman grunted. The voice went on:

"Which brings me to what was originally the purpose for my speaking to you tonight. I am, as you all know, off to Moscow tomorrow myself. It is my hope and belief that in frank, man-to-man discussions with their distinguished leader, Mr Kornoloff, I shall finally lay the ghost of Anglo–Russian enmity. In one of Shakespeare's greatest plays, which many of you will remember from your schooldays, *Hamlet*, there occur the following lines, when Hamlet asks the ghost his nature: 'I am thy father's spirit, doomed for a certain term to walk the night, till the foul crimes done in my days of nature are burnt and purged away!' I am going to Moscow to burn and purge away the crimes committed by others, and to lay once and for all the ghost of Russian–British hostility. Wish me luck, all of you!"

"Too highbrow," said Rupert.

"Much too highbrow," replied Antonia.

"Or not highbrow enough," Page-Gorman added.

"Exactly," said Antonia.

Braithwaite, however, had not stopped for good and all, but simply in order to draw breath and to sip his glass of water. The effect of the Drinamyl was wearing off, and he was beginning to be conscious of the fact that he had a very bad cold.

"And now I have one more word to say to you, before I wing my way eastwards, about home affairs. There has been a renewed outbreak of race violence in London. I refrain from saying who was responsible for this: you have read your papers yourselves. But I will say this, and I say it with all the strength at my disposal: we will not allow our London town to be turned into a second Little Rock or a gangster-ridden Chicago. I, and my colleagues in the government, and particularly my friend John Maynard, the Home Secretary, are determined to root out gangsterism and racial strife once and for all. The police are going to take very large-scale action, just as they did in the case of the public vice campaign, to rid us of this threat to our heritage and to our British way of life. For obvious reasons I cannot tell you exactly what those measures will be, but I do ask you to give the police your full support. Remember, the police are your friends, even if you are sometimes as annoyed as I am when I am given a summons for a parking offence. . . ." Here he gave a laugh. ". . . But the gangsters are your enemies. Support the police in their brave attempt to keep Britain decent and free! Peace, freedom, and decency, those are our watchwords. Goodnight!"

"He didn't say anything about his dead son," remarked Page-Gorman. "Turn the thing off."

She did so. Then knelt down beside his chair again.

"No," he said. "I've had enough massage. Tell me something to cheer me up. A joke, or a bit of gossip."

Antonia was bewildered.

"A joke?"

"What's happened to your sister, the actress?"

"Nora? Why, she's in America."

"Oh. What about that man she lives with?"

"You mean Patrick Clonard? She doesn't actually live with him."

"I thought she did."

"He telephoned me yesterday. He's here."

"Good-looking woman, your sister."

Quite suddenly the joy was drained from the soul of Gretchen–Ophelia–Walewska–Jocasta–Antonia May. And in that moment it was Nora she hated, not Rupert.

PART THREE

10

WHEN Patrick Clonard had flown westward, three days before, he had arrived in New York almost at the same hour as he left London. With Braithwaite's eastward flight the earth's diurnal spin worked the other way. He left London airport shortly after breakfast, and a three-hour flight would land him in Moscow after dark, and just in time for an early banquet at the Kremlin. Rupert Page-Gorman, John Maynard and other members of the Cabinet were at the airport to see him off. So, too, was the Soviet ambassador.

The sun shone from a cold, blue sky, and a sharp breeze snapped at the flags as the distinguished group made their way through the VIP exit and out to the flight apron. The nose of the Super-Comet, too, was decorated with a small Union Jack and a Red Flag, crossed, which fluttered in the wind. Leonard Braithwaite wore an ulster and his old cloth cap, and at the foot of the steps leading up to the plane he stopped, to shake hands with his colleagues, to let the photographers get plenty of pictures and to make a short speech.

"As I leave dear old London town on this historic flight for peace, aaaaah-*choo* . . ." His cold was worse, his speech thick, and two of the evening papers erroneously reported him as having spoken of a 'fight for peace'. ". . . it is of the young people, and of generations yet unborn, that I think. Aaaaah-*choo*. But above all it is to my son, dead these nigh on thirty years, that my thoughts return." A slight expression of strain was visible on the faces of some of his Cabinet colleagues. It was damned cold out there, on the tarmac. "Had he been spared, I know for sure that he would have regarded this historic mission as the climax of my long crusade for peace. . . ." He stopped, expected to sneeze again, didn't, resumed, and at long last vanished into the belly of the big aeroplane, in which his personal staff and the half dozen trade unionists were already installed.

Back in the VIP lounge, the head of London Airport inquired whether any of his distinguished guests would care for a warming drink. Most refused, having urgent business in town, but John Maynard said that a nice cup of Bovril would be delicious. Rupert Page-Gorman and the Soviet ambassador had, in any case, to remain at the airport for a further half hour. The ambassador asked for a small brandy, Page-Gorman for an espresso coffee.

"How's it going?" Page-Gorman asked John Maynard, as he sipped his coffee.

"How is what going?" Maynard replied.

"The police action, of course."

John Maynard glanced towards the Russian ambassador, and that personage, always meticulously polite, said at once:

"Perhaps you would care for me to withdraw . . ."

"Not at all," said Page-Gorman, "not at all. There is nothing secret about our action to round up the race rioters."

John Maynard still looked dubious for a moment, then shrugged his shoulders. He supposed it was all right.

"It's all very complicated. They flushed the King's Cross area last night, as you know. That, incidentally, is the word they use. Can't say I care for it much. They made close on five hundred arrests, chiefly coloured youths with flick knives, bicycle chains and so on. In fact the police stations are overcrowded, and it's doubtful if the magistrates can handle them all today. Tonight they, er, flush the Notting Hill area, along with the anti-vice operation in Mayfair. But where they're going to put them all, heaven only knows."

"Did they pick up the ringleaders?" Page-Gorman asked.

"The trouble is there don't seem to be any ringleaders. Or if there are, they can't be charged with any indictable offence."

"Nonsense," said Page-Gorman. "What about this White British Loyalists group, or whatever they're called? We can't afford to be squeamish with these hooligans, you know."

"But there's no charge on which we can arrest them."

"Conduct likely to cause a breach of the peace. Anyhow,

arrest them first. We'll find the charge afterwards. And while you're at it, how about all those Negroes with placards I saw in Whitehall the other day, asking for protection?"

"They haven't done anything."

"If that is so, we can set them free again soon enough."

"But the police haven't room for the armed ones, as it is."

"It seems to me that the commissioner is being altogether too legalistic, not to say obstructionist, about the whole business. After all, this is a specific operation, not a normal enforcement of the Law." He turned to the Soviet ambassador. "You've had experience of this sort of thing in your country, ambassador. What do you think?"

The ambassador replied, in his usual mild tones:

"Yes, with us the *besprizorniye* were at one time a considerable nuisance. But they are young, they can learn. A good fright often cures them. If not, then a labour camp will usually teach them to behave culturally, besides giving them useful employment."

"Exactly, Maynard. I quite agree with the ambassador. An operation like this requires extraordinary measures. You say your commissioner has no place to put them. Why not make a small camp in Hyde Park? After all, you're planning to seal it off. The army would provide the tents. And a night or two in the open, in January, should cool them off wonderfully."

"I doubt if the commissioner . . ."

Page-Gorman became extremely pleasant.

"My dear Maynard, I quite see your problems. The trouble is, of course, that we have never had to carry out any such operation in this country before."

"The only similar action was the round-up of enemy aliens in 1940, and that is hardly a precedent. Or so the commissioner tells me."

"The commissioner is quite right, of course. But he naturally sees these things from the police point of view, that is to say bureaucratically, while we must act as politicians. After all, what we are doing is to implement one of our two major pledges to the electorate at the last election—cleaning up the streets and putting down hooliganism and racial gangsterism generally. Those are your show, while international affairs are

Leonard's and mine. And as I see it, we must fulfil both our pledges."

"I quite agree," said John Maynard unhappily. "Only we have no precedent, and precious few legal powers."

"The legal powers can be provided, retrospectively if need be, as we are doing with the capital gains tax. As for what you call the precedent, surely you have police officers who have held positions of authority in Cyprus, Kenya, Nyasaland, Malta, and so on?"

John Maynard took off his spectacles, which were misted by his Bovril, and wiped them. Such a conversation, in front of the Soviet ambassador, embarrassed him. It did not appear to embarrass Page-Gorman at all, any more than had the ridiculous accusation in Cabinet that he was dealing with the Russians behind Braithwaite's back. This, John Maynard miserably thought, is yet another proof of Page-Gorman's superiority to myself. I lack aplomb: I am not really suited to lead the Party. Why, I even let the commissioner tell me what I can do and what I can't! Page-Gorman went on:

"Yes, what you need is a man who has had experience in such police operations abroad, and whom you can appoint as special adviser, to act as a buffer between yourself and the commissioner. I believe I know the very man for the job."

"Having myself had no experience along the lines you speak of," Maynard said, "I certainly could do with a special adviser. On the other hand I can hardly expect a police officer from Cyprus or any other of those places to give orders to the commissioner. You know what sticklers they are for seniority."

"Obviously. But the man I have in mind has gained his experience outside the Commonwealth."

At this moment the head of London Airport entered the room. The control tower, he said, reported that the two Russian transports would be coming in to land in five minutes.

"I must be getting back to the Home Office," Maynard said. "And try to sort out all this mess. I must say, I wish I did have a special adviser. Who is this man you have in mind, Page-Gorman?"

"A very sound fellow. An Irishman. I'll send him along to see you this afternoon."

"Experience dealing with the IRA I suppose. That would be extremely kind of you."

"Not at all. A pleasure. Well, ambassador, that looks like one of your planes touching down now."

The ambassador gave a polite little bow towards John Maynard, then adjusted his tie as he followed Page-Gorman through the other door.

Flight 108 took off from Idlewild at the horrible hour of 7 am. Patrick had left Washington, whither he had been summoned by Mr Cuthbertson's friend in the Guards' tie, at four that morning, in order to connect with his flight. He had therefore had some two hours' sleep, for it was, of course, quite impossible even to drowse in the airport lounge, where the loudspeaker was constantly announcing the arrival and departure of planes from and to points all over the globe. In the green imitation-leather armchairs sat other travellers, looking as uncomfortably exhausted as himself; film stars for once uninterested in their appearance, businessmen quite uninterested in the film stars, and the customary two or three nuns. Why, Patrick wondered, were there always nuns at airports?

In the far corner of the lounge was a bar. Patrick walked across to it and asked for a coffee. It was served in a cardboard cup, and the contents tasted more of cardboard than of coffee. The thing to do, Patrick thought, would be to shave. But then he could do that on the plane: it would help to pass the time. And to think that Nora was only a few miles, a few minutes away, sleeping, her hair scattered upon her pillow, her lips parted in a slight smile, as he remembered her asleep on Capri that morning when he had awakened and had watched her, entranced, for one whole hour. So near, while he sat in the dry, stale heat of this airport lounge, waiting to be carried so very far away! Nor had he even been able to tell her that he was leaving, for it had only been decided at midnight that he must catch this flight, taking with him the verbal message for Air Marshal Boreham. It had been too late to telephone then, and it was too early to do so now.

He began to make his way back across the lounge, his eyes on the ground. "Watch out, there," a voice said, and Patrick just avoided colliding with a fellow passenger pushing a hand-trolley loaded with an assortment of suitcases of various shapes and sizes. And immediately behind came Felix Seligman, black overcoat over black pin-striped suit, black homburg hat, dark red silken scarf, rolled umbrella, freshly shaven, the very epitome of an English gentleman; his pigskin gloves matched the suitcases meticulously piled on his trolley which he was fastidiously propelling with one hand. They were, they discovered, both on Flight 108, and they agreed, with only a modicum of insincerity, that this was a pleasant coincidence.

Meanwhile, on the tarmac at London Airport, General Nikitin was shaking hands with Rupert Page-Gorman, with his ambassador (who had of course heard of the celebrated Nikitin, but had never before met him), and with Cockshore (Sir Victor, since the New Year honours) who had only arrived at the very last moment, mumbling excuses about the traffic. From out of the two aeroplanes came the advance party of the Russian inspectorate: twenty scientists, Nikitin's personal staff of eight, and fifty interpreter-secretaries. These latter had received definite orders not to fall in, like soldiers. They looked self-conscious and stood in silence, waiting to be told what to do, while the film cameras whirred and the journalists scribbled in notebooks. Nikitin gave everyone a beaming smile, but said, to the considerable relief of those come to meet him:

"No speeches, no speeches. Too cold. Later. At hotel."

Then the large party walked away towards the waiting buses. One of the interpreter-secretaries forgot, tried to fall into step with the man on his right, and had to be spoken to sharply.

In the public house in Copenhagen Street, where Linc Lee had been mortally stabbed, the landlord had just served the first drink of the day to the British Railways employee who usually stopped in on his way to and from work. The railwayman was enjoying his brown ale, the landlord, his elbows on the bar, reading the *Morning Advertiser*.

"What's the news?" asked the railwayman.

"Nothing," said the landlord. "West Brom have sold Stan Bussey to Spurs, fifty thousand. Nothing else."

There was silence while the railwayman examined the broken mirror behind the bar and the gaps in the ranks of bottles. After a while he said:

"You get the coppers in here last night?"

The landlord did not look up.

"They was in. But none of the Teds was here. They've kept away since Saturday. Good job too."

"That Yank soldier, he didn't half make a mess of your bar."

The landlord swore, turned over a page of his newspaper, then said:

"I should worry. It's all insured. Still, the sooner they clear all the spades out of this part, the better I'll be pleased. I had to waste half a day at that —— Yank's inquest. Black bastards."

"Was it the spades they was picking up last night?"

"The Teds all pulled out. Someone had tipped 'em the wink and they was all in Notting Hill."

"If you ask me, the sooner they put the lot inside, the better."

"Suits me."

"Well, cheerio. Must be pushing along."

The landlord still didn't look up. All he said was:

"Keep your nose clean."

In fact there was some news in the paper. The landlord had had a bloody good tip, from a friend of his whose cousin worked in the Clore stables, for the three-thirty. And the odds, he saw, had lengthened to eight to one. He'd put another fiver on, but he'd be damned if he was going to tell that old bastard from King's Cross about it.

Patrick and Felix also both had newspapers, Felix the *New York Times*, Patrick the *Herald*. The two Englishmen had read in silence for almost half an hour, while in the east, far ahead, the sky began to lighten for the dawn. The principal news item in the *Times* concerned the Russian announcement that a special session of the General Assembly of the United Nations must be summoned to consider the 'act of naked armed aggression' perpetrated by the United States against the People's Republic of China. The *Herald* gave this second billing. It devoted its left-hand column to the new Russian man-carrying sputniks, and to a report from a source close to the White House that these latest satellites, being military machines, might in certain circumstances be guilty of infringing United States territorial space: in which case it might prove necessary to treat them exactly as the United States Air Force would treat reconnaissance planes photographing America for a potentially hostile power, *ie* force them to land or destroy them. Third item in both papers was the earthquake in Japan: when it began some people on Hokkaido had assumed that it was a bombardment of the island by the Russians. Neither paper gave much front page space to English affairs, either Braithwaite's imminent departure for Moscow or the arrival that day of the Russian inspectorate.

The air hostess tapped Patrick, who was next to the aisle, on the shoulder.

"Look," she said, pointing towards the window. Felix also turned his head, and they both craned their necks. Venus was very bright, thirty degrees above the horizon. To the left and below it was another object, equally bright, visibly moving nearer to the planet.

"A sputnik," said the hostess. There was something like awe in her voice. The tiny golden disc closed on the planet. "To think of there being a man in that," she said, and then, after a pause: "Do you want your breakfast now?"

Patrick and Felix said that they did.

"The full English breakfast?" she asked.

"The full English breakfast," Felix said firmly, while Patrick settled for something less substantial. Then they both looked out of the window again. The sputnik was by now to the right of the planet, and fast fading out of sight.

Air Marshal Boreham was that morning at the Palace, to receive a high decoration. He was thus in uniform, perhaps, he thought, for the last time. His Monarch had been most gracious, receiving him in private audience, then, after the little ceremony, inviting him to sit down and inquiring most politely about his plans for the future. The elderly, stumpy air marshal was touched: how he wished Mary had lived, to be here at his side! Indeed he said as much to his Sovereign, who smiled and understood, and made precisely the right reply.

Then, when the short audience was over and he had backed somewhat clumsily from the room, there had followed the other conversation, a man-to-man conversation, with a very distinguished person in whom the Monarch had the most complete confidence. Indeed, as his Sovereign had told the air marshal, it was in order that he might have this conversation—concerning the letter he had written at the time of his resignation—that the private investiture had been arranged.

"Sit down, air marshal. Cigarette? No, of course you're a pipe man." A tobacco jar was pushed across the huge desk towards him. "Unless you prefer your own. Now then, let's get down to brass tacks at once."

Boreham filled his pipe but did not for the moment light it. He said, slowly:

"You saw the letter I wrote at the time of my resignation?" The other man nodded. "I believe that the situation has deteriorated seriously, and rapidly, since then." The other man nodded again. "You are doubtless aware that Page-Gorman has arranged for a very large force of Russians to land in this country, ostensibly to inspect our former rocket sites, and that he did this without the previous agreement of the Cabinet, or, so far as I can make out, even with the knowledge of the Foreign Office. And, as you know, the first contingent of this inspectorate arrives this morning."

"We have been informed about certain documents that were apparently purloined from Page-Gorman's private residence. So far as I can make out, without having myself seen the documents in question, they are genuine and are certainly open to the interpretation that you and your friends put upon them. On the other hand, all that the Palace knows officially is that a Russian inspectorate is due here today. This small group of scientists hardly constitutes the threat that you see. We have no official knowledge of any further Russian force coming here."

"Are you, sir—if you will excuse me being blunt—are you satisfied with your official sources of information on this matter?"

The man behind the desk hesitated, glanced out of the window, looked at Boreham, then said, in firm tones:

"No."

The air marshal breathed a sigh of relief and lit his pipe.

"Which is why, air marshal, I wished to have this conversation with you here today."

"In the opinion of myself and my friends, sir, this government, and specifically Rupert Page-Gorman, are engaged in bringing about the ruin of this country. Which is surely neither more nor less than high treason, and should be prevented with all speed."

"Your friends?"

"I can speak for several senior officers of the Air Force, and of the other services too, as well as a number of other experienced and responsible men." Here he gave a list of perhaps a dozen names, including Sir Charles Duncan, the group of elderly and distinguished men who had met at Jack Beaulieu's flat on the previous Sunday morning and one or two others. "All of us are convinced, sir, that Page-Gorman and his colleagues are leading this country to disaster."

"Your successor as Chief of Air Staff does not, I understand, share your views. In fact quite the reverse."

Boreham gave a grimace.

"That is why he was chosen for the job, sir."

"Yes, I see that, and of course I am not arguing for the sake of arguing. But I would remind you that there have been many occasions in the past when elderly men have believed, with all sincerity, that their juniors were pursuing a policy that must lead the country straight to disaster: the 1832 Reform Bill, Indian independence, self-government for the colonies, and so on. They have usually been proved wrong after the event. The policy of the present government—unconditional neutrality and economic expansion in an egalitarian society—can be defended. After all, if we can no longer be a world power capable of enforcing our will, it is surely best that we should be a happy, small power, prosperous and at peace with all, a second Switzerland?"

"If that were the government's policy, I should never have resigned, sir. But I do not believe it is. In the first place, for

169

economic, geographical, and strategic reasons this country can never be a second Switzerland; in the second, Switzerland is, for its size, the most highly armed state in Europe, with the most efficient defence forces. I quite agree that it would be the height of folly for this country to attempt to act today as though it still had the part to play in world affairs that it had a century ago. On the other hand the alternative to being a great power is not simply to abdicate all power altogether. But that is what they have done and are doing."

"That is what the electorate chose, only some three months ago."

"The electorate were deceived, chiefly by playing on the emotion of fear. They voted for disarmament. What they will get, unless something is done very quickly, is Russian domination."

"Why?"

"I don't quite follow you, sir."

"Why should this government wish to see Russian domination here?"

"Oh, I see. Well, firstly I believe that the Prime Minister and many of his associates are blind to the real nature of the Soviet threat. There are, again, other members of the government who believe that Communism is inevitable, and that therefore it is best that it be brought about peacefully, that a British Communism would be a tolerable or even a desirable state of affairs. And finally there are men who are anxious and willing to exploit such, I am not quite sure of the word, gullibility I would say, who are ready to exploit all that, in their own interests. And specifically, Page-Gorman."

There was a silence. Then the man behind the desk said:

"And what in your opinion should be done?"

"The public should be re-educated, through the newspapers and so on, so that they see the appalling dangers into which they are being led, and then they would presumably throw this government out." The man behind the desk nodded. "But there isn't time for that, even if it is still possible. There are rumours current that the government is planning to impose some form of censorship on the Press, on the grounds that the international situation makes this necessary. I hear that considerable pressure is being brought to bear on the *Daily Telegraph* already. And there is no need for the government to go to the country for another four and a half years."

"If fifty Socialist or Liberal members voted against the government, it would fall."

"I cannot imagine the circumstances in which fifty Socialists or Liberals would vote with the Tories. Or rather, I can, but by the time such circumstances arose I believe it's unlikely that there would be any more voting to be done. Meanwhile the leader of the right-wing Socialists, John Maynard, is actually in the government, and puts Party loyalty above everything. He told me so himself."

"Yes, I heard you'd been to see him."

"In fact, sir, I do not believe that anything can be done to avert the impending catastrophe through the normal electoral and parliamentary means."

"So what do you suggest?"

"I believe that the Crown should act."

"The Crown? How?"

"By appealing first of all to the government, though this would seem a pretty hopeless undertaking. By appealing over the head of the government to Parliament. . . ."

"Constitutionally impossible."

"In the final resort, by dissolving Parliament and appealing directly to the nation."

The man behind the desk smiled slightly.

"I'm afraid, air marshal, that that is quite out of the question. It was for doing just what you advocate that King Charles I lost his head. The country would not for a moment tolerate any direct intervention by the Crown in politics. Even if the situation is as critically grave as you believe, there are only two ways in which the Crown can act. The first is, as you suggest, to advance arguments which may persuade the leaders of the government to alter their policy. This I may say has already been done." He gave a bleak smile. "By me personally, and the effect, so far as I have been able to judge, was nil, even on John Maynard."

"And the other, sir?"

"The other is a last and desperate remedy. This is not

merely a British monarchy. The Crown could move abroad, to Canada, say, or to Australia. There is no telling what effect such a gesture would produce on public opinion here. It would surely be very great. But this must be the final step, and would only be justifiable if your very worst fears were to be proved true."

There was a long silence. Then Boreham said, with some difficulty:

"If, sir, a group of officers were to believe it their duty to act directly, in the name of the Crown . . ."

"No. The Crown can never become party to what must inevitably develop into a civil war."

"Even if . . ."

"In no circumstances, at least not so long as the Monarch remains in England. If the Crown were forced to move abroad, then there is no telling what circumstances might arise here."

"I see. May I ask one more question, sir?"

"Certainly, air marshal."

"What do you suggest that my friends and I do?"

"Prepare for all possible eventualities, and above all be discreet."

The ocean over which Patrick and Felix were flying was black and white, storm-tossed, primeval. To them, when it was occasionally visible through a gap in the clouds, it was only faintly uneven, like the skin on the back of a man's hand, and the lines of foam that topped the clashing rollers gave it a delicately marbled appearance, so high were they above the storm. Patrick, who had been shaving, resumed his seat, and said:

"So you have decided not to settle in America or Canada?"

He could not see how to ask the question that really interested him. He had therefore returned to the subject they had discussed over breakfast, hoping that Felix might volunteer the information he wanted.

"I had never really contemplated settling, emigrating," Felix replied. "I had thought I might try it for a few years. However on second thoughts I've decided against it. I want Toddy to be educated in England, and in certain circumstances it might not be possible for him to get back and forth for his holidays."

Patrick was tempted to smile. Whom did he know, save Felix, who could refer to the possibility of atomic war as 'certain circumstances'? He said:

"I should think Nora would be pleased."

Felix replied:

"Yes," and then, after a pause. "She is getting out of that play, and coming back to England herself. No doubt she told you she's been offered a part in *Lear*?"

Deliberately casual, Patrick lit a cigarette, then said:

"She did mention it, when we lunched together. But surely the American management will never let her go?"

"That's what I thought, but it's remarkable what these agents can arrange. They're letting her break her contract on the understanding that she'll do a Broadway season next year."

"Next year? That's a long time away."

"I gather the theatre is pretty well sold out till then. Seems a bit hard on the people who've bought the tickets, presumably thinking they were going to see Nora. Or so I'd have thought. But a friend of mine explained that *people* don't buy tickets in New York any more, only corporations and scalpers. And presumably the guests of US Steel or Fuelless Energy take what they're given."

The conversation was getting away from the one point that now interested Patrick. He therefore asked:

"I expect they made her give them a fairly long notice?"

"Not at all. She finishes tomorrow, and is flying back on Thursday. As a matter of fact, I'd have waited for her, only little Toddy has mumps, and I want to make sure the house is all ready for him to come home and convalesce in."

Thursday, Patrick was thinking. That means she'll be in London on Friday at the latest, and I shall surely see her then, or at least on Saturday. Three days, four days, why that's *nothing*, nothing at all. However, despite his joy, he remembered his manners sufficiently to say:

"Poor Toddy. But mumps are hardly serious these days."

Felix thought: Well, I've told him what he wanted to know.

And why not? Surely it's better to play the part assigned to me, and that I have accepted, as gracefully as possible? Besides, he's a decent enough fellow, and Nora would wish me to treat him with consideration.

Then that lavishness inherent in his character took control, and he added:

"Why don't you come down to Broadacres for the weekend? I forget whether you enjoy shooting. But if you do, there are a lot of cock pheasants that ought to be dealt with."

Antonia and Mark Vernon had finished their morning's Russian lesson, or rather Mark had drawn it to a close ten minutes early. He had done this because it was her habit to offer him a drink at the end of each lesson, and this morning he wanted a drink very badly indeed. When he had read the list of names of the Russians in the paper that morning, and had seen that they were led by General Nikitin himself, his hand had trembled so that he had spilt half his cup of coffee. Mark Vernon was one of the few people in England who knew the part that General Nikitin had played in crushing the abortive Polish uprising after the assassination of Gomulka three years ago. But it was not this knowledge that made him spill his coffee. Rather was it a purely personal, nervous reaction. Mark Vernon had met Nikitin twice: once, when first Mark had defected to the Soviets, and once shortly before his return to England.

And now he was here. So might a man feel who, pursued by wolves, finds a frail boat on a river's bank, and pushes off in the nick of time, only to discover, five minutes later, that the ferocious creatures can and do swim.

Therefore Mark Vernon stood with his back to Antonia, so that she might not see how much gin he was pouring from her half bottle. After all, once the water has been added there is no telling the strength of a pink gin. He said, over his shoulder:

"Shall I make you one, Antonia?"

"No, no thank you."

He now turned to face her, taking a deep swallow as he did. Better, that was better. But what would Nikitin say when that horrible Irishman told him how little had been achieved by sending Mark Vernon to England? Worse still, what would

Nikitin do? The only person who could conceivably help him was Antonia. And there she sat, gazing into the electric fire, brooding. Women, thought Mark Vernon with disgust, useless, fleshy, emotional, revolting creatures! How did one get them to do something for one? By making love to them, he supposed. The idea almost made him grimace, and besides, he was quite sure he couldn't. Or could he? If his life were at stake could he make love to this plain, emotional *creature* seated there on the sofa, her fat legs stuck out, gazing into the electric fire? And he remembered an anecdote that Pfeiffer had told him.

It seemed that in one of the camps where Pfeiffer had served as an SS officer, there had been a contingent of homosexuals, who were there for re-education. The system was simple. The homosexuals were compelled to commit the sexual act, twice a week, with women prisoners. Those who failed to do so were first punished, then shot as incorrigibles. Pfeiffer said that it was all regarded as a tremendous joke by the guards, a sort of twice-weekly variety show. "And it was marvellous," Pfeiffer would add with a chuckle, "how good they got at it, when they understood what the alternative was! Thousands we cured that way."

Could he, Mark wondered, noting with acute distaste the bulge of Antonia's blouse that hid those well-shaped breasts of which she was so proud? He supposed that in the last extremity he could.

"Antonia," he said, "has Rupert Page-Gorman said anything to you about that job he half promised me?"

She looked up at him, her slightly bulging eyes soulful and sad.

"No, Mark," she replied, "he's said nothing. And the last time I saw him he was so strange. Oh, Mark, I wonder . . . I wonder. . . ."

And suddenly tears began to well up in those poppy eyes of hers, and to dribble out, carrying, Mark noticed, a faint trail of mascara with them. He sat down beside her on the sofa, and after a moment's hesitation he put his arm about her shoulders. Almost at once her head seemed to be resting against his upper arm, and he was conscious of a most distasteful smell, the smell of woman and cosmetics and, he told himself, decay.

"Mark, Mark," she said, as he held her stiffly. "I feel so unhappy. I love him so. But you understand. You're like me."

Mark Vernon nodded, but could not bring himself to agree with this preposterous statement. However, she had no other wish save to go on talking:

"We're both lost. Little children lost in this cruel, cruel world."

At this moment the telephone rang.

Portraits of past Foreign Secretaries gazed impassively over Rupert Page-Gorman's head, their intricate problems forever solved, their robes of the Garter or fine black broadcloth turned long ago to dust, even as were the wearers. The brushwork of Lawrence, the drama of Sargent meant nothing to Page-Gorman. O'Mahony had not even noticed the pictures. Page-Gorman said:

"And quite apart from the very considerable help that I know you can give Maynard, I am all the more pleased to fall in with this request of yours, since I'm not at all happy about the general atmosphere within the police force. I believe they will do as they are told, but some of the senior police officers seem to have acquired very definite ideas about their own importance. It will be a great help to me to have someone like yourself form an independent opinion at first hand."

O'Mahony nodded, as Page-Gorman stretched out his hand for the telephone that was beginning to ring. The voice at the far end said: "Your Flaxman call, sir," and then Rupert was through.

"Antonia? Rupert here."

"Rupert! I'm so glad you——"

He interrupted her.

"I'm afraid I've no time for small-talk. Do you happen to know where Mark Vernon is at this moment?"

"He's here."

"Might I speak to him please?"

Crestfallen, she turned towards the sofa.

"It's Rupert. For you."

Mark Vernon jumped eagerly to his feet.

"Yes, Mr Page-Gorman?"

"Ah, Vernon. I am giving a luncheon for the Russian in-spectorate at Carlton House Terrace. You know where that is?"

"Of course. I used to work there."

"So you did. After lunch I shall be having private talks with General Nikitin. Although I understand he speaks quite good English, he believes and I believe it would be as well to have interpreters along just in case. He is bringing his own. I should like you to do the job for me. Can you be at Carlton House Terrace at two-thirty?"

"Certainly."

"Ask for me personally. Goodbye."

And he had hung up.

Now he turned to O'Mahony, and said:

"You are quite right, it's as well to be on the safe side. Though I still don't see who in the FO could or would have leaked that information to Boreham. You're sure that Vernon is entirely reliable?"

"Quite sure."

Yes, Rupert thought, he is quite sure. But how had the in-formation got out?

Mark Vernon's expression, as he turned back to Antonia, was one close to delight. It would be some moments before he felt the full trepidation of knowing that he must face Nikitin, and interpret for a man who would instantly detect his smallest mistake. But to think that only two minutes ago he had been contemplating imminent ruin or a fate worse than death! He said:

"He's asked for me."

Antonia looked up, sadly.

"He didn't talk to me at all."

"I expect he was busy. Besides, you'll be seeing him tonight at the anti-bomb dinner."

"But not alone."

Femininity! Clutching, possessive femininity!

"Mark, have you ever been in love?"

Of course he had. But what an absurd question for a woman to ask of him! How could these breeding-machines understand what real ecstasy meant? However he was in a benevolent mood.

"Yes, Antonia."

"If you're in love with someone, you'll do anything for them, won't you?" She was twisting her handkerchief between her fingers.

"Of course."

"If you were in love with . . . with someone, and that someone wanted somebody else, and the only way you could keep that person were to try and arrange for him to see that other person, you would have to do it, wouldn't you?"

Mark Vernon had only the haziest idea what it was she was talking about. Nor was he giving her his full attention. What suit should he wear this afternoon? He had bought two new ones since his return to England, but it might be more tactful to wear the one the Russians had given him in Moscow. Or would it?

"Yes, I think so," he said.

"Real love must rise above all jealousy, mustn't it?"

Because he was supposed to be an inconspicuous Englishman, and inconspicuous Englishmen do not dress in square-shouldered, dark grey suits of obviously foreign origin that looked as though they had been tailored with an axe.

"Jealousy is a useless emotion, Antonia."

"You're so right. But it's a very human one, Mark."

There it was again, this glorying in the dirt of humanity. And that was what these creatures called love! A sudden, awful thought came to Mark Vernon. Would Nikitin expect him to know technical terms connected with nuclear weapons? Perhaps if he hurried around to Foyle's he could get a technical dictionary. But to arrive with a dictionary—would that show keenness, or merely incompetence? Oh, it was all so difficult.

Antonia said:

"You know my sister, Nora. Do you think a scatter-brained, frivolous creature like that could attract a man like Page-Gorman?"

What answer did she wish him to give? He said:

"Not for long, Antonia. He might be attracted to her briefly, but he would obviously get much more satisfaction in the long run out of the company of a woman like you—a woman with whom he can talk, exchange ideas."

What rot, he thought. They were all the same, emotional, messy bores. But she had looked up at him with gratitude.

"You're right, Mark. You're quite right."

Yes, he would certainly see if he could get a dictionary.

"Antonia, I must go now."

"Yes, Mark. And thank you for listening to me. You are a good, kind man, Mark. And wise."

He patted her on the shoulder.

The winter sun had risen to meet the jet liner, passed overhead, and was sinking towards the western ocean by the time the plane carrying Patrick and Felix came in to land at London airport. The two men walked together through the cold, raw evening into the floodlit terminal building, where they waited briefly in an imitation, 1945-modern drawing-room, before going through to passport control. There would be a hired car to meet Felix, and he had offered Patrick a lift into London.

At the desk where sat the passport control official, Felix was immediately ahead of Patrick. Patrick thus saw the official examine Felix's passport, consult a thick, black book, look carefully at Felix once again, scribble a note, ring a bell, and when another official in a blue uniform arrived, hand him this note. Then Felix went through to Customs. Patrick's turn came next, and he felt a queer apprehension when the man opened the black book. However, he was let pass at once, and followed Felix through the doorway into the Customs shed.

He looked around for Felix, but there was no sign of him. He had no time to wonder about this though, for almost immediately there were two Customs officials, one in uniform the other a civilian, facing him. The one in uniform said, looking at Patrick's overnight bag and briefcase that stood upon the low barrier:

"Is this all your luggage?"

Patrick replied that it was.

"How long have you been in America?"

"Three days."

"Why?"

"What do you mean, why?" Patrick asked.

"Why did you go to America for three days?"

"On business."

Had it not been for this slight sensation of apprehension, Patrick would have asked the man what damn concern it was of his. However he kept his temper even when the official asked, in cold tones:

"What sort of business?"

"I'm an advertising man. My firm sent me to see a client, concerning an advertising campaign in this country." Then, since the man said nothing, he added: "My firm is Jack Beaulieu, Ltd., and the American company is called Fuelless Energy Incorporated."

"Would you please open that briefcase?"

Patrick did so. The man took out the various papers it contained (and they did, in fact, refer to the advertising campaign for British Fuelless Cars; Cuthbertson had insisted on his taking these with him). Then the man examined the sides and base of the briefcase carefully. Next he took everything out of Patrick's overnight bag, examined that and its contents, still in silence, and replaced them. Patrick said, with a smile:

"You're making a very thorough job of it today."

The man's eyes met his, and in them there was no answering smile. The man said:

"Your wallet please."

"Do you really....?"

"Your wallet please."

Patrick shrugged his shoulders and passed it over to the man, who went through it with care before handing it back. Then he made Patrick remove his overcoat (he went through the pockets) and turn out all the pockets of his suit.

With a definite note of sarcasm Patrick said:

"Wouldn't you like me to take my shoes off? After all, I might be smuggling diamonds in their heels."

The official's voice was entirely cold and impersonal.

"That will not be necessary. You are cleared. You may go."

And with his stub of chalk he made a cryptic sign on Patrick's little bag and briefcase.

Outside the Customs shed, in the foyer or grand concourse

or whatever other ponderous name they may give to those parts of air terminals which are devoted to airlines' desks and the selling of sweets and papers and the purveying of inferior meals at superior prices, Patrick looked for Felix, but again there was no sign of him. Then he saw a small, black notice-board, to which was affixed, in curved white letters, the information: MR F. SELIGMAN'S CAR GATE 8. Patrick hurried down the stairs, hoping that Felix might have waited, and after a little trouble found Gate 8.

There was a long, black car, with a chauffeur in peaked cap standing by the door. The chauffeur saw Patrick looking at him inquiringly, and stepped forward.

"Mr Seligman, sir?"

"No. Isn't he out yet?"

"No, sir."

When at last Felix did emerge, with his large quantity of luggage, Patrick soon realized that what he had been through was as nothing compared to Felix's ordeal. Not only had they examined all the contents of all his bags just as thoroughly as they had Patrick's, but they had stripped him naked and apparently X-rayed his clothes.

"Nor was that the end of it," said Felix, as they sped past the lighted factories on the Great West Road. "There was a man, from the Treasury, I suppose, who asked me the most detailed questions about my investments. It was only by ringing my lawyer that I was able to get away when I did. But I've got to go to the Bank of England for a further inquisition tomorrow."

Patrick said:

"It seems most extraordinary, a man in your position."

Felix did not answer this. He was thinking that what Clonard called 'his position' might well be more of a disadvantage than an advantage henceforth. The Nazis, after all, had showed scant respect for the Rothschilds or the Warburgs, the Russians none for their bankers. Not, of course, that this government was comparable to those. Or at least, not yet. Meanwhile it might not be at all a bad idea to see if he could not take out some insurance with the new masters. The Chancellor of the Exchequer he knew slightly, an intellectual fanatic, quite impervious to everything save his precious theories about real values and the necessity for rigid controls. No help to be found there. John Maynard was an old fool. The people at the Bank would be frightened. What about that fellow Page-Gorman? There was something definitely corruptible about the man, a mackerel-in-the-moonlight quality, a distasteful aura of phosphorus. But for Toddy's sake perhaps he should cultivate the fellow. After all they could make a very nasty case out against him, although he didn't believe that they could take legal action, at least not without passing one of their favourite retroactive laws. But they could always do that. Yes, it might be as well to invite Antonia and Page-Gorman down to Broadacres.

They were in the congestion of Earl's Court now, and Felix was wondering whether in fact he had been wise to come back. But of course he would have had to return in any case, if only to close up Broadacres and fetch Toddy. Far better to get it all sorted out now. He turned his head, and said to Patrick:

"Do you know this fellow, Page-Gorman?"

"I've met him."

"He's a friend of my sister-in-law's. I think I may have to ask them down this weekend, if he's free. Do you like him?"

"No."

"Neither do I. But I think I may have to. Would you come in any case?"

Patrick hesitated. It had been his hope that once he had delivered his message he would be free of Page-Gorman and politics and Jack's plans and Mr Cuthbertson's spies. He certainly had no desire to spend a weekend under the same roof as a man whose flat he had burgled. On the other hand, he told himself, it was probably unlikely that he could in fact extricate himself from all this now. And besides, Nora would be there.

"Yes," he said, "I'll come down to Broadacres. After all, I don't suppose I'd actually have to talk to Page-Gorman."

"You wouldn't," said Felix. "He does all the talking."

The lights turned green, and the car moved on.

Half an hour later Patrick was seated in another car, Jack Beaulieu's Bentley, 'Expense-account Annie' as Jack liked to call it. Patrick had gone straight to Beaulieu's flat, without first going home. He had found Jack in, and also Moyra, as well as a television executive, distinctly worried about the drop in advertising revenue.

"But my dear fellow," Patrick heard Jack say, as he took off his coat in the hall: "I can't find advertisers for you. Can't even find them for myself. Wish I could. We're in for the seven lean years, if you ask me. Patrick, it's good to see you!"

Patrick walked across and kissed Moyra, before being introduced to the television executive. Jack had meanwhile slipped out of the room.

Moyra said:

"His lordship here has just blown in from New York. Good crossing, Patrick?"

"Wonderful till I got to London, where they frisked me as if I was a Messina brother. But it's nothing compared to what they did to Felix Seligman, who was on the same plane. They——"

Jack re-entered the room and interrupted Patrick, to say to the television man:

"Look, do you mind if we leave the rest of our talk until to-morrow? There's a rather important thing on, and I must take Clonard around to see the client in question at once. Forgive me?"

"But naturally."

"And I can promise you that if we're not bringing you the business we did, it's not because we're dissatisfied with your productions. After all," he added with a laugh, "they're really no worse than any of the others, are they?"

In the car, Jack had said:

"Keep it, till we get to Boreham's place."

"Where does he live?"

"Holland Park way. We'll go through the park."

There he was wrong. The Piccadilly end of Park Lane was closed by a wooden barrier, and soldiers were busy blocking the big arch at Hyde Park Corner with rolls of concertina wire. They were waved on by a policeman. At Albert Gate there were more police, and again at Alexandra Gate. Behind the barricade here they could see newly-erected tents in the distance.

"What on earth . . ." Jack muttered, and pulled up beside a police officer.

"How do I get through the park, officer?"

"You don't. You go round," said the police officer. "Now move along please."

"Do you remember," Patrick said, as they slid into the traffic, "that police officer I told you about, the one I reported, or tried to report? Named Prendergast?"

"Vaguely," said Jack. "God damn that taxi, what does he think he's doing?"

"Well," said Patrick, "I believe that was him."

"Looked a real shit," said Jack. "What is the matter with that cab? He must be nuts."

They drove on in silence. Patrick said:

"What are they doing in the park?"

"Search me. Mayfair has been sealed off since lunchtime, and the Notting Hill area too, I understand. It's one of these round-ups."

After a while Patrick said:

"Felix Seligman has invited me for the weekend. Also Page-Gorman."

"*Bon appétit,*" said Jack, and accelerated viciously past a British Railways van. "Have you ever met this air marshal chappie?"

"No."

"He's all right. And hopping mad."

In the great banqueting hall of the Kremlin the heat was tremendous, for the huge cut-glass chandeliers (they had come back from Paris nearly a century ago with the Tsar Alexander III) held several hundred candles. Leonard Braithwaite mopped his brow and attempted to focus on the face of Kornoloff, who was proposing yet another toast:

"To British Socialism!"

Wearily Braithwaite got to his feet and drank. This was the eighteenth since dinner, eighteen little glasses of cold water that had gone down his dry, hot throat since the sturgeon and the wild boar and the venison pasty and heaven knows what else, rich, heavy food, tasteless to a man with a cold as bad as his, lead in the stomach of a man who was normally almost a vegetarian. At least, though, they had compromised about the drinks. His doctor had given him an injection that would carry him through the evening, but had been able to explain, with perfect truth, that alcohol on top of this would be highly dangerous. Hence the little carafe of cold water before him, which was now empty. Suppose he had had to drink that much vodka! (For the British ambassador had told him that it would be regarded as offensive in the extreme if he did not drink every toast, and propose a great many himself, too.) A flunkey was placing a new carafe before him at this moment. Why, Braithwaite thought, if he drank one of those filled with vodka he would be *drunk*!

Now Sspesiatkin was on his feet, flushed and far away beneath the brilliant lights:

"To the British workers!"

Braithwaite drank, and immediately had a coughing fit. Someone had made a mistake. This carafe did contain vodka.

Marshal Ryukin was up now.

"To the British Armed Forces!"

Braithwaite drank again. Slowly the room was beginning to revolve, chandeliers, politicians, diplomats and all.

The air marshal looked closely at Patrick Clonard as he spoke. What he had to say was:

"I have been told to tell you this. The United States government fully share your fears about the probable results of implementing the policy announced by the present British government. And they are extremely grateful for the information supplied which confirms their views. However, they believe that it would be impossible at this stage for America to intervene here in any way, save by those expressions of strong disapproval that have already been voiced. In the first place because America is likely to be fully involved in the Pacific and the Far East. But secondly, and more important, because the United States government must respect the choice made by the British electorate at the last election. As one man in Washington explained to me, they obviously cannot invade Britain because they disapprove of our government, and they presume that neither you nor your friends want them to. In fact, to put it bluntly, we elected them, and it's up to us to get them out. In this, the Americans are prepared to give us every sort of unofficial help short of the use of troops."

"What does that mean?" the air marshal asked sharply.

"Moral support, economic support, information, advice. And if any British government, including this one, were to ask for military support against the Soviets, it would be forthcoming. They have no intention of abandoning Europe, and are planning, so far as their Far Eastern commitments will allow, to strengthen their forces on the Continent and to reinforce the Sixth Fleet. But, fundamentally, the problem is ours. How we solve it is also our concern. If we can keep them informed about developments in this country, they will be grateful. Normal intelligence can be passed through their embassy. Anything considered really secret should go through Jack here, for the time being, to a friend of Cuthbertson's living at the Savoy Hotel. Alternative channels will be established later."

He fell silent.

"I see," said Boreham. "And I can understand their point of view. After all it's much the same as the attitude we adopted to the anti-Nazis under Hitler. Is there anything else?"

"Yes. The American government will continue to regard Britain as a friendly power, but as one that is temporarily incapable of meeting its various treaty obligations. That is to say, its attitude towards us will be much the same as was the American attitude towards Pétainist France. But as was the case with Vichy, such an attitude would be drastically revised in the event of the British government granting the Russians any sort of bases or military or naval facilities in this country."

Boreham nodded. Jack, who had sat in silence while Patrick spoke, now said:

"That's surely inconceivable. Braithwaite would never do a thing like that. After all——"

"There are other men besides Braithwaite," the air marshal remarked. "And even he isn't immortal."

Kornoloff was on his feet now.

"To British culture!" he said, and raised his glass.

186

Braithwaite downed his. The room was spinning faster and faster. Somebody reached out an arm from behind him and refilled his glass. The carafe was almost empty. Braithwaite did not sit down, for he feared that he might never stand again. He raised his glass. There was one more toast that he wished to propose, one that was nearer and dearer to him than any other sentiment, one that these men, here in Moscow, would truly appreciate. For were they not the only ones who understood, who realized what was at stake, who were in fact actively helping the cause for which his son had died, his only son? He raised his glass:

"Arms for Spain!" he said.

The interpreter hesitated. What could the Englishman mean? Monarchist, NATO, capitalist, American-dominated Spain? Arms for Spain? Bombs on Spain? What did the man mean? Meanwhile some of the guests had drunk, others, who knew English, had hesitated, Kornoloff looked extremely attentive. Braithwaite said again, at the top of his voice:

"Arms for Spain!"

The room was spinning faster and faster. Braithwaite reached out to stop it. It was turning upside down. He leaned forward to steady himself. Something crashed against his face. Blackness.

Kornoloff turned to the British ambassador, and said, with a tolerant laugh:

"I believe your Prime Minister is drunk."

But he was wrong. Braithwaite was dead, sprawled across the Kremlin table.

"I think our little dinner went off very well, don't you?" Antonia asked, as Rupert fiddled with the wire cage inside the big front door that caught his letters and those of Mr Kachachurian and the London Gusset Company. Two were for him.

"All right," he said, as he turned towards the stairs.

Canon Christian had been the host, and he had borrowed for the occasion a most handsome room, panelled in age-blackened oak, the property of his cathedral. It had been a small party, the leading half dozen Soviet scientists (General Nikitin had had other business to attend to) and an equal number of members of the Anti-Bomb Committee. The food had been simple and good, and the speeches short and friendly. After the port (Sir Victor Cockshore, who prided himself on his knowledge of port, had explained at considerable length to the Russians both the history and the manufacturing process of this most English of drinks), Canon Christian had taken his guests on a brief conducted tour of his cathedral, which had impressed or perhaps merely bewildered them. It was all over by half past ten.

"Your speech struck just the right note, I thought," she went on, as Rupert opened his flat door, and walked into his drawing-room ahead of her.

· He did not reply, for he was opening his letters. One, she noticed, contained two keys on a ring. He tossed these on his desk, then fished about inside the envelope to see if there was a letter. There was none. The other, in a buff envelope, was obviously either a bill or a receipt.

"Those dinners are quite pointless. A mere waste of time," Rupert said, and walked across to the electric fire, which he switched on. "Cold in here."

"Would you like me to make you a cup of cocoa, Rupert?"

"I'd rather have a drink. There's whisky in the kitchen."

Dutifully she went to fetch it. There was no soda, so she filled a glass jug with water, and also brought in two glasses. Back in the drawing-room she said:

"It *is* cold. You're here so seldom. You should have somebody to come in and light the fires and put a bottle in your bed. Somebody to look after you."

Rupert poured himself a drink, a stiff one.

"Not too generous with their drinks, the clergy. To look after me, eh? Mrs Prince looks after me very well. But I see what you're getting at."

"What do you mean, Rupert?"

"You saw my spare set of keys. I had enough trouble getting them back from Moyra, thank you very much."

"May I sit on the floor at your feet, Rupert?"

He did not reply, and she did so, her legs curled under her, her eyes on the fire. Silence. She did not mind his rebuffs. They were, she told herself, a part of him. And this silence that was slowly unfolding into intimacy was worth, to her, almost unlimited rebuffs. This was their 'thing' together, she thought, their own sort of love, and to preserve this she would do anything. She said:

"Felix Seligman telephoned me this evening."

Page-Gorman moved slightly. She went on:

"He's invited me to his house for the weekend. And he asked me if I thought you'd like to come too."

"I doubt if I'll have the time. His wife's in America, isn't she?"

"She's coming back. She'll be there."

Was there a faint note of bitterness in Antonia's voice? She hoped not, and therefore added quickly, in almost sugary tones:

"I do hope you can, Rupert. It would be a rest for you. You know how comfortable it is at Broadacres."

"I'll think it over. When do you go?"

"Friday night or Saturday morning."

"I might be able to get away in time for lunch on Saturday."

"Do try, dear Rupert. It would be such fun."

The telephone rang.

"Oh, Lord," he said, as he got up to answer it. She watched him.

"Yes, speaking." He was frowning, the public man, the other half of the man she loved. But their budding silent intimacy was broken. "Yes. You're quite sure? No, don't inform anyone till I get there. Right."

He put down the receiver and stood for a moment, his fingers to his forehead.

"What is it, Rupert?"

"Eh?" He had obviously forgotten that she was in the room. This was simultaneously hurtful and yet a further proof of intimacy, so that she was pleased.

"I have to go to the Foreign Office," he said. "Leonard Braithwaite has died suddenly. I must take charge at once, before the Palace has a chance to send for Maynard."

He hesitated, as though about to speak, thought better of it, opened the lower right-hand drawer of his desk, and took from it a slim brown folder, which he tucked into his briefcase. Then he walked to the door, and out of the room, and into power.

11

In FLEET STREET the pubs were closed, the journalists scattered, and pallid, harassed night editors busy putting their papers to bed, while printers swore, and huge machines clanked and whirred.

The first interruption to this cheerless routine was a series of telephone calls to the leading newspapers (and also to the BBC) from the Foreign Office information desk. These announced, quite baldly, that renewed hostilities had broken out between the United States and China, that atomic weapons had already been fired, and that a State of Emergency had therefore been decreed in Britain. In order to ensure that nothing which could be interpreted as a breach of neutrality occurred, the leading papers were requested to refrain from partisan comment.

Rapidly the journalists returned to Fleet Street, some from their dinners, some from their tellies, a few from their own or other people's beds, some drunk, one, who had been to a dance, in a tail-coat. By the time they arrived the second item of news had come in, that Leonard Braithwaite had died of a heart attack in Moscow. (The Tass news agency, which was only fifteen minutes behind the Foreign Office, reported quite bluntly that he had died 'of drink', but this was naturally discounted, since all in Britain knew of his teetotal views.)

While the sub-editors were ripping out pictures of the pitched battle between the hooligans and the police in the Notting Hill area, and the obituarists were putting the final touches to their brief lives of Braithwaite, the editors and other distinguished persons attempted to get more and harder news concerning the outbreak of hostilities between China and the United States. Here, however, they drew an almost complete blank. The Foreign Office had nothing to add to its bald statement, the Foreign Secretary himself was unavailable even to the editor of *The Times*, and when they attempted to contact their correspondents in Washington they were informed, politely but firmly, that all telephone and wireless links with America, Ireland, and the Continent were temporarily disconnected, 'owing to the emergency'. Nor had the American Embassy any comment to make, which was hardly surprising, since this item was as much news to them as it was to Washington. The American ambassador was as unable to contact the Foreign Secretary as was the editor of *The Times*.

Where, all Fleet Street wanted to know, was Page-Gorman? Fascinating items about fiscal reform in Italy were ready to be ripped from some papers, about HOUSEWIFE DEFENDS KIDDIES AGAINST SEX-MANIAC from others, as the journalists awaited his expected statement. Then he was seen leaving the Hertford House Hotel by two newspapermen who had been collecting material, necessarily scanty since they were not allowed inside, about the temporary detention centre in Hyde Park. But he refused to talk to them.

"Sorry, boys, nothing. I'm off to the Palace."

By the time he emerged from the Palace a crowd of journalists was waiting, anxiously, as were their superiors in the now brilliantly lit Fleet Street palaces. For the minutes were ticking past. Meanwhile leading articles had been written on the assumption that Page-Gorman had been sent for in order to assume the premiership.

This was, as yet, untrue. The Sovereign had decided that such an appointment could not be made in these circumstances. And indeed Page-Gorman had not been sent for, but had requested an audience. However he told the newspapermen that there would be no announcement until the morning and did this in such a way as to convince them that he was, in fact, the new Prime Minister.

John Maynard, out at Harlow New Town, had taken a very strong sleeping pill only half an hour before the Press began to telephone him. Eventually Mrs Maynard simply left the telephone off the hook (since her husband was clearly not making any sense at all) and an hour later was busily repulsing the journalists at her door. She was a forceful woman. They went.

Certain facts were unknown to the journalists.

One was that General Nikitin had sent a wireless message, over his Embassy's transmitter, to Moscow, which contained only the figures 39745391. The result of this message was that the men of the special RKK battalion standing by in Moscow

191

were awakened from their sleep, while seven large transports were made ready to take off at dawn. (Page-Gorman did not know this either.)

Nor did they know that after Page-Gorman's request for an audience at the Palace, Air Marshal Boreham received a telephone call which necessitated his making several calls to various friends in the RAF. As a result of these a Super-Comet of the Royal Flight would be standing by, ready to take off, from Prestwick airport at 0800 hours next day.

Finally, they were unaware that after a lengthy conversation between Page-Gorman and a certain O'Flaherty, who had earlier that day been appointed special adviser to the Home Secretary to deal with racial crime, some seventeen senior police officers were that afternoon relieved of their appointments (all on the charge of accepting bribes from brothel-keepers) while an equal number of hitherto unknown junior officers were given triple or quadruple promotions. One of these was named Prendergast.

At eleven-thirty that evening the BBC Light Programme—television and the other sound programmes had as usual closed down at eleven—interrupted its popular programme of music called *Waltzing into Space* to give its customary news summary.

"It is with deep regret that we announce the death of the Prime Minister, the Right Honourable Leonard Braithwaite, PC, OBE, MP. Mr Braithwaite, who was visiting Moscow, succumbed to a heart attack while attending a dinner party given by Mr Kornoloff. The dinner party was immediately discontinued. Mr Braithwaite, who was suffering from severe nasal catarrh, had left London airport only this morning for personal conversations concerning peace with the Russian leader.

"After receiving the news of Mr Braithwaite's death, Mr Rupert Page-Gorman, Secretary of State for Foreign Affairs, was summoned to the Palace. It is expected that an announcement will be made in the morning.

"Her Royal Highness the Princess Alexandra today visited the Hainault College of Art, where she distributed prizes to the most successful students. Her Royal Highness wore a blue dress.

"The Foreign Office announces that war has broken out between the United States of America and the People's Republic of China. Nuclear weapons have been used by both sides. In order to safeguard British neutrality, a temporary State of Emergency has been declared. This is unlikely to affect daily life.

"The unofficial strike of seventy-two sock cutters at Wolverhampton has now entered its third month. A further ninety thousand loom operators are likely to be affected in the Burnley area.

"In the fifth round replay, Scunthorpe Wanderers defeated Canvey United three–two. Scunthorpe now meet Maid o' the Valley in the quarter finals. All three of Scunthorpe's goals were scored by Ron Bussey, the younger brother of Stan, the England centre-half.

"We return you now to *Waltzing into Space*."

Carleen's father had taken the girl 'up West', hoping, as he explained to his wife, that a sight of the bright lights and a visit to the pictures might 'get her out of herself a bit'. Since the magistrate had released her, on payment of a £5 fine and after a fairly protracted homily in which he had seen fit to bully her for what he called her immoral and un-British ways, Carleen had been living at home, red-eyed, silent, and apathetic.

Bermondsey is a cheerless borough at night, the streets largely deserted, the cinemas closed under pressure from television, the huge pubs—built for thirstier, lustier generations of dockers and workers—half empty, filled with bright neon strips, the customers frozen before the flickering pictures of commercialized sport and music from Radio Luxemburg. Besides, Carleen had a dull antipathy to entering any pub at all.

"Take the girl up west, Jim," her mother had said. And he had done so, sitting beside her on the top of the No 1 bus that took them over Waterloo Bridge, changing in the Strand, and finally to Piccadilly and the bright lights. When asked what film she would care to see, she had been listless.

"I don't mind, Dad."

So he had chosen for her, which had meant getting on yet another bus that took them to the new cinema near Marble

Arch. The film which he had chosen with the express intention of cheering her up, of making her laugh, was called, *After You, Constable*.

He soon realized that he had chosen badly. The audience about and below them might laugh and whistle, the comic policemen on the screen throw themselves about, make simple sexual jokes, and work themselves into grotesque situations, but he was aware that the girl beside him was sitting rigid and motionless, silently twisting her handkerchief between her fingers. It did not occur to him that the very sight of policemen, comic or not, might be distressing to her, nor that the scene in which these persons arrested a coloured man who was, in fact, a woman police officer disguised, could upset her deeply. But he was sensitive enough to see that the evening was a failure. Some fathers would have blamed their daughters for this, but Jim Fisher was a kindly man. He was merely saddened himself, and a little bewildered, and so forced himself to laugh all the harder, in the hope of evoking answering laughter from her.

When the show was at last over, and they were inching their way out through the crowded and brilliantly-lit foyer beneath the enormously improbable photographs of stars, he glanced down at her shiny, yellow head.

"What'd you like to do now, girl?" he asked.

"I don't mind, Dad."

Take her home? Or for a stroll along Oxford Street? He himself would dearly have liked a beer, but then this was her outing.

They started down the north side of Oxford Street. Both deep in their own thoughts, hers of sorrow, his of concern for her, neither noticed the subdued commotion up at Marble Arch, nor the large numbers of police cars in evidence, nor even the wire barricades blocking Park Street and North Audley Street, and the other entrances into Mayfair. Even if he had noticed, the West End was so strange a place to Carleen's father, the behaviour of its inhabitants—of which he knew only from the more spectacular Press—so foreign, that Jim Fisher might well have regarded the 'flushing' operation by the police as perfectly normal, and certainly as no concern of his. They

194

walked slowly on. From time to time she would stop briefly and gaze into a brightly lighted window filled with cheap shoes, or mass-produced dresses, or underclothes. This was a reflex action. They had thus progressed for a couple of hundred yards, when they reached a corner pub, and her father's reflexes also came into action.

"Fancy a drink, girl?"

"No, Dad, no. I . . . I don't feel like it. But you go in. I'll wait for you here."

"You're sure you don't mind?"

"No, no, Dad. You go in and have a pint."

"Right."

It took him a little time to get his pint, but when at last it was placed before him, he downed it in one. For he felt slightly ashamed of having left the girl out there. After all, this was her evening. He therefore wiped his mouth quickly with the back of his hand and went out into Oxford Street.

There was no sign of his daughter. A black van was moving off, and two policemen were standing on the corner, talking together. Carleen's father glanced up and down. This great street had suddenly become almost deserted, and she was not, as he thought she might be, looking into any shop window within sight. He moved closer to the two policemen and heard one say to the other:

"That makes eight so far. Two more and it's our quota."

Then one of the policemen turned and saw the middle-aged docker.

"What the 'ell do you want here?"

Carleen's father was immediately on the defensive.

"Nothing, guv. Just looking for my daughter."

Both policemen laughed.

"Daughter? That's a good one. Hop it."

Carleen's father now began to feel frightened.

"I went in there for a pint, and——"

They were both standing over him.

"You 'eard what I said. 'Op it!"

But the docker went on:

"Did you see her? She was waiting for me. A fair-haired girl. Sort of slight. Did you see her?"

Now the policemen exchanged glances. After a moment's pause, one of them said slowly:

"There was a bird standing here, might answer your description. But she's not here any more, see. Now 'op it."

"A bird? That wasn't no bird. That was my daughter. My Carleen."

The younger of the two policemen sniggered:

"They've all got fathers, haven't they?"

"Where's she gone? Where've they taken her?"

The older policeman now spoke.

"They've taken 'em all up into the park."

"The park?"

"What's the matter with you, you drunk or something? Hyde Park, that's where they've taken them."

Carleen's father hesitated, then turned and began to run up Oxford Street, back towards the Marble Arch. Behind him he heard the younger policeman call:

"Heigh, where do you think you're going? You can't go in there."

But he ran on, past the bright windows filled with shoes, and dresses, and underclothes.

Jack and Patrick exchanged glances as Boreham reached for the ringing telephone.

"Speaking," he said, and then seemed almost to come to attention in his chair.

"Yes, sir," he said, and there was a long pause. "Yes, I see." He scribbled something on a pad, while the person at the other end spoke. "Yes, I believe I still have sufficient, er, influence with the RAF to arrange that. Right, sir. Immediately." He rang off.

For a moment he sat in silence, holding the bridge of his thick nose between finger and thumb. Then he stood up.

"It seems, gentlemen, that I have a difficult job to do this evening. I'm afraid I cannot say what it is. But I can tell you this. Page-Gorman is making a play for power, and in a very strange fashion. I shall know more in a few hours' time. I may be being alarmist, but I believe it would be as well if I were not to sleep here, or at my club. Can you give me a bed, Beaulieu?"

196

"Certainly."

"I shall be with you in about two hours. Meanwhile, please get in touch with Cuthbertson's man and tell him . . ." He hesitated. Then sat down again and scribbled briefly in silence. He folded the sheet of paper into an envelope. "And give him this. He's at the Savoy, isn't he?"

General Nikitin had difficulty in controlling his fury. He strode up and down the room, before the armchair in which Rupert Page-Gorman was seated, at times breaking into Russian, and then glancing at Mark Vernon who stood nervously in a corner. Mark translated.

"It is preposterous," he was saying, "monstrous, this so-called BBC news broadcast. It is to make a laughing-stock. . . ." He went on in Russian.

Page-Gorman looked at Mark.

"The general says that so to present serious news, mixed with inane items about a Royal princess and reports of quite uninteresting sporting activities can only be construed as a puerile joke."

"But," said Page-Gorman, "that is the way the BBC always presents the news these days. They always bring in about the Royal Family, and football."

Nikitin looked at him closely, then said:

"It could be construed as sabotage."

Mark Vernon glanced at Page-Gorman, and saw that he was smiling very slightly as he replied:

"Sabotage is not a word that we use here. And even if we did, I don't believe that anyone could ever accuse the BBC of committing so heinous a crime."

"Heinous?" asked Nikitin, and glanced at Vernon, who translated. This brief moment gave Nikitin time to regain his self-control. He now said, quite calmly:

"Why was the text of this stupid broadcast not checked with me first?"

Page-Gorman shrugged his shoulders, as he said silkily:

"Should it have been?"

"This lie about war between the United States and China. Who invented that?"

"Information in the possession of the Foreign Office——"

"Please be serious, Mr Page-Gorman. You have declared a State of Emergency. In certain circumstances this could be construed as an action hostile to the Soviet Union."

"Really? In view of the fact that our declaration of a State of Emergency is intended solely to safeguard our neutrality, I fail to follow your argument. Furthermore, General Nikitin, I was not aware that you were entitled to speak for the Soviet Union in such matters."

To Mark Vernon's consternation Nikitin now grinned. He walked over, slapped Page-Gorman on the shoulder, and said:

"We understand each other, you and I. But . . . be careful. Come, Vernon. The Foreign Minister has many matters to attend to. We must waste no more of his valuable time."

He laughed again heartily, while Vernon, who after all was employed by Page-Gorman, glanced nervously from one master to the other. Then, after a nod from Rupert, he rose and followed the Russian from the room.

Rupert Page-Gorman waited for the door to close behind them before he got to his feet and walked over to the big desk in the corner of the room. His eyes resting speculatively upon the thin brown folder that he had brought from his flat, and that now lay in the centre of his blotter, he put through a call to Scotland Yard and asked that Chief Superintendent Prendergast be sent around to Downing Street at once. He was in Hyde Park? Then he must be fetched from Hyde Park immediately. After which Page-Gorman returned to his armchair and gazed into the red eye of the deep coal fire.

This, he thought, was the ultimate moment of decision. The next step would be irrevocable, but now it was still possible to jam on the brakes, even to go into reverse. Furthermore, from his own point of view would it not be best to stop now, since he had proved that which he wished to prove, namely that he could outwit them all, that total power was his as by some right of nature? He had read enough and seen enough to know that the actual exercise of such power, delicious as it could be, was a satisfaction incomparably inferior to its achievement. The reward was now, tonight, not tomorrow nor next week.

Yet to whom could he relinquish it? Nikitin and those others had always assumed that it would be to them, not only because, in pursuit of his own ends, he had deliberately led them to believe this, but also because they regarded themselves as the representatives of an absolute power, an historical imperative, in which all transitory and temporary power must eventually be merged as the rivers flow into the sea. But he would not surrender his power to Nikitin, and for three reasons. It had never been his intention to be a sort of *gauleiter* of their Britain. Such a role was quite incommensurate both with his capabilities and with his desires; besides, it would be dangerous and, in a way, humiliating. Secondly, as a patriotic Englishman, he had no wish to see his country a Russian satellite. Indeed, the wish to see a strong and determined England, created in his own image and playing a leading part in world affairs, had always been one of the mainsprings of his motivation. That was one reason why he had been determined to break the American influence. But if Britain had to be dominated by a foreign power, then he would really prefer it to be the Americans. And his third reason for refusing to surrender what tonight lay within his grasp to Nikitin was basically a moral and philosophical one. Nikitin and his friends might represent a very real impersonal force: Page-Gorman represented, or rather incarnated, an equally real personal force. Marxist-Leninism was true enough in its way, but Page-Gorman was even truer in his. He could not surrender to it. Or at least if he did, he must die. And he had no wish to die.

The fire hissed softly.

There was another course, another route for withdrawal that still lay open to him. The old system of government, moribund though it might be, was not yet dead, and would linger on were he not to give it the final euthanasia. What had been done so far could still be explained away as a normal implementation of a somewhat abnormal policy demanded by the electorate. Maynard could be permitted to form a government to carry out the will of the people. But could he? Had the people a will? Had John Maynard a will? It was this declension of will that had long ago nauseated Page-Gorman with political Britain. They talked, and satisfied their appetites, and left others to make the decisions. And the result of this was that they ceased to be subjects and became objects, that they found themselves, inevitably, in false positions, performing actions that were out of character for interests that either did not exist or were irrelevant. He had seen this as long ago as the Suez fiasco, when the Tories had behaved as though they possessed a power that no longer existed, and the Socialists and Liberals had lamented the loss of some moral world leadership which was equally imaginary. Nor was it only in politics that this declension of will had become more and more apparent through the 1950s and into the '60s: it was evident in the private lives of almost everyone he knew—adulterers who not only talked about but actually believed in the sanctity of marriage: pacifists quite prepared to use violence to attain their personal ends: atheistical clergymen not even aware that they had no God: millionaire socialists: semi-illiterate corner-boys accepted as leaders of culture by highly literate critics: drunken teetotallers: expatriate patriots. Foreigners might regard it as hypocrisy, but Page-Gorman had long ago recognized this malady for what it was: loss of will.

But he had not lost his will. Indeed he had strengthened it, fortified it, and used it as a lever to force himself into the very centre of this crumbling mansion, into the seat of power itself. He was no half-crown tourist, but rather a robber baron, a modern Goetz von Berlichingen. Could he now abdicate to what he despised? For years he had given all his strength, all his life really, to this effort of will. The next stage was to change that instrument into another tool, to strengthen and rebuild the shaky mansion, to clear out the lumber and put new bulbs into the dead lamps, mend the fuses, and show the tourists the door. Britain must be recreated. Then it could resume the place that belonged to it, could take the opportunity that those others had simply thrown away, and become the leader of a united Europe and of a united Commonwealth. He had had, he knew, to follow devious paths to get even this far, and the rest would require high subtlety and cunning too, but he possessed both qualities in abundance, did he not? A united and rejuvenated Europe, led by a Britain steeled with the will of Rupert Page-Gorman, working in close amity with a united and rejuvenated Commonwealth—why, there was nothing they could not do!

No, he would never surrender the keys of the house to Maynard and his sort. All that they would do with it would be to let it fall down tomorrow, or the day after, in the name of their favourite parlour game, parliamentary democracy, marching through the lobbies as their whips ordered, terrified of the unions, lost in their unreal dreams, acting their ill-written and ridiculous roles upon a worm-eaten stage to a half-empty theatre, while the decisions were being made elsewhere. No, he would never surrender to that.

Therefore he must act quickly and at once, checkmate the Russians (after having used them for another twenty-four hours), present the country with a *fait accompli*, call in the Americans as and when he needed them, impose his pattern upon Britain. If the people had no will, if they preferred to be objects, then he would treat them as objects, but solely in order, eventually, to turn them into subjects once again. When that had been done, and not before, it would be time to talk about a new and revived democracy. Until then, his will was all that must count.

There was a knock on the door.

"Chief Superintendent Prendergast to see you, sir."

"Show him in, please."

A policeman held up Jack Beaulieu's Bentley at Marble Arch, just outside the Cumberland Hotel. A man was being half dragged, half carried from the direction of Hyde Park by four other policemen, shouting as he came:

"I tell yer she's done nothink, I tell yer she's a good girl!"

Jack wound down his window and leaned out.

"My God!" he said, "I do believe that's Jim Fisher. Wait here, Patrick."

The struggling little party had reached the Oxford Street side of the road now, where other police were gathered, and the traffic policeman was waving on the Bentley. But Jack had already got out.

Patrick was in a position both to hear and see what happened next. Jack strode through the knot of policemen up to the four men holding the small cockney. They appeared to be taken aback by his authoritative manner or perhaps merely by the way that he ignored them. In any event they stopped pushing and pulling at their prisoner, who showed considerable astonishment when Jack said:

"Jim Fisher, what in heaven's name are you up to?"

"Mr Beaulieu, sir! God bless you, sir! They've taken my Carleen, my youngest, and they've shoved her away in there, and she's done nothing, sir, nothing. She——"

An elderly police sergeant now interrupted:

"Do you know this man, sir?"

"Indeed I do, sergeant. We used to firewatch together, back in '44. You get to know a man pretty well if you spend a year alone on a roof with him. What is all this about?"

The police sergeant explained that among the prostitutes rounded up earlier that evening there was one whom this man claimed was his daughter.

"Carleen," said Fisher. "You remember Carleen, Mr Beaulieu."

"I remember her being born. In fact my wife and I came to the christening."

Incoherently Fisher told about his pint in the pub. Jack said to the sergeant:

"Sergeant, I'm sure Jim Fisher is telling the truth, and that there has been an unfortunate mistake. Can we go and see the girl?"

The sergeant, an honest, red-faced man, hesitated. Then he said:

"There's no one allowed in the park, sir, while the operation is in progress. But I'll phone through."

He called over yet another policeman who, Patrick saw, was wearing walkie-talkie equipment. This man did the actual talking, repeating the replies from the other end to the sergeant. From this complicated conversation it transpired that Chief Superintendent Prendergast was not where he was expected to be: he had gone to Downing Street. There was nobody else entitled to admit unauthorized personnel to the park. Sorry.

Again the sergeant hesitated, glanced from Fisher to Beaulieu, and finally said:

"Come on, sir. I'll take you in on my own responsibility."

Jack said:

"Shall we go in my car? It would save time."

"Yes," said the sergeant, "we'll do that."

So Patrick sat in the back with Jim Fisher, while they followed a Black Maria full of yelling Barbadians through the swung-back barricade, where the sergeant had had a quick word with the policemen on duty. Then they were in the dark and empty park. Jim Fisher sat rigidly upright.

The sergeant said:

"The women's camp is down to the left, on the north side of the Serpentine at the far end. You know where that is, sir?"

"I can find it," said Jack. The Black Maria had turned the other way. "What goes on here?"

"It's a big operation to clear the streets of these women and the 'ooligans. The prisons are overful, so they're putting 'em in the park for a couple of nights, to cool off. Though I can't say . . ." He stopped himself.

"Neither can I," said Jack. "Is that the camp?"

Through the trees they could see a score of bell-tents, surrounded by coils of dannert, and with bright lights strung on wires overhead.

"I reckon so," said the sergeant.

They drove almost the whole way around it before they found the entrance, then pulled up. Immediately, as Jack and the sergeant jumped out and as Patrick was fiddling with the door catch in the back, two men in plain clothes stepped forward. These were heavily-built men in long, dark overcoats, with hat brims pulled well down over their eyes. The bright lights from above nevertheless caught on snub noses, on broad and prominent cheekbones.

"This the women's camp?" the sergeant asked.

Neither of the men replied, their hands in the pockets of their overcoats. By now Patrick and Jim Fisher were also out of the car.

"Don't you speak English?" asked the sergeant. But he had no need to await a reply, for at once a young, fresh-faced policeman appeared from the shadows. The sergeant said to him:

"This the women's camp?"

"No, sergeant, this is the Special Camp. There's no one in it yet. Are these . . .?"

"Where's the women's camp?"

"About five hundred yards along there, on the left."

"Come on, quick," said the sergeant, and they all got back into the car. The two Russians watched impassively, their hands still in their overcoat pockets, as the car moved off.

"Ah, Prendergast, come in, come in." Rupert Page-Gorman was at his most affable. "Sit down, won't you? Would you care for a whisky and soda?"

"No, thank you. I'm on duty, you know."

"Yes, of course. But do sit down."

Prendergast did so. Page-Gorman held out his cigarette-case, but the police officer who was wearing, Page-Gorman noticed, an unusually well-cut uniform of dark blue barathea, merely shook his head.

"No vices?" remarked Page-Gorman with a smile. Prendergast said nothing.

"Then let's get down to business. You will recall the occasion some months ago when I sent for you, about a footling complaint made by a certain Lord Clonard?" Prendergast nodded again. "Let me say at once that I was impressed both by your attitude towards your duties as a police officer, and, if you will excuse me so putting it, by your manner generally. You may or may not have guessed that that is why you have been promoted so very rapidly. And that is why I have sent for you tonight."

He paused, to give his words their full value, before going on:

"We live in very difficult times, Prendergast. You have heard the news tonight?" The police officer nodded once more. "You will also have drawn your own deductions from the drastic re-shuffle of the police force as a whole, and also from the appearance of certain strange individuals in your sphere of activities. I do not wish to be more explicit at this point. But you follow me?"

"You mean those Russian detectives?"

"Them, and a certain Irishman called . . . er . . ."

"O'Flaherty?"

"That's right. Now I want to ask you this very important

question, Prendergast, though I suspect it is quite unnecessary. I can, I know, rely implicitly on your patriotism, but can I also rely one hundred per cent upon your loyalty to me—I naturally do not mean to me personally, but to myself as head of the government, which, incidentally, I am?"

"Of course."

"Good. The next question is a little more complicated. Until yesterday you commanded a column of the Mobile Guard. How strong was that column, and for how long had you commanded it?"

"Four hundred. Two months."

"You know the men of that column well?"

"Very well. I had previously been second-in-command of the column. For over a year."

"They would obey your orders implicitly, as you have said that you would obey mine?"

"Certainly."

"Even to the extent of ignoring orders from any other source if you instructed them so to do?"

"Yes."

Page-Gorman now got to his feet, and walked over to the desk. Prendergast followed him. Page-Gorman opened the folder. He said:

"Here is a list of eighty names, with addresses. I want all these men picked up tonight, and put into the Special Camp in Hyde Park. This is to be done as unobtrusively as possible, but it *must be completed by dawn*. You will ensure that there are enough men of your own column in and about the Special Camp to ensure that they are not released by any other police officer or, of course, allowed to escape. You will not inform O'Flaherty or anyone else of this action until it is completed. Do you have any questions?"

"What about warrants?"

"This is a national emergency. I'm afraid we have to waive the formalities. The warrants will be available tomorrow."

"Can I use force?"

"If need be."

Prendergast now read the list of names. Page-Gorman said:

"As you will see, most of them are in London. There are a

few at Oxford and elsewhere, but I imagine you can manage to pick them up within the next seven or eight hours."

Prendergast murmured:

"Harlow New Town, that's no problem either."

"You can guarantee me that you will be able to do this?"

"If they are all at the addresses listed."

"Quite. Now once this is done you will, of course, be at full liberty to discuss the operation with your colleagues as necessary, and also with O'Flaherty who, I imagine, will be very interested."

Prendergast was looking at him impassively. Page-Gorman went on:

"You are to tell him that you carried out these arrests on the direct orders of the government as represented by myself, to forestall a possible pro-American action. What you are not to tell anyone is that I enjoined you to secrecy. Right?"

Prendergast nodded.

"And one last word, Prendergast. Arrange your day, and that of your men, tomorrow so that you and they will be available to carry out a considerably more difficult assignment of a similar nature tomorrow night. If you meet any difficulties, I rely on you to take what steps you may regard as necessary to brush them aside. If you require my help, I am of course available. Have you any questions?"

"No, I don't believe I have."

"Then please report to me personally, tomorrow morning, at No 10 at, er, let's say ten-thirty. Goodnight."

General Nikitin had Suite A of the Hertford House Hotel. His large drawing-room was furnished in a delicate shade of very light brown, the sofas and armchairs being upholstered in an extremely soft leather of that same colour. O'Mahony, seated in one of these leather chairs, was wearing a jacket of a similar material, only black, the black *Lederjacke* which for the past thirty years had been, as it were, the evening dress of the senior Communist. (This formal attire had 'frozen' *circa* 1932, in imitation of the Berlin workers, the *Rotfrontkaempfer*, much as the capitalist tail coat and top hat had frozen *circa* 1820. Now, in the fashionable gathering places within the Communist Empire, the *élite* were easily recognizable not only by sight but by sound. In the Café Warschau, the Hotel Metropole, the better restaurants of Warsaw and Budapest, a faint creaking emanated from men dressed like proletarians who, in real life, were senior civil servants, the conductors of symphony orchestras, film stars or the managers of large industrial undertakings.) General Nikitin, on the other hand, wore a lounge suit, and stood in front of the triple-bar electric fire, his hands behind his back. He said:

"You have still not explained to me why neither I nor Moscow was informed of the probability of this development."

O'Mahony's attitude towards Nikitin was ambivalent. On the one hand he feared him and therefore respected him. On the other, he regarded him as a mere technician, as his social inferior in the Communist world: after all, O'Mahony had been acquainted with Brecht and Ulbricht and Brodz and even with Molotov, in the long distant days when Nikitin was merely a junior officer in the MVD. Nevertheless, in the past decade O'Mahony had quickly learned that the power lay now with the Nikitins, which was why he had tried to identify himself with them, an endeavour in which he had, to a certain extent, succeeded. He replied:

"Page-Gorman is an opportunist. That is his strength, and of course also his weakness. He is of no world-historical importance. How could I warn you of the probability of a development which is dependent solely on circumstances?"

"He thinks that he can use us for his ends."

"Perhaps. If so, he is more of a fool than I believe."

"I do not wish to use force unless and until it is essential."

"Naturally."

"On the other hand, I cannot allow this *bourgeois* individualist to confuse our policy by measures of his own. This announcement of war between America and China. . . ."

"It will have to be denied tomorrow. And tomorrow you will have troops here."

"But I have no wish to use them."

"Of course not. Nor need you. Their presence will be enough."

"You seem extraordinarily satisfied with a situation which, to me, appears both obscure and potentially unsatisfactory."

"You will forgive me, General Nikitin, if I point out to you that we are dealing here with the British, not, say, the Germans. Obscurity is the air they breathe. You were no doubt brought up to believe that this city of London was lost in a perpetual fog. That is no longer true. But the fog persists in their minds. There is, I think, no need to remind you of Kornoloff's statement that we must forward our ends with the means to hand. Here we have a perfectly clear example of that. Foggy minds have led them this far. Let the fog thicken. We can only gain by it. History is on our side, and our task is in reality only to give it a helping hand. The more confused the situation here, the better for us. Because, after all, we are the only people who know exactly what we are after."

"That would sound very well in the *Literary Gazette*, comrade. I am interested in what we do tomorrow."

"So am I. Let me remind you that I control the police. You will have an adequate military force. We can act as and when we choose. But in my opinion we must not act yet. We must allow the situation to obfuscate itself still further. And we can rely on Page-Gorman to do that for us."

Nikitin nodded. Then he said:

"But let us get down to details. . . ."

Patrick had left Jack Beaulieu at the Savoy Hotel and had himself driven the Bentley down into Bermondsey. Carleen had sobbed, quite noisily, all the way, while her father, also seated in the back, had tried to help her with muted words of encouragement, as though he were talking to a very sick person or were perhaps in church. "Cheer up, girl. Soon have you home, girl. Your Mum won't half be pleased to see you, girl." Patrick frowned as he drove the big car whose mechanism he did not know. The girl sobbed on. He would be glad to deposit them.

It had been a shocking scene in the women's camp, shocking because it had been so utterly unlike what Patrick would have expected. A screaming, Hogarthian Bedlam of half-naked, half-drunken whores would have seemed almost normal, almost healthy. Instead they had walked through these long tents, with the plank beds a foot apart and two uniformed policewomen at each end of the tent, between banks of silence and bitter eyes. Only once had a woman hissed: "*F——!*" at them, and immediately the woman police officer who was escorting them in their search for Carleen had ordered a subordinate on duty to take that woman's name. For the rest it had been silence all the way while the women, some young, a few quite pretty, but mostly fortyish, fiftyish, or more, stared at them impassively from cold, closed faces. Their expressions were not predominantly those of fear or even of past greed, but of hatred and resentment as authority walked past—the resentment of the animal in the trap for the trapper on his rounds. And Patrick had recalled with a shudder of distaste that it was such depersonalized women who in Russia were given authority over the female political prisoners, the innocent wives and sisters of arrested men, and over their children.

"Which way now?" Patrick called over his shoulder to the couple in the back of the car. Jim Fisher hesitated, before replying:

"Next on the left, guv'nor. Down the Spa Road."

After a couple of misdirections Patrick found the cottage.

"I'll never know how to thank Mr Beaulieu and you for what you've done, guv'nor, never. My Carleen here——"

But Patrick cut him short, accepted Carleen's thanks offered in a tiny voice, and was soon headed back through the silent, sleeping slum towards central London and—what? What was the meaning of the Special Camp? Special for what? Special for whom? He wished now that he had taken the trouble in years past to find out more about the Russian concentration camps, yes, and the German ones too. How had the Russians created their camps when they had occupied Hungary and Poland? How had the Germans established theirs in France and Italy? Was there a pattern, a system, a standard procedure of which this was the first stage? Or was it perhaps simply what it pretended to be, a temporary administrative measure for dealing with criminals and prostitutes without choking the prisons and police stations? But in that case, why the Special Camp?

On Waterloo Bridge he passed a Black Maria, with shrieking siren, escorted by four black-helmeted Mobile Guards on roaring motor cycles. Although he did not know it, this was one of Prendergast's detachments, on its way to Bromley, Sevenoaks, and Goudhurst, there to arrest, respectively, a very senior trade union official of uncompromising views, the vice-chief of the Imperial General Staff, and the editor of a well-known Sunday newspaper.

Patrick drove along the Strand, and past the silver-shiny Savoy entrance. (Jack had had no idea how long he would be with the American, and had arranged to go to his flat by taxi.) Finally he parked the Bentley in Arlington Street. He was feeling less tired now than he had three hours ago. After an almost sleepless night and a transatlantic crossing he had reached that second phase of weariness, when a man carries on by nervous energy. But he was hungry. Still, Moyra would give him something to eat.

And so she did. Neither Jack nor the air marshal had arrived yet, and Patrick therefore accompanied her into the huge, white kitchen where she produced a bottle of very cold champagne from the fridge. He sat on the white enamel table and drank, while she scrambled eggs and fried bacon upon the electric stove and the healthy, homely smell filled the clinical kitchen.

"What is it all about, Patrick? What are you and Jack up to?"

"I think, Moyra, that it would be best if Jack told you."

"Yes, I see." She turned and faced him, the fork with which she had been stirring the eggs in her now motionless hand. "It's something to do with Rupert, isn't it? With Rupert Page-Gorman? No, don't bother to deny it, I know it is." She took a step towards him now. "He's a terrible man, Patrick, a horrible creature. You know about him and me?"

Patrick nodded, and she quickly looked away, turning back to the little saucepan of eggs. With her back to him, she said:

"You wonder why I ever let myself get involved with a man like that, don't you? You think I must be rotten or crazy, or both, don't you?"

Patrick said gently:

"I·learned long ago, Moyra, that we have surprisingly little

210

choice in whom we get involved with. And I certainly wouldn't dream of condemning anyone——"

She interrupted him.

"That's almost exactly what Jack said. But you must admit it's strange, a man like that, and me."

"Yes, I do."

"I hate him, Patrick, I really hate him, and in a way I always have. Perhaps that's what it was. Perhaps I'm really just a messy little masochist. But there is something more."

"What?"

"He's so certain of himself, so completely self-assured and ruthless. And so few men are these days. And that sort of, I don't know, that sort of hypnotizes women."

Patrick thought, immediately, she is making excuses. She is saying she is no worse than any other woman, nor worse, for example, than Nora. Would Nora be hypnotized by a vulgar careerist such as Rupert Page-Gorman? No, no, he must not allow himself to speculate upon so horrible a thought. He must not. Moyra was talking again, as she examined the toast under the grill:

"And now he's doing it in politics too. If some woman doesn't pull a gun on him, I hope some man will. He's a terrible person, Patrick."

She had said this quite placidly, the simple re-statement of a firm conclusion reached long ago, and even as he had been shocked by the silent hatred in the women's camp, so now he was once again shocked by the utterly matter-of-fact tone in which this highly civilized woman discussed murder. All very well to dismiss it as the verbal revenge of a woman no longer desired, but somehow Moyra was not that type of woman. Her voice was quite cold and firm now. And as she scooped the eggs out of the saucepan and on to the toast, he thought: how little we know of them, how little we understand our civilization, how weirdly thin the ice is, everywhere.

"Here you are, Patrick. Tuck in. Tell me, how was Nora . . .?"

Save for the rustling fire all was quiet in Page-Gorman's room at Downing Street. He had given orders that he was on no account to be disturbed, for he was busy drafting the short speech that he must make, on the radio, tomorrow. Often before had this room held just such a scene: the solitary figure at the desk, in periwig or frock coat or black jacket or lounge suit, and silence save for the deep fire and the faint scratch as quill or fountain pen or pencil moved across white paper, noting down the words that tomorrow the nation would hear, and the next day all the world. But Page-Gorman had for the moment laid aside his pen.

Nora May, for example, Rupert Page-Gorman thought. There are many rewards, power, luxury, money as a symbol of power, beautiful objects, but the ultimate is women or rather the love of women. Money meant little to Page-Gorman, for he was too energetic to be truly luxury-loving and works of art held only a limited appeal for him, while as a symbol of power, what was money to a man who had chased and caught the reality? But women were something else again. Hitherto, in his almost monastic pursuit of his ends, he had had little time to spare for love. He had taken the easy ones, had not bothered with those who resisted his advances. But now that he was on the point of achieving his ambitions he required, as by right, the award. And the award, for him, must be Nora, the famous actress who was also one of the most beautiful women in England, with wit and charm and tenderness as well. And the fact that when they had met, in the past, she had treated him with what he could only call a gentle disdain, why this merely added flavour to what he now intended to do! She could not, she would not despise him now. She was his equal perhaps in every way except in two; she was a woman, and he had power. As for Patrick Clonard, that nonentity with a title, nothing would be easier than to brush him aside. And when he looked Nora May straight in the face . . . no, there could be no question but that she would surrender, reluctantly perhaps, but surrender nonetheless. Because, after all, he was strong and she was not.

Yes, that would be his true reward for all the struggle. Power has its uses after all. He would pin her like a butterfly, a warm and living butterfly. The time was over for the Moyras and the Antonias and the rest. Henceforth it must be nothing but the very best. He would certainly go down to Broadacres that weekend, to celebrate in his own fashion what, by then, should be a completed triumph.

With a sigh and a smile he picked up his pen, and wrote:

"For us in Britain, a great and glorious future knocks upon the door. Not the stale greatness of Empire nor yet the wicked glory of conquest, but a finer future, a future of achievement in peace and love. . . ."

Nora, Felix thought, seated at the piano in the drawing-room of his London flat that he so seldom used, Nora. He had just played, with a certain hesitancy, Brahms's *Variations on a Theme of Handel*, and the plangent music still filled the great Edwardian room. The piano needed tuning, almost as much as he needed practice. But then it was a sad business, playing for oneself alone. Perhaps during Toddy's convalescence at Broadacres he could interest the boy in music. Mr Rubinstein, the boy's music teacher, had said that Toddy had talent. 'A definite ear', had been his exact phrase, which had struck Felix as absurd. Was he too young? Surely not for music? At nine the prodigies were filling concert halls. And for that matter he could remember enjoying music at that age himself. He must have been nine, for he was only ten when his mother died, yet he could quite clearly remember her seated at this very piano, and himself upon the floor, looking up and watching as her shoulders moved from side to side to the music she created. He could almost remember the tune, or at least a tune, that she had played. Idly, with one finger, he picked it out upon the Bechstein. Chopin, of course it would be Chopin. And her dress, too, with a sort of fringed skirt, grey. And her rings, which she had taken off, glittering brilliantly upon the little rosewood table. Those rings Nora now had. He wished that she were here to hear him play.

He looked at the ormolu clock and subtracted five. Not quite seven in New York. She would have had her bath, and now in dressing gown and fluffy slippers would be eating the boiled egg and drinking the tea which she always had before she went to the theatre. He wished that she were here, not only to hear him play but also because there was something here that was all wrong. It was not merely the extraordinary insults to which he had been subjected at the airport—his lawyers should know how to deal with that—but rather the attitude of his lawyers themselves, of Gerald Quigley when he had rung him from the airport. There had been something cautious, reserved, distant in the man's manner. And the drive into London, too, had seemed heavily strange: even Clonard had noticed an oddness about the atmosphere. Felix shook his head, raised his hands over the keyboard, then stopped.

Had he known it, an ancestor of Felix's had felt just as he did this evening, in a village at no great distance from Minsk, one hundred and forty years ago. The causes then had been equally trifling: an insult, which normally he would have taken for granted, from the village hetman: the failure of a bale of cloth to arrive as promised: a cold, strange, and heavy atmosphere. Felix's great-great-grandfather had had even more sensitive fingertips than his descendant. He had called his family together, had packed whatever valuables were easily transported, and had moved west next day. Three days after he had gone, screaming, drunken cossacks had poured into the village, burned the houses of the Jews, and massacred most of their inhabitants. But by then the little Seligman family had covered fifty miles of the road that was to lead them to fifty years in Frankfurt.

Even so, Felix now felt that his wife should be with him, that this was a time when his family should draw close. He therefore went out into the dark, wood-panelled hall and picked up the telephone.

"I'm sorry," said the operator, "there is indefinite delay to New York."

He tried the telegrams service.

"Delivery of cables to New York is indefinitely postponed."

"Why?" Felix asked.

"Because of the national emergency."

Felix replaced the receiver.

When Boreham had begun to talk, Moyra had offered to leave the room, but Jack had insisted that she remain, and Boreham had nodded his approval. Had Mary been alive, he would have expected her to be with him in everything, in every secret. Quite right that Mrs Beaulieu should know exactly what her husband was doing.

And so he had told them about the imminent departure of the Royal Family for Canada, and, in slightly veiled terms, about the conversation that he had had at the Palace that morning, and of the deductions which he had drawn from it. He told them of the certainty that the story of war between America and China was a deliberate lie, put out by Page-Gorman to enable him to issue his emergency powers decree. He told of the rumour that others than prostitutes and criminals were being arrested this very night. And finally he told them what he believed should be done.

"In my opinion," he said. "I believe that we should act at once."

"In what way?" asked Jack Beaulieu.

"I believe that this man Page-Gorman should be arrested. If that is impossible—then he should be shot."

There was a long silence. Then, as from an immense distance, Patrick Clonard heard his own voice, or was it his own voice? What it said was:

"If you haven't managed to take care of him by Saturday, I believe that I might be able to murder him then."

12

As STATED earlier, Antonia May was assistant editor of a magazine called *Minos*, which appeared once each month. Originally a literary and scholarly publication, it had, with the years, become more and more the mouthpiece of the extreme left wing, the pacifists and of the Anti-Nuclear Bomb movement, though ostensibly preserving its original purpose. For the past two years the editor had been a certain Raymond Buler, who made little pretence to hide the fact that literature as such, in his own phrase, bored him stiff. He therefore employed Antonia May to run that part of the magazine, safe in the knowledge that she was unlikely to let anything get in that might have an effect contrary to his policy. The work involved was scarcely one day a week, and the pay proportionate, but for Antonia there was one great advantage to her position: it gave her a sounding-board of her own.

Writers inevitably have a quantity of thoughts which, while unsuitable for the currently fashionable forms of novel, play, essay or short story, are doomed to perish, unless the writer be so famous that he can persuade a publisher to produce volumes of trivia. Writing down these smaller thoughts in a diary gives them at least the simulacrum of permanency, but of course a professional writer likes to publish what he puts on paper. During her girlhood Antonia had been a great admirer of the celebrated Huguenot writer, André Gide, and it was perhaps in emulation of him that she kept a very full diary, extracts from which were published monthly in *Minos* beneath the rubric 'Pages From an Uncompleted Journal'.

It is impossible to say whether she would have chosen these extracts from her January diary for the March number of *Minos*, but to judge by the somewhat studied style, and the impersonal nature of her references to Page-Gorman, it seems a possibility: on the other hand the whole diary was written to be published posthumously—the Goncourt Brothers had also provided a formative influence in the years when Antonia was at Somerville. The first entry, that for Wednesday, was made on the day after the events described in the previous chapter.

Wednesday. Having spent the later part of yesterday evening watching a performance of *Mutter Courage* on Eurovision from East Berlin (of which more later), I had missed the announcement on the BBC and the morning papers therefore came as a complete surprise to me (though I had had private information about Leonard Braithwaite's sudden death—also of which more later). But first to the events of the day.

A great many harsh things have been written about the British Press in recent years, most of them in my opinion justified, but today they really did fall down on the job. Even the dear old *Guardian* seemed quite unable to handle news of this scope: one Prime Minister dead in most romantic circumstances, another taking his place, the apparent outbreak of a

Third World War and the news of this denied and the truth apparently smothered (Wall Street?), the arrival of the Russian inspectorate, and the rumours of an attempted pro-American *coup d'état* nipped in the bud. It was all too much for them. It reminded me of nothing so much as the sickly newspapers of wartime. One of my earliest memories—I can only have been eight, because it was before we were sent out to the country—was of a newspaper describing a German bombing raid on a 'large city in South-East England', and even we tiny, tiny children clutching our anti-gas helmets knew that it must be London!

So fed up was I trying to find out what had happened from the papers (though I liked the description in one of them: Rupert P.-G. 'a Napoleon of peace') that I allowed my egg to boil as hard as a boss's heart. Memo to self: must buy an egg-timer. I wonder if they still make those miniature hour-glasses, through which sand trickles oh so slowly, and which so delighted us as children—though now perhaps we would sadly envisage a tiny old man standing beside it, a miniature scythe upon his bent shoulder, ready to snip the gossamer thread that is each mortal life!

Mark Vernon rang me up, to tell me that he could not give me my Russian lesson this morning. Rupert needs him, he said. Well, a mere woman can hardly complain, but I must say I did feel a little disappointed. I derive a great deal of pleasure from my Russian lessons, even from drawing the large, stiff letters, so strange to us, almost half way to Chinese ideographs. The complicated grammar, too, enchants me. How do we manage in English without a future pluperfect, or rather, how is it that we never notice its absence? I shall had had—there must be occasions when we would like to be able to use it? Surely at some time in the future I shall had written my last entry in this diary? Besides, I had prepared a little surprise for Mark, a light luncheon here—lamb's kidneys and aubergines stewed in Greek wine—and afterwards a visit to the great Sodoma exhibition at Burlington House. Still, world affairs must take precedence.

So out I hied me upon my shopping. A cold, bracing day, with sunshine and clouds like January lambs skipping about against the blue. The sort of day that makes one glad to be in England! I suspect that our great variation of climate plays a not negligible role in the development of our national character. After all, we have to be prepared for everything! Hence our adaptability. In America, where the governing class (the rich) live in a completely steady and predictable climate, either out of doors (Florida, California) or indoors (central heating, air conditioning) they inevitably lose that flexibility and quickness of response which is one of our saving graces. When a political policy becomes outworn, we can discard it, just as we can put on or take off a woolly depending on what Mr Weatherman promises for the morrow. But they, and to a lesser extent the Russians, are stuck with their bikinis or their quilted jackets as the case may be. The political advantages of a maritime as opposed to a continental climate? An interesting subject for speculation, though I must remember not to write political policy, a tautology!

Great excitement at Mr Muggs the greengrocer's. He had sold right out of potatoes! It seems that a lot of silly women, frightened by the news, have been laying in stocks of everything they can lay their hands on, as though this were 1914 or 1939. Mr Muggs says that if this goes on, there will have to be rationing all over again, and an old woman in the shop, with a face like a New England witch, said that it would be much fairer. I am inclined to agree. Mr Muggs has started a sort of voluntary rationing already. It seems that a rich and presumably hysterical woman in a large car tried to buy fifty tins of diced carrots. Mr Muggs told her firmly that the diced carrots were for his regulars, but that she could have three. I wish I'd seen her face!

Then to the wine shop, for a bottle of *retsina*, if that is how it's spelt. Luigi, the nice Sicilian boy, was also much worried by a silly rumour that all aliens from the Common Market countries are to be interned. I told him that this was nonsense, but he only shook his head sadly. There seem to be rumours galore today, and so far as I can make out there does seem to have been some sort of an American conspiracy to seize power, or at least to prevent Rupert P.-G. from being Premier. But Rupert seems to have acted with commendable speed to checkmate this. They were saying in the post office that John Maynard has been arrested, as well as several firebrands in the Tory party and the armed forces. It all seems most strange and in a way un-English. On the other hand, we mustn't forget what happened in France in 1958. If Maynard has been arrested, or more likely taken into some form of protective custody, it will be no great loss to the country as a whole. Presumably our local Soustelles and Debrés would like to use him as a sort of Pétain or Eisenhower, which would never do. I used to have a certain affection and even respect for the man, but I can well see that he would provide an excellent staking-horse for the *ultras*. Meanwhile, I ran into Betty Foreman, Canon Christian's sister, pushing the twins along the King's Road. She seems to attach a great deal of significance to these arrests, although I told her we have no evidence in fact that anyone has been arrested at all. She has heard that the Americans had deliberately put out this story about armed conflict between themselves and China in order to spread confusion here, so that they could seize control, rebuild the rocket bases and all the rest of the horror. Could cynicism go further! We both agreed that it was a mercy Rupert is at the helm. But it seems the canon is very worried.

So back to a solitary lunch. The kidneys were delicious, but I was more interested in the news over the BBC. It seems that there is in fact no war in the Far East. I am inclined to agree with Betty Foreman that this is a Wall Street trick. Meanwhile we have obviously got to tread very delicately here at home. No mention of the 'arrests', which probably never happened. There was a curious item about the Royal Family who, it seems, are planning a state visit, *en masse*, to Ottawa in the near future. It doesn't seem a very tactful thing to do at this particular juncture, but if the Americans are being difficult, the immense prestige that royalty evokes in their snobbish hearts might pour oil on troubled waters over there. I just don't know. Some of my friends are anti-monarchist. My own feeling is that so long as they keep out of politics, the pageantry does no harm and of course is good for the tourist trade. But is not the whole business really a futile anachronism?

After luncheon, to the Sodoma exhibition. Beautiful!

Those greenish flesh-tints are really remarkable. I was surprised at the size of the crowd, but then I always am these days when I visit a first-rate exhibition or attend a really good concert. Whatever the foreigners may say about us, they certainly can no longer accuse us of philistinism. I was particularly impressed by *Lazarus Emerging from the Tomb*, the man who has seen and felt death even to the extent that his flesh seems to be decaying, emerging once again into the sunlight and life, dazed, fearful perhaps, his mind clouded with past horror. Is there here some comparison with this new England (*not* New England!) of ours, as we too emerge from the tomb of fantastical armaments and the death-race, into the sunlight of neutrality and peace? The story of *Lazarus* as a play, with political overtones? Rupert was speaking to me the other day about *will*. Substituting will-power for the childish 'miracle'? A definite possibility.

Then walked around to the Hertford House Hotel, as I was anxious to catch a glimpse of the Russians again. Indeed I even thought of calling on one of those nice scientists I had met at the canon's last night and perhaps having a *glass* of tea. But was frustrated by a bobby in Curzon Street, who told me that that area is sealed off. I can understand that they don't want a lot of 'rubberneckers' about, since after all they are here on serious business, but I am surprised that one cannot get to the hotel. However, the bobby (a member of the Glasgow police force, sent specially to London to deal with the disturbances) told me that a lot more Russians had just arrived, and that the whole hotel has now been taken over. I suppose these are probably the Soviet delegates to the Youth Against the Bomb Congress which opens next week, though I should think I would have heard of it if they were arriving early, since after all I am on the committee!

By this time I was beginning to feel like James Forsyte, and that 'nobody ever tells me anything', so I bought an evening paper. It contained almost no news, apart from a fine piece about poor Leonard Braithwaite and his struggle for peace. But the main item was that Rupert is to speak in the House of Commons at eight, and that his speech would be broadcast. I realized then that there was no chance of seeing him today. A pity, as there is so much I would like to ask him.

It was getting dark by this time, and I hadn't had my tea! Hyde Park is still cordoned off, and the streets seemed strangely empty as I made my way home on the dear old 22 bus. Read Sartre's latest for a couple of hours. What a mind that man has! I am still hoping, vaguely, that Rupert might telephone, but of course I realize that he is hopelessly busy. However, I did have the privilege of listening to his speech. Meanwhile, Felix Seligman called and seemed very worried about the international situation. I told him firmly that the country was in good hands for once. He repeated his invitation that I come down for the weekend and bring Rupert. I pointed out to him that Rupert is Prime Minister now, but that *en principe* he had accepted. Nora returns tomorrow evening.

Rupert's speech was magnificent. "A future of achievement in peace and love," he said, and what could be finer than that? His reference to the royal tour of Canada struck me as obscure, but his assurance that the emergency regulations will be lifted at the earliest possible moment must have gone a long way to reassure Mr Muggs and the others! Curiously enough, there was no applause at all. Perhaps the MPs were ordered not to clap. After all, this was the first time that a British Prime Minister had spoken both to Parliament and to the People simultaneously.

Since when I have been writing this long entry in this diary. And now—Bedfordshire! My comments on poor Leonard and the Brecht play will have to wait.

Mr Kornoloff was in the very best of spirits. While Antonia May had been speculating concerning the effects of climate on national character he, together with Sspesiatkin and two of their closest advisers, had been drafting a flamboyant APPEAL FOR PEACE. This took the form of three letters, slightly different in wording, to the Secretary General of the United Nations, the President of the United States, and the President of the Chinese People's Republic, and the essence of all three letters was that he, Mr Kornoloff, was prepared at any time to mediate between China and America in the interests of peace, and so great was his and his country's devotion to this aim that he was prepared to fly anywhere, day or night, for a Big Three Conference to remove 'once and for all the roots of world tension according to the principles expressed in the Charter of the United Nations.' The draft of these letters was now complete, and copies on the way to their destinations as well as to Radio Moscow for immediate transmission to world public opinion.

Mr Kornoloff leaned back in his chair and rubbed his hands together.

"And now for Britain," he said.

At a very early age Kornoloff had been an instructor of Marxist-Leninist-Stalinist theory at the Smolensk training centre for Comsomol leaders. From those distant days he had retained a certain fondness for lecturing and for the didactic method of approach. He now proceeded to give Sspesiatkin and the two advisers a brief résumé of his views concerning Britain:

"At the conclusion of the Great Patriotic War against Nazi Germany, Britain found herself in a position that was dialectically of the highest interest: on the one hand she was the greatest power in Europe apart from ourselves, and simultaneously the leader of a loose conglomeration of States known as the Commonwealth, and the closest ally of the world's most powerful state, America: on the other hand she was, in relationship to ourselves and the United States, a second-rate power. She therefore was faced with three choices—at least in theory. She could become the leader of a unified Europe, the junior partner of an omnipotent Atlantic bloc, or she could forge the Commonwealth into a true political unit. The first two choices required some measure of relinquished national sovereignty, a course highly unpopular in an old-fashioned imperialist capitalist State: the third involved a return to a form of imperialist expansion and investment no longer possible for a country lacking the necessary finance capital."

Mr Kornoloff paused, and glanced at Sspesiatkin, whose expression was painfully attentive, painful because he had a stomach ache, attentive because even though he had heard this particular lecture more than once it was wiser to be so. Mr Kornoloff continued:

"However, it was not to be. First Britain withdrew from, and then quarrelled with, Europe, in the interests of obscure groups of merchants and manufacturers in the antipodes. Next, as Lenin foresaw long ago, Britain quarrelled with the United States. Having thus no longer any real power at all, she found that her Commonwealth was a mere sentimental dream. All this, of course, we foresaw and encouraged. Finally, in a fury of self-destruction, she abolished her own defences. The plum was ripe to fall."

Sspesiatkin winced.

"Do you not agree, Sspesiatkin?"

"Indeed I do."

"Very well then. Now, it is not in our interests to occupy Britain as such. What we require is a strong base in a weak country, thus isolating Europe, which will then in its turn become ripe for us to deal with as we choose. I believe that the first stage has just about been completed in Britain. But I fear that Nikitin may overplay his hand."

He frowned, and Sspesiatkin nodded quickly.

"I have therefore taken certain measures. In the first place, I ordered that the RKK battalion which is at present on its way to Britain by air must go in civilian clothes. Secondly, that they must not be used save in an extreme emergency. Thirdly, that we must establish one large airbase of our own. Fourthly, that Page-Gorman is to be kept in power temporarily while he continues the task of demolition of the British institutions and system. We can remove him at any time that suits our convenience once his task is accomplished. Meanwhile we are to give him what help he may require from us. But the only occasion on which I can see that the use of troops might be necessary is if there were to be either an American attempt to regain control of their bases, in my opinion highly unlikely in view of the recent perfection of their ICBMs and their feverish building of rocket bases along their Eastern seaboard, or, alternatively, if there were to be some sort of an armed uprising or insurrection against the Page-Gorman government. If either of these contingencies arose, then we would intervene, *at the request of the British government*, a purely internal affair comparable to the American intervention in the Lebanon some years ago and one therefore not amenable to discussion at the United Nations. You follow me so far?"

"Brilliant," said Sspesiatkin. *Old fool*, thought Kornoloff, but he went on:

"Therefore we must acquire this base with all speed, station a picked force of highly mobile troops on it, and continue to hold, as we are doing, an airborne force of six divisions in readiness should the Page-Gorman government require our assistance. So far so good."

He leaned back in his chair, gazed for a moment at the ceiling with his fingertips together, then said rapidly:

"You have all seen Nikitin's message of midnight last night. He complains of Page-Gorman's actions and advocates his immediate arrest. I can only say that General Nikitin, brilliant administrator as he is, has failed to appreciate the full dialectical significance of what is happening in Britain. He is not, after all, an expert in such matters, and his knowledge of that portion of the globe is in parts deficient. For example, he seems to be quite unaware of the importance of the Irish Revolution of 1916. On the other hand as a commander of police troops he is first class. But I am reluctant to leave the implementation of our policy solely in his hands. Meanwhile I have been making certain inquiries about a man named O'Mahony who is at present in Britain working closely with Nikitin, and although of *bourgeois* antecedents . . ."

He frowned at Sspesiatkin whose grandfather, as everyone knew, had been a wholesale corn chandler.

". . . of *bourgeois* antecedents, he is well grounded in the principles of Marxist-Leninism and has worked closely with the Party for over thirty years. I believe that he is a reliable man, and extremely well informed. Finally we have our ambassador in Britain. I therefore propose that these three men establish a *troika* to implement our policy in Britain. Sspesiatkin, make the necessary arrangements."

Then Kornoloff smiled.

That afternoon, while Antonia May was admiring the flesh-tints of the Sodomas, Rupert Page-Gorman had a brief and formal conversation with O'Mahony-O'Reilly-O'Flaherty, who had already been informed of his new and elevated status as a member of the British *troika*.

"Who exactly are these men who arrived by air this morning?"

"General Nikitin felt that in view of the rumours of a pro-American *putsch*, rumours verified by the arrests that you found necessary to order last night, his inspectorate required a certain measure of self-protection. They might be described as the equivalent of the marines who can be seen outside the American Embassy in Grosvenor Square."

"They are policemen?"

"I'm afraid that they come under General Nikitin, as I am not fully conversant with their exact status. But in general I would say that you are correct, that they are roughly the equivalent of policemen."

"Do you not think that General Nikitin should have secured the approval of the British government before importing this large body of policemen into the country?"

O'Mahony shrugged his shoulders.

"General Nikitin was worried by your action of last night. I am not kept fully informed, either by you or by him."

"I'm sorry, I had to act very quickly to avoid a most dangerous situation."

"I quite understand. I also understand that you have Prendergast's column standing by for a similar operation tonight."

"There are certain recalcitrant elements within the police force itself that must be neutralized. It was to tell you this that I have asked you to come here."

"In which case, these Russian police will be useful to you."

"I should like them to take over the responsibility of guarding the prisoners, particularly those whom we plan to arrest tonight."

"That is a sensible suggestion. I will see if it can be arranged."

"You doubt this?"

"No, it will be arranged. However, it will deprive General Nikitin of the security guard that he deems necessary for his inspectorate's own safety. I therefore believe that the best arrangement would be for General Nikitin to be given one of the large and now deserted bases to the north-east of London, so that security guards can be flown in as required, and also that the political prisoners be moved there."

"I am strongly opposed to the importation of any more Russian personnel without previous consultation between the Russian authorities in this country and HM government."

"Of course. The ambassador is anxious to speak to you on the matter. The base I have in mind is ten miles north-east of a town called Bishop's Stortford."

"I shall instruct the appropriate department to be in touch with General Nikitin about this, after I shall have seen your, I mean the Russian, ambassador."

"Thank you. And I presume that you would like me to see Prendergast concerning the police operation this evening? And now I have a personal message for you from Mr Kornoloff. Would you care to have me read it to you?"

"Most certainly."

O'Mahony took a piece of paper from his pocket, unfolded it, and read in a flat voice:

"Personal to Mr Rupert Page-Gorman, MP, Esq., from K. V. Kornoloff, First Secretary the Communist Party the USSR etc. by the hand of F.X. O'Mahony. Comrade, my best wishes accompany you in your great fight for peace and freedom in Britain and my assurances that in pursuit of this great ideal you can rely on the full support both of myself and of the Union of Soviet Socialist Republics. It is my hope that you may care to associate yourself and your country with my initiative for peace in offering to mediate between the United States and the Chinese People's Republic. Meanwhile be assured that you can rely on myself should your and our enemies attempt to sabotage your great work for peace in Britain. F.X. O'Mahony, the bearer of this personal message, has my full confidence and I recommend him to yours. Kornoloff."

"That," said Page-Gorman, "is extremely gratifying." And after a pause he added: "To both of us."

To his surprise, the Irishman did not now leave the room.

"There is something else?" Page-Gorman asked.

"Yes. Something that concerns you directly and personally."

"Oh?"

"You will recall that certain, er, tentative arrangements made between yourself and me became known some days ago to a number of men who, in fact, had no business knowing them at all. I have been surprised at your equanimity in this matter."

"It was worrying, but it's old history now. That knowledge is valueless today."

"You may think so. For myself, and for the people with whom I work, it is a matter of considerable importance to know how such a leak took place. All the more so, since I have reason to believe that it was directly connected with the flight of the Royal Family to Canada."

"I can only assume that some clerk in the Foreign Office——"

"So you told me. Did you know that certain documents, annotated by myself, had been photostated? Documents which were not normally kept in the Foreign Office?"

Page-Gorman's manner, which had been almost off-hand, now changed.

"No, I did not. I did keep certain papers at my flat. But they haven't been stolen."

"They were stolen, and replaced after being photographed."

"How do you know this?"

"As I told you, the people with whom I work have a strong antipathy to unsolved mysteries of this sort. As interrogators, your British police are children. Fortunately General Nikitin's inspectorate contains a number of men who have been trained in the extraction of secrets—even from reluctant senior officials and politicians. I myself ordered the intensive examination of several of the men arrested last night. One of them had actually seen the photostats in question, a capitalist peer named Closehaven."

"You are quite sure of this? I should like to question Closehaven myself."

"You cannot."

"Cannot? What on earth do you mean?"

"He died under questioning."

"He . . . ?"

There was a moment's silence. Then O'Mahony went on:

"His story has been confirmed by the others, none of whom I may say, held out for more than two hours. Who had access to your papers beside yourself, to the papers you kept in your flat, I mean?"

"Why, no one."

"Mr Page-Gorman, I must ask you to tell me the truth. You have a mistress by the name of Moyra Beaulieu who possesses a spare set of keys to your flat."

"I did have, and she did, but . . ."

"She was still in possession of those keys last Saturday?"

"Saturday? Yes, I believe she was."

"The mystery is not a very difficult one to solve, when I tell you that it was her husband who showed the photostats in question to Boreham, Closehaven and a group of other men on Sunday morning. Three of these men are still at large, and must be arrested tonight. I have already added their names to Prendergast's list. I take it you have no objection to this? One of them was on last night's list, Air Marshal Boreham, and is, as you know, the only man on that list who has not so far been arrested. I have instructed Prendergast that an intensive search be made for him, all the more as I have reason to believe that he is attempting to organize some childish resistance movement. Finally, I have also ordered the arrest of Moyra Beaulieu and of her husband."

"The arrest of Moyra? Look, I suppose it's necessary, but I must insist on one thing. I will not have Moyra maltreated."

O'Mahony looked at him coldly.

"I was under the impression that you said she is no longer your mistress. Furthermore, she betrayed you. Finally, she may possess valuable and even vital information. Such *bourgeois* sentimentality seems strangely out of place."

Page-Gorman opened his mouth to speak, but no words came.

For Jack Beaulieu conspiracy preserved a faint romantic novelty, even in Llewellyn Street, SE 16; or perhaps the utter strangeness of Jim Fisher's home added the final touch of dramatic improbability to a situation which Jack could still not accept as fully real.

The news of the arrests had reached him and the air marshal early, for Boreham had started the day attempting to telephone various of his friends, and on five occasions a strange, suspicious voice had answered and had inquired, with the unmistakable accents of the police, the name of the caller. Finally he had telephoned his own flat, and again a strange voice had replied.

It had taken Boreham a little time to persuade Jack of the probably serious nature of the position in which they, and also Patrick Clonard, now found themselves. When he had succeeded in doing so, Jack had suggested that they visit the East End. Jim Fisher's gratitude was once again overwhelming, and although Mrs Fisher was quite sure that her front room would never do for such as Mr Beaulieu's friend, her protestations of inadequacy had at last been overcome. Since his face was the less well known of the two, Jack had found a room at the corner pub. Their story was that they were doing a little field research into the living conditions in one of London's few remaining slums for some unspecified purpose connected with Jack Beaulieu's advertising business. In order to disarm his competitors, Jack explained, he did not wish his name to be known. Patrick, meanwhile, had at last, after a lengthy argument over the telephone, agreed to move round to Nora May's place for a couple of nights. Francesca, the maid there, would certainly let him in without question. As for Moyra, she was to go down to her mother's at Bognor next morning, until the situation should have become clarified.

Now the three men were seated in Mrs Fisher's front parlour, beneath the china dogs and coloured mugs from seaside resorts, in a room crowded with furniture, a television set and the narrow bed that would be the air marshal's. They had all been out all day. Boreham said:

"Did you see Seligman, Clonard?"

"Yes. I lunched with him. Rumours in the city bear out your worst suspicions. Nobody knows quite how many arrests were made, the figure varying between thirty and over two hundred. But it's apparent that several of the most active and reliable men in business were not at their desks this morning. Among others, Lord Closehaven. It is hard to work out a pattern, or even a motive, in these arrests. Seligman himself had been at the Treasury and the Bank all morning. There is a rumour of a huge capital levy, but he is inclined to discount this, as it would wreck the country's exports completely. I don't pretend to understand much about that sort of thing. In any event, there seems no question that if the Stock Exchange hadn't been closed by order and all dealings in foreign currency suspended, there'd have been a panic which would have made last November's seem like a picnic—that was Seligman's expression."

"Did you remind him about your weekend at his house?"

"Yes. And he understands Page-Gorman will be there."

"And are you still prepared . . . ?"

Patrick Clonard glanced down at his hands, resting upon the rough maroon tablecloth. He was silent for a moment. Then he looked up.

"Felix spoke again of shooting pheasants. He said that he believes Page-Gorman will be there. At what range can you kill a man with a shotgun?"

"Point-blank would be best, of course. But not more than three yards, in the back or side of the head."

Patrick's eyes returned to his fingers. His index finger, he noticed, the one that would be ordered by his brain to pull the trigger, was faintly discoloured by tobacco smoke.

"Meanwhile," said the air marshal slowly, "I have made the necessary arrangements, as best I can, for this end. I shall not give you details or names, since it is as well that none of us should know more than is strictly necessary. But I have arranged that a unit of the Royal Air Force Regiment will be available in central London to neutralize these Russians in Hertford House, occupy the BBC, and certain key positions in the Whitehall area. They will go into action half an hour before dusk, by which time your, er, shoot down in Hampshire shall and must have been completed. I believe that the whole business can be put right in a matter of hours now. Next week it might be too late."

"Look here," said Jack. "I probably have even stronger

reasons for loathing this Page-Gorman fellow than either of you. But is it really necessary to bump him off? I mean, it seems a bit hard on old Patrick here. If you can do your stuff in London, couldn't Patrick and Felix and whoever else is there simply tie him up or something?"

"Naturally I'd much prefer that myself, but it's too dangerous. In the first place, he's bound to be accompanied by security guards. Even if you could lock him up somewhere, he might be let loose by his own people. And if he were in action when we act in London, he could quite well stymie the whole thing, or at least create a situation that might amount to civil war, with Russian intervention a certainty. I'm sorry, he's got to be killed. I only regret that I must ask you to do it, Clonard, and that I can't take the responsibility on myself."

Patrick said nothing. Nora, he thought. If only I could ask Nora what I must do in this horrible situation. But could he? She would be back tomorrow night: they would doubtless sleep in one another's arms as they had so often done: and yet, could he ask her whether he should do this? Could he burden her with this awful knowledge that the man with whom she had laughed and made love and walked up from the Faraglioni rocks, a basket of wet bathing things swinging between them, was a volunteer murderer? Could he? He could not.

There was a knock on the door, and the three men stiffened. It was only Carleen, red-eyed as ever.

"Mum says, would you gentlemen like a nice cup of tea?"

"That is very kind," said the air marshal.

"Not for me," said Jack, glancing at his watch. "I promised to ring Moyra at six-thirty, which I shall now do from my hostelry. Coming, Patrick? I believe a drink would do you good.'

"Don't be long," said the air marshal. "We have various other matters to discuss, and I have an appointment at a quarter to eight."

Patrick ordered himself a whisky and soda, and was drinking it in the huge, 'contemporary' and almost deserted bar. Eight men were watching the boxing on the telly, which was turned up very loud. An old man was looking at the racing form. Two women in improbable hats whispered together over their stout. That was all. Jack came out of the booth in the corner.

"All right?" said Patrick.

"I think so. She's off first thing tomorrow. I couldn't talk for long, as there was somebody at the door."

"What door?"

"The flat door."

"Oh, I see. Jack, I hate this."

Jack looked at him shrewdly, and said:

"You wouldn't be doing it, if you didn't. Do you follow that remark?"

"I think so. But . . ."

"Come on, we'd better be getting back."

There was no entry in Antonia May's diary for Thursday. The next one was dated Friday. It ran as follows:

Friday. Such a lot to write! As a trained observer and clerk (in the French sense) I feel that it is my duty to preserve something of the atmosphere of these momentous days for posterity. And yet it is all so complicated and confusing and, of course, though perhaps better informed than most, there is a great deal going on behind the scenes of which I am unaware.

The very atmosphere in which I am writing is incongruous. Here, at Broadacres, who would guess that the history of England is being, perhaps has been, completely changed in the last three days? It is now half past five, and I am in my bedroom, seated at my desk, with a coal fire on my right. (Quite unnecessary: the house is if anything too hot already, as the central heating has been turned up on account of my nephew Toddy, who is recovering from mumps.) While we were having tea (and Felix was advancing political views which I found quite intolerable, so that I was glad to escape up here) one of the maids had unpacked my bag. Now she has just been in to ask me what I would be wearing for dinner, and when I would take my bath, her eyes averted as though to make herself quite impersonal, so that I felt she would have preferred to communicate her inquiry in some less human way than by means of vocal cords. When I told her that I was quite capable of choosing my own dress, and of running my own bath in my private bathroom, she looked almost hurt. Such servility is surely humiliating to all! But there you are, that is the bad old England. Bad, but I must say extremely comfortable, provided one can blinker oneself, as can my sister Nora, to the essential degradation of human values upon which it was based. In any event, it is a thing of the past.

But why am I writing all this, when I have matters of so much greater importance to put down on paper? Yet London seems so very far away, in this artificial cocoon world.

Well, first of all, the flight of the Royal Family. The news got about with astonishing speed yesterday morning, though there was nothing in the newspapers. The first I heard of it was on the bus. I had to go to my literary agent's, so boarded a 22 as usual, and noticed at once a very strange atmosphere. People were talking to each other, just as I've heard they did in the war! And very soon a fierce argument broke out. Since I didn't know what had happened, it was a little time before I understood what this was about, but a nice old woman explained to me that everyone had heard that the Royal Family had fled to Canada, 'because of the politicians' she explained. I burst out laughing at this, but it seems it was quite true and that it had been announced on the BBC at nine o'clock. They've all gone to Canada in three aeroplanes, no doubt taking plenty of money with them. It all seems most incongruous, as though this were the French Revolution. If it was done without the permission of the government (as I now know it was, but of that more later) it seems odd that nobody stopped them, like the flight to Varennes (and a lot of good that did *them*). But back to my bus. A middle-aged man in a dirty turtleneck pullover, who looked like one of the Angry Young Men we all used to admire so a decade ago, was holding forth loudly about how it was a good riddance, since all they did was to spend other people's money and encourage snobbery. People began shouting back at him, and he shouted:

"Well, what's any of them ever done for you?"

To which a little old woman, replied:

"More than you ever have, gingerbum!"

I had to laugh at this, but no one else did, and the angry man got angrier and angrier, and I thought there was going to be a free-for-all right in the middle of Sloane Street. But the conductor came down from upstairs, and ordered the man off. I thought that this was unfair, and said so. As I pointed out, we're all entitled to express an opinion. But to my surprise, and, I may say, chagrin, nobody agreed with me. Indeed they all stared at me with the greatest hostility, and then to my great indignation the conductor said if I felt that way he didn't want me on his bus either. I was livid! All the more so when all those sheep-like passengers sort of cheered. I think I blushed scarlet (for the first time in how many years?) and got off too. I looked for the angry man, to congratulate him on the stand he had taken, but he had vanished.

But that was not the end of it. I caught the next 22, and found there was a diversion, since it seems Knightsbridge is closed to traffic (owing to the internment centre in Hyde Park?), and we soon found ourselves going down Constitution Hill, but slower and slower. The reason soon became apparent. A huge crowd had collected in the front of the Palace and in the Mall, which the police could scarcely control, so that the traffic could only crawl through. Well, this was too good a chance to miss, so I got off again, even though this would make me late for my appointment. Believe it or not, there were people in tears, though these, I noticed, were mostly old people. If the angry man had made his speech here, I do believe they would have lynched him. Surely such popular hysteria is almost inconceivable in the second half of the twentieth century, and psychologically it is extremely unhygienic, to say the least!

I tried to talk to people, but needless to say this was an extremely uneducated crowd, real *lumpenproletariat*: and all I got out of them were silly rumours. For example, the guards behind the railings were not in scarlet but in air force blue. One man told me that the guards had been disarmed and 'confined to barracks', because, as he put it, they regarded it as their duty to guard the Royal Family. Well, I said, if the Royal Family had run away, it was still their duty to guard the Palace, which after all belongs to the People. He didn't seem to understand this, and another man who was standing there said it was all a stunt. I don't know what he meant. Another man said we ought to have a general strike. That was the level of comment! But at this point some people on the far side of the crowd began to sing 'GOD SAVE THE QUEEN', as the mounted police arrived. The police, so far as I could see, behaved very efficiently on the far side of the Victoria Monument, charging the crowd and breaking up what might have become a really nasty demonstration. I thought it was time to slip away.

My agent, old Sowerby, was in a blue funk. It seems one of his most successful authors, Kit Croninshield, has vanished, and perhaps been arrested. I said that anyone who wrote such immoral and irresponsible novels in favour of violence, religion, and class-prejudice deserved to be arrested, but this did not go down at all well with Sowerby. I suppose he was thinking about his ten per cent, as usual! He was very gloomy about the chances for an American sale of my play. Even if it were to be put on over there, he said, there was now some doubt about whether I could be paid. So the Americans seem to be about to go back on the International Copyright Agreement, and we're back in the days of Dickens and the pirates! He said that it was something to do with currency restrictions, but this does not make any sense at all. Just because the new government has made it impossible to convert sterling into dollars, there is no reason why the Americans should prevent the fair payment of royalties over here. But it was a gloomy interview, and I left old Sowerby shaking his head.

I had arranged to lunch with Mark Vernon at a dear little Chinese restaurant, very reasonable and friendly, near Covent Garden. As I had a half an hour to kill, I went to a pub, a thing I haven't done, and certainly not on my own, for many years, but after the extraordinary demonstration outside Buckingham Palace, I was anxious to hear what the real workers were saying. (Because of course I had realized that the people outside the Palace, by reason of the time of day alone, could not have been the real workers of Britain.) I would have liked to buy a midday paper, and did so, though it seemed to contain no news at all, except the list of horses for the afternoon races. (The morning papers, too, had been even worse than the day before, and my *Daily Express*, which I read for laughs, had not been delivered at all.) Anyhow, I went into this pub, which was apparently chiefly patronized by workers from the market, a thoroughly British crowd. I can only describe the atmosphere as subdued, and there was certainly nothing like the outpourings of emotion that I had seen on the bus or in the Mall. I ordered myself a lager and then, taking my courage in both hands, I asked the man behind the bar what he thought of the day's news. He did not seem to understand my question, so I repeated it. His reply surprised me:

"You from a Gallup poll or something?" he asked, with justified suspicion. I laughed and assured him I was not, though I felt rather self-conscious, as I could feel that the other men in the bar were watching me. I did not get a chance to repeat my question, because a most interesting thing happened.

Two Russians walked in! I suppose that they must have been from the inspectorate, great big men in long overcoats. They walked straight over to the bar and asked, in very broken English, for *kvass*. The men in the bar were completely silent by now. And then a most amusing mistake occurred. The publican gave them Bass! They looked at this and seemed surprised. So I thought, here's my chance to practise my Russian! Speaking slowly and clearly, I explained to them that there had been a mistake. But they did not appear to follow me, and stared at me in silence, then exchanged a few words in a language I did not understand. Is my Russian too pure? Or were they speaking some altogether different tongue? They certainly looked extremely Oriental, perhaps from Outer Mongolia or somewhere of that sort. In any event, they simply swallowed their beer in one, after having had some trouble with the currency, and left. I felt a bit of a fool! Nobody in the pub said anything, no comment at all.

Over lunch with Mark I asked him about this, and he agreed that they probably came from Outer Mongolia. Mark was in a thoroughly depressed mood, which struck me as curious, as after all working with Rupert like this is what he wanted. He refused, quite rightly I suppose, to tell me exactly what it is he does except interpret and naturally he wouldn't say anything about what it is that he has to interpret. In fact he gobbled up his chicken *chou-minh* almost in silence, and muttering something about an urgent appointment, slipped me ten shillings and left. What a strange, sad man he is! One feels that he has been through a great deal.

I had planned to work that afternoon, but instead thought I would go to the pictures. I excused this to myself, because I chose a Russian picture (not dubbed, but with sub-titles) so that I felt that by only peeking at the sub-titles from time to time, I was really working at my Russian. And I was surprised how much I understood! And then home, and to the most interesting part of the day. But I see that it is seven o'clock, so I suppose I had better run my own bath (if I dare!) and finish this entry after dinner.

Dinner that evening at Broadacres was a constrained and unhappy meal. Without its central leaves the dining-room table laid for four was a small pool of light beneath its candles, in the centre of the big, dark dining-room, where the brilliant Cézanne, the Manet and the two Renoirs, each lit from below, were like windows opening on to a brighter, more real world.

As a result of Antonia's violent outburst at tea they avoided the subject of politics, but since the political situation in its various aspects was the only subject that interested, and indeed preoccupied, them all, this imparted a strained and artificial quality to their conversation, as they discussed Toddy's mumps, Nora's crossing, the shoot arranged for the morrow, and other apparently innocuous topics.

Patrick thought: I wish I were not here, eating Felix's food. Even more, I wish I were not here to do what I have come here to do tomorrow. But perhaps most of all, I wish that Nora had not driven straight here from the airport, that I had been able to see her alone in London, if only for an hour or two, to regain in this nightmare world the assurance of truth that only she can give me and that she always does.

He looked at her, through the swan-like necks of the silver candlesticks, and she smiled quickly back. And he thought: Would she smile if she knew that I were an assassin? Or am I even that? Will I have the courage, if that be the word, to kill an unsuspecting man? What am I, in this topsy-turvy world?

Felix had seen the quick smile cross his wife's face, and while the insipid conversation wound slowly on, he thought:

No, I must not allow myself to feel the smallest flicker of jealousy, for that way lies complete disintegration and chaos. After all, if he is here, it is because I asked him. And she would smile thus at any dinner guest, wouldn't she? Now, more than ever before, appearances must be kept up, the façade preserved, the family kept together. Because what on earth is happening to this country of ours? How is it conceivable that in England men like Closehaven and Stoneham and Jungk could simply vanish? Why are the papers so censored as to be meaningless? The French radio spoke of an attempted general strike in the Midlands, broken by force, with the union leaders arrested. But when I rang Ullman in Leeds a couple of hours ago he refused to talk about it, and then we were cut off by an operator saying that all conversations are now limited to three minutes. But where are the union leaders, where are the politicians? Why this extraordinary silence, and these fantastical rumours? Was it like this in Berlin, in 1933? But the English aren't Germans. This can hardly be a Russian take-over, with the handful of troops they have, unless one accepts the rumour that they have occupied the whole of East Anglia. And in any case, if we're in the middle of a revolution, it seems hardly likely that the Prime Minister could spare the time to come down here and shoot. And besides, what about the Royal Family in Canada? Why have they said nothing? At least I should be able to get some idea of what is going on from Page-Gorman, if he comes. Though I wish he weren't, really. A horrible man: if only a fraction of these rumours are true, even more horrible than we have hitherto believed. Nor do I imagine that he can or will do anything for me. I might as well resign myself to the loss of my property here, one way or the other. And as soon as Toddy is well enough to travel, then we must try to get out. Did I do wrong to ask Nora to return? No, it is better that we should be together. Where I did wrong was not to trust my own feelings weeks ago. I should have taken Toddy to America then, because is it in fact possible to get out now? But it must be, via Ireland or some other way. It must be possible to . . . to what? To run away from England, and leave my home to be pillaged, strangers wandering through deserted rooms, silently fingering the curtains, walking upstairs, opening the bedroom doors, picking up objects and putting them in their pockets? No, no, it cannot come to that. But I must try to find out tomorrow what is happening, and then I must follow my instincts. My instincts? My instinct would be to die here, in defence of my home. But Toddy must come first.

"I'm sorry," he remarked, turning to Antonia. "I didn't quite catch what you said."

"I only asked you if you have had the Cézanne cleaned. It looks even brighter than when last I was here."

"No," he said, "no. But I think it always looks brighter by artificial light."

Antonia thought: What a very dull man he is. I bet he's thinking about his beastly stocks and shares. No wonder Nora prefers Clonard, though he too is a pretty ineffectual sort of man. But then of course Nora has no brain at all. Rupert, would realize that quickly enough. Attractive perhaps, gay perhaps, amusing perhaps, but superficial. Rupert would soon tire of her stagey chatter and come back to her, to Antonia, who was really his soul-mate. But oh, she thought, her eyes going down to her plate, it would be difficult tomorrow. She would have to keep a very tight rein on her emotions, and smile and look tolerant. At least she would have Mark Vernon to talk to, since Rupert had announced that he intended to bring him along too. But still she wished, in a way, that Rupert wasn't coming, because she could hardly hope to see him alone, to establish that wonderful intimacy which, lately, had seemed to be slipping from her. In fact she wished that instead of being here she were in London, in his Bloomsbury flat, with the curtains drawn. But then, she told herself, she must realize that he was Prime Minister of England now, that he was a very important man indeed, and she must be grateful for any scraps of time or affection or intimacy that he could throw her way. Yet all the same, she wished she was not here, at Broadacres. It all seemed wrong, and strange, and what would happen tomorrow?

Nora thought: I am tired, and I do hope I don't become irritable, but really Antonia is impossible. What on earth is this dinner all about? Why am I sitting here, with these people whom I know so intimately, making small talk? Why aren't I alone here with Felix, dining off a cup of *bouillon* in my bedroom? Or, better still, in London, alone with Patrick. And this horrible man arriving tomorrow, and Toddy's illness, and this endless talk about politics, politics, politics, and Felix obviously frightened, and Patrick more glum than I ever remember seeing him, and I *know* that at any minute Antonia is going to make some perfectly asinine remark as she did over tea, when I had hardly been in the house five minutes. Oh I do hope that if she does I won't allow myself to snap at her, because the poor woman has such a dreadful, dreary life. Oh dear, this is *all wrong*.

Antonia said:

"I expect you'll have to close up part of the house now."

Nora said, quickly:

"These guards or policemen or whatever they are that Rupert has to take about with him, where do they eat? I mean, are they servants or what?"

And at the same moment the butler appeared.

"Lord Clonard is wanted on the telephone."

When Patrick came back his face had somehow changed both its colour and its shape.

"What is it, Patrick?" Nora asked.

Patrick sat down and picked up his crumpled napkin, which he laid across his knees before replying.

"That was Jack Beaulieu. He said . . . He said that he has been unable to get in touch with Moyra, and he has reason to believe she's been arrested."

Antonia sniffed.

For a moment nobody moved or spoke. Then, in silence, they returned to their meal.

From Antonia May's diary (continued):

. . . so that, I suppose, explains why Rupert was so gloomy when he came round to see me last night. Theoretically he came to discuss the great Against the Bomb Youth Congress, but even when he rang me and told me this, I did not quite believe him. After all, he is very busy, and even in the old days he used to leave such routine matters to others. I assumed,

240

with joy in my heart, that it was my company he wanted, that he needed the sort of relaxation which, I believe, only I can give him.

Of course the whole visit was strange. To begin with, he was accompanied by a policeman, who first looked through the flat, and then waited outside. I asked Rupert what was the reason for this, and he said, with a shrug, that it was routine, that plenty of people would 'like to see him out of the way'. When I asked him what people, he just shrugged his shoulders again and said 'lots of different sorts', and that he had plenty of enemies and no friends. I told him firmly that this was nonsense, that he was simply overtired. After all, was not I his friend?

He had been walking up and down the room. Now he stopped, and stared into my eyes for a long, long time before replying, so I began to feel almost creepy. Then he said:

"Would you betray me?"

I shook my head, and he went on, with great intensity:

"No, I don't believe you would. But I might betray you. And it is even worse to be the traitor than to be the betrayed."

I thought then that he must be referring to private matters, and perhaps specifically to my sister Nora. I was about to tell him infidelities meant nothing or very little to me, that my love for him was of a higher and nobler order than that. But then he said, more I think to himself than to me:

"I would never have done it, never, despite everything. . . ."

So I said:

"Can you tell me what it is that is worrying you, Rupert?"

He stopped, and it was almost as though he had forgotten I was there. He said, after a while:

"No, I don't believe I can. But power carries horrible responsibilities, Antonia."

I told him that his shoulders were broad and strong enough to bear the burden, to which he replied:

"It isn't what I do, but those others."

When I asked him if he meant his political enemies, or the Americans, he said, much to my surprise:

"I wish to God the Americans had never gone."

So I could only assume that he was having difficulties with

the Russians, which seems most odd in view of everything that has happened. After all, they must be immensely grateful to him.

Then, after only twenty minutes, and no mention of the Youth Congress, he left. I didn't know what to make of it. But now I imagine, after what Patrick said over dinner, that he knew the Russians were arresting, or planning to arrest, Moyra Beaulieu. But why? What could that feather-brained socialite nonentity mean to them? It is all most mysterious.

Meanwhile, to continue with events, chronologically, the principal rumour in London yesterday was that screams could be heard coming from the detention camp in Hyde Park. Needless to say, I met no one who had actually heard the screams himself. I myself went as far as the wire barricade at the top of Sloane Street, but of course could hear nothing, though I could see the outline of the tents far away. Presumably, if there were screams, it was the hooligans and the prostitutes fighting among themselves. I said as much to Mr Muggs the greengrocer, but he said . . .

Downstairs at Broadacres, Felix had retired to his study, to work on the extremely complicated report that the officials had demanded of him concerning his finances. Nora and Patrick were thus alone together in the big drawing-room. She said:

"Does it annoy you to see me knit?"

"Annoy me? How could anything about you ever annoy me?"

She gave a somewhat puzzled laugh.

"Well, it annoys some men. It used to drive my poor old father almost wild when mother knitted. Patrick, why are you looking at me like that?"

"Because I love you with all my heart, because every breath I draw is for you, because you are the only thing that matters, and you matter absolutely. And I want you to remember that, whatever happens."

"Patrick, you . . ."

He interrupted her.

"Nora, will you promise to remember that whatever happens, what I do will be done for you, and that no matter what the consequences, so long as there is breath in my body I shall love you completely and absolutely?"

She was quite serious as she replied:

"Yes, Paddy, I'll remember."

Mr Kornoloff frowned at Sspesiatkin over the top of his heavy, horn-rimmed spectacles, and thought: the man is quite useless, a real old dunderhead. As soon as this British business is satisfactorily tidied up, I really shall have to get rid of him. A public trial would be best, so that he can be blamed for the poor harvest and anything else that has to be explained away. *Silly old fool!*

But what he said was:

"You do not express yourself at all clearly, Sspesiatkin. That *bourgeois* education of yours clearly left a lot to be desired. However, let me see if I have correctly followed your train of argument through the mass of verbiage in which you saw fit to entwine it."

He paused for effect, then went on:

"Nikitin informed you by telephone twenty minutes ago——"

"Not Nikitin, the Irishman, O'Mahony."

"Ah ha, a very important point. O'Mahony informed you that a certain woman who is or was this man Gorman's mistress has made certain confessions under intense interrogation. The principal fact to emerge is that the Fascist warmongers in Britain are planning a *putsch* for tomorrow, using air force troops, presumably under command of an elderly air marshal who has vanished. Am I correct so far?"

"Quite correct."

"Not very interesting so far, either. But now we come to more interesting facts. O'Mahony informed Nikitin, who visited this man Gorman and in his turn informed him of this statement for which, incidentally, there was corroborating evidence from quite independent sources. Right?"

"Right."

"But to Nikitin's considerable surprise and subsequent annoyance, Gorman not only refused to attach any credence to this, but was extremely angry that the woman should have been interrogated at all, stated that he had no intention of taking any counter-measures to frustrate this intended *coup d'état*, announced his intention of visiting a notorious capitalist at his palace in the country and ended by ordering Nikitin out. Right?"

"Right."

"The conclusion that Nikitin drew from this was that this man Gorman is playing a very deep game, is almost certainly implicated in this Fascist plot, and in any event will henceforth be more of a liability than an asset to us in Britain. Further interrogation of the woman extracted an admission from her that Gorman was, as Nikitin expected, implicated in this plot, the purpose of which is neither more nor less than a complete reversal of British policy to what it was six months ago. However, during this second interrogation the prisoner was in a very weak state, and too much reliability cannot be placed upon the statements extracted from her."

Kornoloff paused, then said:

"The logical sequel to this not altogether surprising development, as Nikitin sees it, is that he should be allowed to use his forces to deal with this *putsch*, having first issued a proclamation in the name of the British government, in which that government requests Soviet help in dealing with internal disturbances. Meanwhile, in the course of the *putsch*, he will see to it that Gorman disappears. His death can be blamed upon the Fascist warmongers, but in fact he will be flown here for questioning. After which, Nikitin will set up a government comparable to the Kadar régime in Hungary. Nikitin will of course remain in charge of Great Britain. That is what he wants, is it not?"

"That is what he wants."

"And what are your views, Sspesiatkin?"

"I . . . It is all so sudden. . . . But if what Nikitin says is correct, then it seems the best course to take."

"Quite. But O'Mahony, to whom you spoke, while agreeing that an attempted *coup d'état* is likely to take place tomorrow, is convinced that this man Gorman is not privy to it. The conclusion I would draw from that is that Nikitin, who has only a superficial knowledge of the British Isles, may be acting from personal motives. After all, he is asking that we send him a parachute division in order to make him neither more nor less than dictator of Britain. I don't like that."

"Neither do I."

"Oh you don't, don't you, Sspesiatkin? Then what do you suggest? That we allow this *putsch* to succeed, the American bases to be rebuilt, Western Europe no longer to be isolated? Use your brains, Sspesiatkin."

Sspesiatkin said nothing. Kornoloff went on, quite benignly now:

"The proper course of action is as follows. We shall give Nikitin full permission to act as he sees fit to deal with this emergency, and will drop the parachute division north-east and south-west of London, as he requests. In fact we shall do more than he asks. We will drop two airborne divisions in the first wave, with a follow-up of two more to be put down on the East Anglian bases, and with a further two standing by here. That should deal with any English attempt at resistance quickly enough. And if this man Gorman is taken alive, then Nikitin is to bring him personally to Moscow for interrogation. If Gorman is not taken alive, then Nikitin will in any case come here at once to report, leaving this Irishman, whose name I have difficulty pronouncing correctly, in control. You have that?"

"Yes, I have it. It is a brilliant solution. Meanwhile I shall prepare the appeal for help from the British government, to be issued when the parachute divisions are airborne."

"Exactly."

"There is only one question."

Kornoloff frowned.

"A question?"

"Suppose the Americans . . ."

Kornoloff cut him short:

"They won't. After all, they have their own ICBMs for their hemisphere defence. Just because the British have chosen to commit suicide, why should they do likewise? No, they will not start a world war for Britain any more."

EPILOGUE

WHEN THE guillotine comes down, it comes down fast.

January

In Washington, on the following Monday, the President, the Secretary of State, the man called G.W., and a man with an English accent who wore a red and blue striped tie, were alone together. The President said:

"If what you say is correct, Page-Gorman cannot have issued this appeal for Russian help, because according to the Russians he was dead by then."

G.W. looked towards the man in the Guards' tie, who now spoke:

"What exactly happened at this country house is not quite clear. We know that Lord Clonard went down there with the express purpose of killing Page-Gorman while on a pheasant shoot. Page-Gorman left London by car at eleven-fifteen on Saturday morning, and almost immediately afterwards, perhaps as a result of his departure, the Russians threw a cordon around the RAF barracks and disarmed the men intended for the afternoon's operation. Our people in London did not become aware of this development until one o'clock. Attempts to get in touch with Lord Clonard by telephone failed. As we now know there had been some sort of a quarrel between himself and Page-Gorman before lunch, apparently something to do with his hostess whom Page-Gorman appeared to have insulted. As I say, what exactly happened we don't know. In any event our people in London immediately sent two men down there by car, but they had some difficulty in getting past the road blocks, and did not arrive until it was all over. It is their evidence that we rely on for what happened."

"So Page-Gorman was certainly alive at one o'clock?"

"Apparently. At least it appears that they all had lunch, including a police officer by the name of Prendergast, but

246

minus Clonard, who, it seems, had gone for a walk. So far as I can discover, Page-Gorman was in good spirits over lunch, which would imply that he knew nothing of the attempted rising in London, and therefore that he had not then issued the appeal for Soviet intervention."

The President nodded.

"What happened after lunch is even more obscure. The men of the party with the exception of Mark Vernon went out with their guns, and it seems that by this time Clonard was back—or perhaps he joined the shoot later. Mark Vernon and Antonia May stayed in the house. Mrs Seligman, the hostess, went shooting with the men. This was at about two-thirty. They were passing through a small wood, when it seems that Mrs Seligman shouted: 'Look out!' Almost immediately there were two shots, one of which killed Lord Clonard. This, incidentally, is what they were saying later that day in the village, though who could have heard this cry of 'Look out!' I do not know. Nor do we know to whom Mrs Seligman addressed it. So far as we can tell, she was not informed of the plan to kill Page-Gorman. She may have seen Clonard pointing a gun at Page-Gorman, or she may have seen Prendergast, the policeman, draw a revolver. We just don't know. But we do know that Clonard did not murder Page-Gorman, as the Russians say."

"What time was this shooting?"

"At about three or three-fifteen. The shooting party now made their way back to the house, with the exception of Mr and Mrs Seligman, who remained with the body. Our people arrived at four o'clock, but by that time the whole place was swarming with Russian and British police. One of our men managed to get in, pretending to be a newspaperman. He says that Page-Gorman had definitely returned to the house, shaken but unhurt according to an Italian maid, but had left almost at once in a Russian car. There was considerable confusion, and some of the Russians seemed to be looting. Then the police began rounding everyone up. There was even a child, who was sick in bed, brought down in his pyjamas and bundled into a van. Finally, he saw Mr and Mrs Seligman coming across the lawn towards the house, he with his arm around her. He heard Prendergast order two of the British police to arrest them. At this point our man decided it was best to slip away."

"What time was the first announcement of Page-Gorman's death?"

"Six," said G.W. "Six their time, that is."

"So if he was alive he could have issued this appeal for Russian help?"

"He was alive all right at four, I should guess. But whether he issued the appeal is another matter. He certainly had not issued it before the Russian parachute divisions were airborne."

The President sighed.

"Not that it really makes a great deal of difference. All we can do is to take the case up at the United Nations, whether or not the appeal was phoney. Now tell me about this man O'Mahony, who appears to be in charge over there. . . ."

February

Owing to a Russian veto in the Security Council, the debate took place in the General Assembly of the United Nations. The resolution, sponsored by Canada and Ecuador, deplored recent events in Britain, and called for respect for the fundamental human rights of the British people and for their distinctive cultural and social life. The representative of the British People's Republic maintained that what was happening inside Britain, and, specifically, the large shipments of British volunteers to Irkutsk and other industrial centres of the Soviet Union, was a purely internal British matter and therefore beyond the competence of the United Nations. The voting was 45 in favour of the motion, with 19 against and 26 abstentions. (It was commented on, but regarded as purely coincidental, that the wording of this resolution was almost identical to that sponsored by Ireland and Malaya at the time of the Tibetan genocide of 1959: only a single, and presumably embittered, French journalist noticed that the United Kingdom, as it then was, had abstained from voting for or against the Tibetan resolution, on legalistic grounds.)

On this same day, extract from the admission lists to Camp 56 (Juveniles), Grantown (Nairn):

Sainsworth, J. W., f., 8, mother convicted prostitute.
Salmon, W., m., 14, incorrigible delinquent convicted sex crimes.
Seligman, E. G., m., 9, orphan, parents politically undesirable.
Seth-Jones, K. L., f., 15, delinquent, convicted prostitute.
Simpson, G., f., 3, orphan, parents pol. undes.
Sustermann, K., m., 17, delinquent, drug addict. . . .

Toddy, however, was not an orphan. Felix Seligman had escaped from prison, and had joined a small group of men, living rough among the Welsh mountains. These men, led by an elderly air marshal, had a weak radio transmitter over which they broadcast to the people of Britain, urging them to do as they were doing—to refuse to co-operate with the Russians and to murder any Briton who did.

March

Raymond Buler, deputy Prime Minister of Britain, announced a drastic undertaking in order to 'streamline the British economy to meet the changed conditions of the late twentieth century'. Since it was clearly illogical to attempt to feed fifty millions of people on an island designed for less than half that number, the Soviet Union had graciously decided to make available large areas of rich virgin land in southern Siberia to which a portion of the British population would be transferred. This 'grandiose act of far-sighted social engineering' would solve once and for all Britain's export problems.

The British government claimed that the government of the Republic of Ireland was being consistently hostile, in that it was sheltering enemies of the British Republic on its soil, and had given support to the abortive revolution attempted by certain Fascist and reactionary elements in Northern Ireland. It claimed, further, that Ireland was harbouring American spies and the agents of 'other war-mongering countries' and demanded the right to send an inspectorate to examine the report that there were rocket bases in Wicklow and Wexford.

In the same month, Pfeiffer, still brigadier of the Foreigners' Hundred on Novaia Zemlia, was delighted to see his old friend Mark Vernon being marched through the camp entrance. With him was another prisoner of nordic descent, by the name of Page-Gorman. "Good," said Pfeiffer to himself. "They will help me to control this Jewish filth."

April

The *New York Times* reported that the re-activation of the rocket bases in Britain was now believed to be complete. Russian forces in Britain were estimated at 180,000 men, the majority of whom had arrived within the last six weeks to replace the last of the six airborne divisions that had landed in January, and to crush the unofficial general strike organized with so much difficulty and at such risk in the North and Midlands in protest against the mass evacuations.

Antonia May was one of three hundred women and four thousand men to be moved in the Soviet prison ship *Red Dawn* from Hull to Kolyma, via the Arctic Ocean. To her considerable surprise a familiar and still just recognizable face was the first that met her eyes in north-eastern Siberia: Moyra Beaulieu had already been in this camp for a month.

May

Air Marshal Boreham was captured in Wales. Though his trial was held in secret, it was announced that he had implicated the former Foreign Minister of the Soviet Union, Sspesiatkin, who was thus proved to have been for twenty years a paid agent of the Fascist warmongers. As for Boreham himself, the British Home Secretary, one Prendergast, announced that the death penalty had already been carried out.

But despite the employment of large bodies of Mobile Guards, supported by Russian troops, the attempt to round up the Fascist bandits in Wales was not wholly successful. The weak broadcasts from Radio Free Britain were still being picked up from time to time in the Midlands. It was said that these outlaws were now commanded by a certain Captain

250

Felix, an almost mythical figure known for his extreme dourness and the utter ruthlessness with which he dealt with any traitor who fell into his hands.

The great Youth Against the Bomb rally, which had had to be postponed, was at last held in Britain. Ten thousand youths and maidens from Russia, Bulgaria, Korea, Albania and the other countries of the Societ bloc marched down the Mall, with banners flying, and Braithwaite (formerly Buckingham) Palace was the scene of many impassioned addresses calling for peace, freedom and co-existence.

The monthly death roll at Camp 82 (Females), Dartmoor (Devon) included:

Sackville-Stuart, Lady Edwina, 56, Pneumonia.
Seligman, Mrs Nora, 30, Cancer.
Simpson, Mrs Patricia, 25, Pneumonia.
Sturtevant, Mrs Olive, 83, Cancer.

Throughout this list the cause of death was alternately cancer and pneumonia. It was known in Princeton, however, that the women had staged a hunger strike that had lasted for four weeks, their principal demand being that those with children should be allowed to have them with them in the prison. When this hunger strike proved unavailing, they marched, arm in arm, to the house of the prison governor. He, however, had already warned the Russians of this probable development, and tanks had been summoned. As had happened with the Latvian women at the Kingir camp, in Central Asia, on 26th June, 1954, the tank crews waited until the prisoners were crowded together outside the governor's house. Then the tanks crushed the women.

June

Mr O'Mahony announced a stupendous new training programme for scientists, 'in order that Britain might hold her own in this modern world.' This training would be available to every schoolboy and schoolgirl who, on reaching the age of 15, was deemed to have sufficient aptitude for further instruction. It would take place at the great universities of the Soviet Union.

In preparation for the visit to Britain of Mr Kornoloff, the Russian and British police made an extensive round-up of possibly subversive elements. In so doing, they picked up one or two men they had long been looking for. One of these was Jack Beaulieu. Others arrested as a purely precautionary measure included Sir Victor Cockshore, Canon Christian, and a young woman named Carleen Fisher.

It was decided, however, that Mr Kornoloff would not now visit Wales as originally planned, for yet another attempt to capture Captain Felix and his men had failed.

July. . . .
August. . . .
It was a wet autumn and cold winter, in England.

Constantine Fitz Gibbon

ADULTERY UNDER ARMS

A deliciously hilarious cad's-eye view of gay abandon among the bombs and bottle parties of wartime London. Tommy Phipps, though a Guardsman, is no warrior at heart. The only fortress to which he ever admitted laying siege was the person of desirable Lola. (2/6)

Al Morgan

ONE-STAR GENERAL

A riveting, caustic novel of American professional soldiers—and their wives. Bronson is a man trapped by the 'army game'. He has stopped at nothing to achieve his silver star, sacrificed his wife, his friends, the men who died under his command—all on the altar of his ruthless ambition. (2/6)

Al Morgan

CAST OF CHARACTERS

Hollywood with the lid off. A bitter, brilliant satire exposing the false world of filmland and the lives of stars, directors and technicians. 'Such a saga of tragedy, treachery, jealousy and petty-mindedness is revealed that the reader is left reeling'—*Yorkshire Evening Press*. (2/6)

Walter Macken

SEEK THE FAIR LAND

Cromwell's armies are ravaging the hungry land of Ireland in an orgy of death and destruction. A few brave men, relentlessly pursued by the tyrant invader, journey in search of freedom. A magnificent novel on a vast canvas. (3/6)

THESE ARE PAN BOOKS —

Saul Bellow

HENDERSON THE RAIN KING

A powerful and unusual novel—its hero a big, blustering misfit of an American millionaire. Among primitive African tribes he becomes not only Rain King but a man in his own eyes. 'Rippling with energy, sizzling with invention, comic as Quixote'—*Daily Telegraph*.　　(3/6)

Niven Busch

CALIFORNIA STREET

A lusty, tempestuous saga of a ruthless San Francisco press lord and his rebellious daughters. 'Ferociously efficient writing'—*Observer*.　　(3/6)

Niven Busch

THE ACTOR

Love and hate behind the scenes in Hollywood. Compellingly readable story of a star who dreams of a comeback. By the author of *Duel in the Sun*.　　(2/6)

Gillian Tindall

NO NAME IN THE STREET

A young girl's ecstasy and disillusionment in love among the students and bistros of Paris. 'There is no clinging to innocence by this heroine. It is a story of first love, but a love experienced with joyous abandon, accepted to the full'—*Times Literary Supplement*.　　(2/6)